Devastated

DELTA FAMILY ROMANCES #10

CAMI CHECKETTS

D1004508

Birch River
PUBLISHING

Free Book

Receive a free copy of *Seeking Mr. Debonair: The Jane Austen Pact* at https://dl.bookfunnel.com/38lc5oht7r and signing up for Cami's newsletter.

Chapter One

Jessica Delta had to escape. She had no idea how she would accomplish such a feat, but she needed to run out of the back door of her beloved grandfather's house and keep running until she somehow outran the pain, the emptiness, the responsibility, and most of all her acute awareness that she could never complete her assignment and was in fact doomed to fail.

When Papa had appointed her Secret Keeper, he'd explained something she hadn't shared with anyone—she was not only destined to protect the weapon, but she would have to fire it. Soon. She, Jessica Delta, the youngest and weakest of the elite Delta family, would be responsible for killing King Frederick, and anyone within approximately twenty feet of him, and she'd have to do it at the exact time she was inspired from heaven above.

No pressure.

Forget the fact that Jessie didn't want to kill anyone, no matter how evil and deserving of death Frederick and his associates were.

What if an innocent maid or someone Frederick had captured was in the room when she fired the weapon? She had no way of knowing who she might kill when the time came.

The only thing Jessie knew for certain—she was the wrong person for the job.

It was ... maybe Thursday evening. The entire family, minus the newlyweds Hudson and Kelsey who were taking a couple days to themselves, and Greer, Alivia, Klein, and Colt who were on duty monitoring the cave, and Emery and Bailey who were on duty watching the cameras and sensors downstairs, were gathered in Papa's spacious living room. Everyone was chatting and eating leftovers from the wedding earlier today.

She'd lost track of time since Papa had been shot and killed. Though Papa had told her it was coming, there was no way to prepare to lose him and be the Secret Keeper and future executioner. Her life had upended.

Had that only been yesterday morning? It shouldn't be hard to keep track of one day, but it felt like a heart-wrenching lifetime of pain had been driven through her head and her heart between then and now.

"You okay?" Her next older sister Maddie sat close to her on the couch and nudged her with her shoulder.

"Not really." Jessie shrugged and forced a smile again. "But what do you do? Keep putting one foot in front of the other, just like Papa taught us."

Papa. She touched the pendant hidden under her shirt as tears stung her eyes. She missed him—his insights, his spirituality, his toughness, his teasing, his smile. If she was honest with herself, she was ticked at him for leaving her. Which was selfish in light of everything going on, but there you were.

Jessie wanted to prove to everybody, especially a particular elite special ops demolitions expert who had joined them last week, that she wasn't selfish or immature. Maybe she was, and she was in no way someone Chief Petty Officer Zander Povey would be interested in. And good heavens, why was she caring about *him* when the world was falling down around her and she was expected to save it?

"You've got this, beautiful sis." Maddie put her arm around her and hugged her. "Papa made you the Keeper because of how incredible you are." Jessie didn't know if it was simply Maddie being insightful or if her worries were revealed on her face, but her sister added, "And you've got all of us backing you up."

Looking around at her accomplished family members, Jessie realized many of them were sneaking glances at her even as they conversed with each other. Shelly sitting on Thor's lap. Aiden and Melene snuggled close. Her parents, aunt and uncle, Kelsey's mom Lori, and Granny Vance teasing with little Mo as they played Chutes and Ladders at the table. Chandler, Kylee, Esther, and Reed cleaning up the kitchen.

Any of her incredible siblings or cousins should've been made the Keeper and final line of defense for the world instead of her. Aiden was a Navy SEAL for crying out loud. Esther was a lawyer for the Air Force and excelled at everything she did. Greer could wrestle a mountain lion with his bare hands. Her big brother Colton was as serious and impressive as any man she knew. Maddie was like Black Widow and protected children and families

3

throughout the world taking out human traffickers and drug lords.

Why on earth was she the "chosen one," as hilarious Thor had dubbed her? She knew he was only trying to make her smile, and she appreciated his humor, but she didn't want to be chosen. She wanted to be the happy peacemaker and keep everybody smiling and do her part to guard the secret. She sure as heck didn't want to be the one to fire that weapon when the time came. She had trouble killing spiders or snakes. She second-guessed if all of God's creatures shouldn't be allowed to live, even if they were creepy.

She should stand up and share Papa's instructions that she wasn't just the Keeper but the one who would fire the weapon. They were already overprotective of her and probably second-guessing if she could fulfill the responsibilities as Keeper. Knowing that she'd have to kill Frederick would flip them all out.

There were too many people she loved in this room. It felt like her beloved family were all as worried as she was, and they were using up all the oxygen.

"I'm going to go outside and get some fresh air," she whispered to Maddie, instead of stepping up and facing everybody's questions and fears when she dropped the bomb.

The bomb. Would Frederick really rain nuclear warheads on America if he got the weapon or if Jessie didn't kill him? She was responsible to keep her family and the world safe from Frederick and his threats of nuclear warfare. Her stomach flipped over and her palms got sweaty.

"I'll come with you," Maddie said, grabbing her hands and tugging her to her feet.

"Sorry, sis, I just … want to be alone. Can you cover for me?"

Maddie nodded and whispered, "Make sure one of the SEALs is watching you."

An elite SEAL team had invaded their valley a couple weeks ago in a Blackhawk helicopter. They'd been assigned to retrieve the Delta weapon and take it to Area 51. They'd brought Maddie's Braden with them and Braden had begged their EOD, his friend Zander Povey, to trust him that Admiral Davidson Delta and his family were the only people who could protect the weapon and not use it for their own means.

Surprisingly, the entire team had trusted him. They'd disobeyed orders, and joined the Deltas. It was a huge blessing, but Jessie couldn't help but wonder if the SEALs were questioning their decision now that Papa was gone and "sweet little" Jessie was the appointed leader.

No. She wasn't the leader. Her dad and uncle had seamlessly taken over that role and Papa's many other responsibilities together. They'd been trained for their parts, just as she had. They'd included her in decisions, correspondence, and information like Papa used to. Of course, keeping her name out of the conversations with anyone but family. As the Keeper and executor of the weapon, she had to know and be part of everything. No matter if she'd rather go work with adorable children learning how to form their r's and s's with their tongue's movement and placement in their mouths.

The SEALs had been patrolling the Deltas' valley during and since the wedding. Reed, Esther's fiancé, was the sheriff, and his men had also been invaluable and trustworthy. They'd guarded outside the cave and the mountains during the wedding but were now home with their families or getting some much needed rest and downtime. The sheriff's department also had to keep patrolling Summit Valley, so the deputies and Reed were working overtime. Great guys. Men they all knew and trusted who had their backs and could keep a secret, even from their wives or friends.

Jessie nodded to Maddie that she would make sure one of the SEALs was close by, but she knew they'd follow her as soon as she exited the house. They all seemed extra diligent around her, and she felt like Chief Petty Officer Zander Povey was always watching her. Zander was the epitome of tall, dark, and handsome with a quick smile that made his cheeks crinkle in the most appealing way. His dark eyes seemed to glint with humor. Jessie had fantasized about getting to know him since the first moment she'd laid eyes on him. He'd climbed out of the Black-hawk helicopter holding an A.R. like he was born to be a military hero. She'd been holding aloft an 84-pound .50 caliber machine gun, pointing it right at him as he'd seemed the natural leader to her.

He'd been focused on Papa as her grandfather strode confidently to the five men, the four-man SEAL team, and Povey as their EOD expert. On that crisp, terrifying morning, afraid she'd have to gun down American heroes to save her Papa and protect the secret, Zander Povey's dark gaze had zeroed in on her. It had been brief, but she'd seen appreciation and longing brighten his deep-brown eyes before he'd focused back on Papa.

She shook her head. She was going nuts. Chief Povey, as she needed to think of him, appreciated and respected her family, but lately she worried that he'd eyed her with concern, not interest. If she glanced around this room again, she'd see the same concern in her family members' eyes as well. They worried if she was capable of being the Secret Keeper.

Well, join the club, she thought.

"I have a question," Maddie called loudly to the group, walking away from Jessie and toward Thor and Shelly snuggled in a chair hardly big enough for Mo.

Jessie edged toward the laundry room, her shoes and jacket, and hopefully a quiet exit.

"Is Thor or Aiden the biggest simp?" Maddie demanded to know.

Jessie actually smiled as Thor roared his protest. Her male cousins liked to call any man a "simp" who tried too hard to capture a woman's attention. Thor and Aiden were both tough and outstanding but they'd do anything for Shelly and Melene. It was cute to see all the strong and impressive men in her family so gone over their loves. Her sisters' and Esther's men were the same —so tough but "simps" for the women they loved.

"Thor's the biggest simp," Aiden called out, "but it's because he's so ugly. Give the guy a break. He had to pull out all the stops to get Shelly with a face like that."

Jessie made it to the laundry room as the room exploded with laughter, and Shelly and Thor's rebuttals floated behind her. She slipped her shoes on and grabbed her jacket, then quietly opened the door and crossed the dark garage. She dodged dark shadows that she knew by heart—Papa's truck, Razor, dirt bike, and Harley.

Her foot caught on something and she sprawled forward, but caught herself before hitting the concrete. She looked back and saw the outline of Papa's mountain bike. It must've somehow gotten knocked off the wall where it always hung, and in the craziness of the past two days, nobody had stopped to lift it back up.

Tears sprang to her eyes looking at that mountain bike on the garage floor. Out of place. Never to be picked up and ridden by Papa again.

Everything felt out of place right now. Even inanimate objects missed Papa.

Especially her. She was out of place and missing Papa. Unfortunately, nobody could pick her up and put her back where she was supposed to be.

Papa would argue that she was exactly where she was supposed to be.

"Well, it's dang sure not where I want to be," she shot back at the empty garage.

She waited. No response. Quiet. She was alone.

No Papa. Just emptiness and her pain.

Tears pricked her eyes, but she blinked to stop them from forming. She was sick and tired of crying. Grasping for something positive, she thought about Papa on that mountain bike.

She and Papa had loved to explore the gorgeous mountains surrounding their homes, using deer tracks on their rides together. He'd always claimed she was fearless. Not anymore. She had so many fears without him here to teach her and smile at her and encourage her.

The rest of her family would be even more concerned if they knew she'd have to fire the weapon soon and also how lost she felt without Papa. Her parents would probably feel hurt she didn't trust and turn to them as she had with Papa. The rest of the family seemed heartbroken, but it was natural for them to step up and keep going. They'd all sworn their allegiance and were focused on protecting the secret and now protecting her as the sole keeper of the weapon. Jessie had no clue how everyone else seemed able to go on with life when she felt devastated, empty, and scared.

Really, really scared.

What was coming? Who was coming? She didn't know, but she knew it would be intense. Dangerous. The mercenaries, Frederick's soldiers, and even America's best, their own military special ops, would probably be assigned to go after the secret. They'd be looking to manipulate and force her to give them the weapon. She shivered. If only she could give someone else the power to fire it. But no. She didn't want anyone to feel as overwhelmed and terrified as she felt.

She picked up the mountain bike and hung it on the pegs on the wall. Touching it, she whispered, "Love you, Papa."

Forcing her legs into motion, she went out the side door and embraced the sting of the crisp fall night. Lights danced on the lake from the boathouse, the moon, and Greer's house across the way. She slowly walked along the grass, hopeful Maddie would stop anyone from coming after her.

A shadow moved from behind the pavilion where Papa had held so many parties for the family and the entire valley. She could easily picture him at the barbecue grill or dishing meat out of his prized smokers. He loved and welcomed everyone, and some greedy, despicable mercenaries had shot him multiple times to steal the Delta weapon and make themselves millions of dollars. Anger hit her then, red and hot. She welcomed it. The anger felt a lot better than the sorrow.

The shadow lifted a hand to her, thankfully not speaking. She recognized Petty Officer Manuel Leandro and wondered where the rest of the SEALs were. All watching her and feeling bad for her? Or maybe not. They were ultra-tough and experienced warriors who'd probably seen many violent deaths, and administered even more. She was certain they all knew how devastating and huge the loss of Papa was, but they probably didn't waste time on simple emotions like sorrow and grief. She couldn't understand or relate to them if that was the case, but she was a little envious. She wished somebody would teach her how to eradicate the hurtful emotions so she could be tough and be the Secret Keeper the entire world needed right now. It was so heavy she felt her shoulders bow under the pressure.

She plodded along the thick grass. Sometimes they'd had snow by the end of September, but this year there hadn't even been a hard freeze, so the grass was still green. Papa would've cut it by now, but nobody else had time for such trivial pursuits as cutting grass. Not that Papa had been focused on trivial things, ever, but he'd worked harder than anybody and kept up on everything.

Right now it was more than enough keeping the secret safe and trying to feed and clean up after the crowd now gathered in her parents', uncle and aunt's, and Papa's house. Thor, Colt, Alivia, and Greer also had beautiful homes nearby and had offered to have the SEALs or any of the other family members stay with them. Maddie and Braden were staying with Colt as he and Bailey weren't married yet, but the other three were newlyweds and nobody wanted to interrupt any alone time they might have together in their homes.

The dock stretched out into the calm, peaceful lake. Jessie walked to the end of it, lay down on her back on the smooth wood planks, and stared up at the stars and the half-moon in the navy-blue sky.

"Papa? Are you up there?" she asked.

Immediately she felt silly. Of course he was up there. She wished she could see him and Granny together. That would ease the pain a lot. Was that really asking too much? Just to see them and know they were happy? If she couldn't even have that miracle happen, how could she be expected to spiritually know when she should fire the weapon?

Hot tears stung her eyes and trailed down the sides of her cold cheeks, wetting the hair at her temples. It was hard to close her eyes and not see that evil man shooting Papa right above the bullet-proof jacket, then the unexpected shots from the trees hitting him above his hip, in his leg, and multiple hits to his jacket.

Jessie had been in those trees seconds before. The two snipers must've been on branches, and somehow she'd missed seeing them and saving Papa's life.

She hated the memory of Papa hitting the ground, blood seeping from his wounds. She hated it so much.

She'd gotten to him first, pressing her palms into the wounds until Thor had ripped off his T-shirt and offered it. Papa's eyes had opened, filled with pain, but he'd ignored it like the tough, experienced military man he'd been. He'd focused on her and whispered, "My girl. It's your time. I'm so proud of you, and now I'll be your guardian angel."

Jessie blew out a breath and squeezed her eyes tight, but all she could see were his blue eyes focused on her, so proud, unquestioning, thinking she was the answer to the Delta secret's future and believing she could rise up and kill Frederick at the right moment.

If only she believed that.

Footsteps on the dock yanked her to her feet. She saw black for a second going from lying down to upright so quickly. She responded like she'd been trained, knife out of her pocket and open, ready to fight, cussing herself for not carrying her favorite 9mm Smith & Wesson that was small and easy to conceal.

Her gaze cleared and she focused in on the beautiful deep-brown eyes of one Chief Petty Officer Zander Povey, EOD. Braden had told her and Maddie about all his friend Zander's extra training stints and accomplishments. Zander was highly decorated and impressive. Jessie wished she could only focus on the benefit of having him and the other SEALs here and simply be grateful they'd given up their lives and careers and some of them their families to join in this battle.

But she didn't focus on any of that. She reacted like a girly-girl and felt her stomach do a little flip as she met his dark gaze.

He strolled toward her, an A.R. strapped to his back, pistol on his hip, and she could only imagine the knives and other weapons concealed in his cargo-type pants. The strap of the A.R. across his chest and the T-shirt that fit him perfectly emphasized his well-built chest and arms.

He was incredible. And she needed to control her girlish reactions to him. This wasn't a man who would be drawn to a twenty-three-year-old girl fresh out of college—well, almost finished with the master's program that would benefit many children. Ever her choice of career wasn't tough and impressive like his.

Zander had to be at least thirty to have the ranking and experience he did. But wait ... Braden was only twenty-eight, and they'd both joined as eighteen-year-olds and done their basic training together. Twenty-eight was only five years older than her. This man seemed to have a lifetime of knowledge and experience in those eyes and those hardened muscles. She shivered just looking at those arms and wondering what it would feel like to touch them.

Sheesh, she needed to get a grip. She was acting like a moony teenager, not the responsible granddaughter of the famed Admiral Davidson Delta and current Secret Keeper of the most sought-after weapon in the world and the only thing preventing nuclear warfare from exploding worldwide.

"Are you okay?" Zander—Chief Povey—asked in a husky but soft voice that seemed to penetrate through her.

He stopped a couple feet away, studying her. Was he doubting her ability to be the Secret Keeper, or was he offering his support?

"I don't know," she answered honestly. "Everything's pretty heavy right now."

"I bet." He offered a grim, understanding smile. She appreciated that smile, but she wished he'd offer a hug.

She rolled her eyes at herself, closed and pocketed her knife, and turned to look out at the water before she did something stupid like try to touch him. Just one touch on that smooth, rounded bicep? *No. Stop it.* He would think she was insane if she trailed her fingers along his arm, then cupped the bicep muscle and appreciated each striation. Goodness, she needed to focus. But it was actually a nice distraction to be worried about his arm muscles and not death and dying.

They stood there in silence for a few beats, her studying the water, him studying her. Would he say something about being sorry for her loss? They'd told Pastor Sam to spread the word through Summit Valley that the Delta family appreciated their prayers and love but wanted privacy at this time. They were planning a small graveside service Sunday afternoon for family only and would have a large memorial service soon. So luckily she hadn't had to endure friends from school, church, or the valley stopping by to offer condolences. She'd tried to keep up with the messages on her phone, but her response most of the time was simply "loving" the message with an easy-to-click heart.

She could feel something like nervousness radiating from Chief Povey. That made no sense. This man had traveled the world as an accomplice to elite special ops teams and either diffused bombs or set them. Bullets probably rained around him in situations she couldn't even imagine. What could he be nervous about right now? In the past day and a half, everything had been as quiet as it could be with Papa's loss. Maybe the storm was gathering to take them out and he could feel it with his long experience.

Risking a sidelong glance at him, she saw he was still studying her. He looked away quickly and the silence and tension between them grew. She should head back to the house to get away from this uncomfortable yet stimulating interaction. But she wanted to see why he'd approached her and hear what he wanted to say. Was he going to declare his allegiance like her family had to her as Secret Keeper? That seemed laughable. If her family, who knew how diligently Papa had trained her, were concerned, this guy was probably wondering how to lobby for a new Keeper. He was probably trying to figure out how to keep her safe and keep her from dooming the free world.

"I wanted to say ..." he began, then paused.

Jessie looked at him again, and her pulse quickened. Moonlight glinted off the smooth planes of his face and his dark, wavy hair. He was so handsome. She wanted to run her fingers over his expressive lips, along his strong jawline and then twist them into his hair, tug his head close, and ...

Goodness sakes, she was doing it again. Immature girl with a crush on the experienced, hot military guy who was completely out of her league. A stupid emotional reaction that she needed to stop.

He met her gaze and everything around them disappeared. Her body felt hot all over and she found herself edging closer to him. He reached out and his fingertips grazed her cheek, setting off so much warmth in her chest that she feared she'd explode. The touch was simple yet gave her so much—acceptance, longing, desire.

His eyes widened. He quickly pulled his hand back and flexed it into a fist, then relaxed it. A muscle ticked in his jaw. He looked out at the peaceful lake and said quickly, "I just wanted to say that death sucks and crap happens, but it's all inevitable and part of the plan."

What? She almost laughed at the unexpected words but this wasn't something to laugh at. Death sucks and crap happens? How insensitive was that?

"Your grandfather was one of the best men out there, so I'm pretty sure the devil didn't get his soul. Right?"

Devil getting his soul? Heck no, the devil better stay far away from her Papa. If Papa wasn't in heaven she didn't want to go there. She glared at Chief Povey. How dare he joke about Papa's death and soul like this? She'd wondered earlier if these elite military men were calloused to death and dying. Apparently she'd been right. And far from wanting to become calloused herself as she'd thought, she wanted to hit him.

Chief Povey gave a hollow laugh and then pushed a hand through his thick hair. "Sorry, this isn't coming out right. That's kind of a joke with Cap and I." He drew in a breath. "I just want you to know that we're all on your team. We're all standing by your side right now. We're all hoping you can buck up, put the death behind you, and focus on the mission."

She blinked at him. "Excuse me?"

He looked back at her, but he was focused on the top of her head as if afraid to meet her eyes again. "That's how you'll get through it. That's how we do it. Focus on the mission. Don't let the emotion affect you. Joke about it and, you know, someday soon the bullet will get one of us."

Her eyes and mouth both widened. What kind of sadistic, awful jargon was this? She'd been wanting someone to help her get through, but not like this. Forget Papa, push away all emotion, focus on the mission. And the bullet coming to get one of them? She'd take a bullet for any of her family members, but she couldn't handle anyone else dying. It was the furthest thing from a joke she could think of. She wanted it all to stop. She wanted peace, not more death.

The only way the world was getting peace was if she inflicted the death.

"But not you." He finally met her eyes and gave her that smile of his that she'd found herself looking for over the past two days. She'd thought before that it made his cheeks crinkle so irresistibly and made her feel like they were sharing some inside joke. She still liked his smile, but she didn't like his jokes much right now. He should probably keep them to himself.

"Not you." His smile fled, and he breathed out the words in a deep, husky tone, his voice and his gaze suddenly turning to a caress.

The frustration disappeared like somebody had waved a wand, and she instantly wanted him to hold her.

He'd told her to not let the emotion affect her, but he was affecting her and making her feel like she was on an emotional roller coaster—upset at him one moment, wanting him to touch her the next.

She didn't need this complication right now. Her emotions were a big enough mess already.

"We'll protect you." His eyes swept over. "I'll protect you. You're the focus of my mission now."

The moment stretched between them and electricity seemed to arc through the air. This man would protect her. She was his personal mission. He'd never, ever desert her no matter who came after them.

She felt that deeply. Despite his weird humor attempts, she was drawn inexplicably to Zander Povey. Maybe Papa was orchestrating this from heaven. Making sure she was taken care of, protected, but most importantly supported and no longer alone. Her family were each willing to step up and take this single-minded protection of her role that Zander was offering, but they all had a significant other to worry about now and Jessie didn't want to take any of them from the beautiful people they'd found and relationships they'd developed.

As she was wondering how to respond to his declared allegiance, he shifted his weight and then declared with the kind of smart-aleck smile Thor would happily wear on his face, "It's all you now, Jessica Delta. You're the man, or, um … woman, and …" His grin grew. "You got this."

"I've got this?" She felt like she had whiplash. From beautifully declaring he'd protect her to giving her the lamest pep talk tripe she could think of? She didn't know if she should laugh at him, hug him really tight, or slug him. His comfort, encouragement, allegiance, or whatever he thought this was, made her want to cry, laugh, kiss him, pummel him, and ticked her off and made her long for him alternately. Was it just that her emotions were completely out of control, or was it that this impressive man might be ultra-accomplished, but he was also a scattered goofball? Could she possibly make him nervous? Maybe the military stud wasn't an accomplished ladies' man.

He kept smiling at her. Was he encouraging her or placating her?

She stepped closer and poked him in the chest. It was as hard as it looked and she might've jammed her index finger, but she didn't give him the courtesy of knowing that. Instead, she unleashed all the angst and frustration building inside her. "Was that your idea of a pep talk?"

"Sure, I mean …" He pushed a hand through his hair. "If it worked."

"No! It absolutely didn't work. Crap happens? The bullet's going to get one of us? Declaring that you'll protect me and then saying 'you're the man' and 'you got this?' My Papa died yesterday and the devil did not get his soul!"

His face tightened, but he didn't back up. He might be an elite weapon, but she would shove him off this dock if he didn't watch what he was saying and stop toying with her raw emotions.

"You might be immune to death and be able to joke about it," her voice escalated, "and put it behind you and focus on the mission, but I am not an elite soldier, Chief Povey. I am a woman. I have a heart." She should stop talking now so he and the SEALs didn't realize the truth: that she was far too emotional and she really didn't want to complete this mission. Maybe they'd walk away or take the weapon and put it in Area 51 like they were supposed to in the first place. They'd all given up a lot staying here and supporting Papa.

But now Papa was gone.

"I don't even care," she found herself screaming at him.

He stared at her with his dark eyes wide and every muscle tense.

"I don't care what you think about me," she yelled. "I don't care if you leave. I don't care if I lose your 'elite support.'" She made air quotes with her fingers. "I will protect the stupid weapon and at the exact right moment, I will kill Frederick with it exactly when I'm suppo ..." She trailed off as she realized what she'd just admitted to him, what she should've told her family already.

"Did you just say ..." His dark eyes filled with understanding and concern. "You're not only responsible for protecting the weapon, but you have to fire it at ... the exact right moment?"

Jessie's stomach churned. As she met his gaze, she found herself saying, "Yes, I do. And yes, I have no idea if I can kill someone, no matter how evil Frederick is."

His gaze was very, very concerned. "Can't someone else fire it?"

How she wished someone else could. But Papa had made certain ... the transfer to her was to be the last weapon transfer. If she died, the weapon died with her. She'd almost prefer that. Except then Frederick would kill everyone with nuclear weapons.

She sighed and shook her head at Zander. She'd happily protect the secret, give her life for it and her family, but to take life ... it made her feel like she was wrenching her soul apart.

Of course this ultra-tough man questioned if she could do it. She questioned it herself. Yes, she was a Delta and had been trained and molded for a time such as this, but she wanted to crawl in bed and have a good cry. She'd just lost her mentor, grandfather, and one of her closest friends. She needed Chief Povey to just declare he'd support her and give her a hug. Was that too much to ask? Yes, it was. This man wasn't the hugging type. He was the let's focus on the war and the mission, kill the bad guys, and not let emotion creep into it type. Good for him. That wasn't her.

"You don't understand." She rolled her eyes. In what Pollyanna world had she imagined this guy could understand when her own family wouldn't. "Of course you don't, Mr. Macho, Brave, Tough, and Untouchable."

He opened his mouth to say something, but she overrode him.

"Don't worry about it. Nobody understands. I certainly don't expect you to be the exception."

She pushed past him and up the dock, heading for the house. Tears streamed down her face, and she was humiliated and hoping she hadn't already messed up her fabled assignment by losing the support of the SEALs who everybody looked at as a gift from heaven.

She was going to fail at protecting the weapon, or firing it at the right moment. Papa had claimed she'd "know" the exact moment. Yeah right. She knew nothing right now.

Crazily enough, she was more upset about hers and Zander's first private conversation imploding. She wished he had lived up to her unrealistic expectations from the looks and smiles he'd given her before tonight. She'd built him up to be perfectly tough but also perfectly understanding. A man like that didn't exist. Not outside her family, at least.

At the moment, her idealistic dreams of Zander being smashed hurt almost as much as the pain of losing Papa. And that ticked her off even more.

Chapter Two

Zander pushed his hand through his hair and watched the woman he couldn't get out of his head run up the dock and across the grass. From the moment he'd seen the small, dark-haired beauty with the impossibly blue eyes hefting a .50 caliber machine gun that most men would have trouble lifting and pointing it at him with no fear and also compassion in her eyes, he'd lost his heart and his head. In that tense moment, one trigger slip away from a firefight that would have wiped out him and his four close friends, he'd imagined how fun it would be to tell their children about the first time they met.

Finally, after almost two weeks of being here in Colorado at the Deltas' valley, he'd *finally* gotten his chance to flirt with her, talk to her, help her with the heavy burden she was carrying and somehow show her how attractive and impressive she was to him.

But nope. He'd gotten so nervous being around the beautiful

sweetheart that he'd fumbled his words and his encouragement had come out all rambling, disturbing, and weird.

Instead of offering her a hug like he was dying to do, he'd ticked her off and she'd revealed that she not only had to protect but fire the weapon and she didn't know if she could. That was concerning, to say the least. Then he'd made her yell at him and run away. He'd messed this one up. Badly.

His gaze followed her progression across the sweeping lawn. She avoided the crowd in her grandfather's house and ran into her parents' back door, slamming it shut. Pushing out a breath, he trudged off the dock and across the grass.

"Well, that went nicely," Captain Zeke Hendrickson said, stepping out of the shadows of the pavilion.

Zander nodded. "Right? She'll probably be asking me to sneak away and make out by tomorrow night."

"Yup. I was thinking to myself, 'There's a woman who is gone over my buddy Demo.' How do you keep them at bay with all those sweetly impressive lines?" Cap grinned, enjoying mocking him. "You must practice in the mirror at night."

"I do. And yes, it's rough to keep the women from attacking me. The good looks, the impressive bio, the smooth tongue. I mean, charm just oozes from me." At least he could joke with Cap. Sadly, his attempts to joke with Jessie Delta had come across flat, weird, and offensive. He'd never been so nervous and uncertain of himself. When he'd focused on her blue eyes, the chaos seemed to settle and he thought he could conquer the world with her by his side, but then he'd started spouting crap that he'd meant to be helpful or inspiring but had the opposite effect. He spent too much time around men.

"Seriously, man, I'm sorry you messed that up so bad." Any of his other friends would've slapped him on the shoulder, but he'd never seen Cap initiate physical contact, unless it was to tackle somebody or start a wrestling match. "I've seen you looking at her when you think no one's looking."

"Can you blame me?" Zander pushed his hand through his thick hair. He needed a haircut, but it was like the sloping grass of the Deltas' beautiful valley that needed to be mowed. Who had time for stuff like that right now?

"Nope." Cap pumped his eyebrows. "She's not only beautiful, but it's a great combination, the sweet but tough thing she's got going on. Sensual and innocent. That's as irresistible as anything I've seen in a long while."

Zander's thoughts exactly. Jessie Delta was so beautiful he got nervous looking at her, so sweet you could feel it radiating from her, yet she'd been trained to fight. Though she was small, every line of her body was strong, appealing, and yes, sensual. He didn't appreciate Cap noticing that and thought it would be quite a shame if he accidentally bumped his buddy into the lake right now.

Jessie seemed like the perfect woman, facing a crazy obstacle that no twenty-three-year-old should have to face. She'd lost her beloved grandfather and now the youngest Delta was assigned to protect the secret weapon, and someday soon fire it.

Had Cap really overheard the conversation? Zander actually doubted it or he would've said something about Jessie not knowing if she could fire the weapon. He was just teasing about the sweet lines. Was it Zander's place to reveal what must be a secret Jessie was keeping? The SEALs had chatted about how and when the weapon might be used, but the Deltas had never confirmed anything but they were to protect it. He highly doubted her family knew what was resting on sweet Jessie's shoulders.

Zander and his SEAL buddies had sworn allegiance to Admiral Delta and to keeping the weapon out of King Frederick's blood-stained hands. Their sources said as soon as Frederick had that weapon it was lights out for America. They'd had to allow the Navy to presume them dead. Zander had been able to get a message to his family that he was on a mission and to keep it quiet that he'd contacted them and was in fact alive. Manuel "Wolf" Leandro, Kyle "Preach" Christensen, and Braden Moyle had done the same for their families, so that was a load off. Zeke "Cap" Hendrickson and Van "Chaos" Udy didn't have families.

They all knew they'd probably kissed their hard-earned military careers goodbye and would most likely be stripped of rank, court martialed, and thrown in prison when they resurfaced from the dead. Unless some miracle happened. With the highly-revered Admiral Davidson Delta being killed it seemed miracles were on short supply this week.

But protecting the Delta weapon had been the right thing to do. Zander and each of them knew it. Zander had his friend Braden Moyle to thank for opening his eyes, and luckily the SEALs either trusted him implicitly or had felt the rightness of this mission themselves.

How to show Jessie that they'd now transferred their allegiance from Admiral Delta to her? Zander wasn't questioning that, despite how she was obviously struggling. Would the other men?

"If I didn't hate touching people, maybe I'd go after Jessica Delta myself," Cap said.

Zander felt a rush of gratitude that Cap shied away from touching anyone and a man could get laid out flat for forgetting that and initiating contact. Zander did not want to compete with the ultra-handsome, highly-decorated, and impressive captain. Cap had been engaged and then dumped a couple of years ago. Besides that emotional damage, nobody knew why Cap was so averse to anyone touching him. They were just careful not to. And they didn't ask.

Instead of shoving Cap into the drink, Zander asked, "Hey, what exactly did you overhear?"

Cap's bluish-gray gaze sharpened. "I was giving you a hard time. I heard your initial lines, but then I backed away. I did hear her yelling that you didn't understand and nobody understood before she ran off."

Zander ran a hand through his hair and lowered his voice. Cap needed to know what the Deltas either didn't know or could possibly be hiding from them. "Jessie not only protects the secret, but she's supposed to fire it at a certain time, and she doesn't know if she can do it." He felt a sting as if he'd betrayed her, but shouldn't knowledge of the weapon and how it works be common knowledge amongst the Deltas?

"You think they all know that?" Cap rubbed at the back of his neck.

"I would think so, but ... maybe not? I'll ask Braden."

"Okay." Cap squinted back up at the huge houses above them. "Why would they hide something like that from us?"

"No idea. They're some of the best people I've ever met. I

don't see them being deceptive. At the same time they've hid this secret from the world for years so maybe it's hard to trust anyone from the outside? Jessie said she didn't know if she could fire it, but she also said she didn't care if she lost our support." He met Cap's eyes and his shoulders tightened. "Maybe they're afraid we'll leave if she's not decisive?"

"Possibly."

Zander respected and liked the Deltas. He wasn't going anywhere, and he didn't think any of the SEALs would change their minds. But it was frustrating to have key details held back.

"It's been a rough couple days for this family," Cap said slowly. "Her screaming that nobody understands ... maybe only Admiral Delta and now Jessie know what the weapon's capable of and that she needs to fire it at a certain time."

Zander liked that theory better than the Deltas keeping them in the dark, but it meant he may have just betrayed a secret Jessie had shared with him in her anger.

"Talk to Braden and then we'll chat with Joseph and Keith."

"Okay."

Cap turned to walk away.

"Cap." Zander stopped him. "What do you think of assigning me as Jessica Delta's personal bodyguard?" The idea had come to him as he'd spouted the other stupid stuff tonight. That was the one thing he said that he'd liked—she was the mission now, and he'd protect her. Yes, he'd messed up tonight, but he could help her with this emotionally challenging time, keep her safe no matter who came after her, and support her now and when she had to fire the weapon.

There was the slightly selfish thought of wanting to get to

know her, be close to her, and hold her when she needed a shoulder to cry on. But he convinced himself it was a small part of the equation. And if he was her bodyguard, he'd have to be in control of himself and not get romantically involved until the mission was over.

"Not a bad idea," Cap said. He rubbed at his neck. "Actually, a really good one. You can keep her safe and make sure we have all the details from the Deltas." He smiled despite the heaviness and worry pressing around them. "You could also get her to fall for an impressive guy who has no clue how to talk to beautiful women."

"I'll probably mess that part up." Not that Cap would do any better. Women chased the tough, unapproachable, but natural hero, and he'd never seen Cap engage or flirt.

"Probably." Cap's grin grew. "But at least I can try to help a guy out. I'll officially assign you so it's not your idea."

"Thanks." Zander's pulse skyrocketed at the thought of around-the-clock protection of Jessica Delta. Yes, he liked this idea a lot.

"Okay. You talk to Braden and see if Jessie using the weapon is common knowledge. I'll set up a time for us to chat with Joseph, Holly, and Jessie. We'll work out the details of you protecting her and call them out about keeping stuff from us if needed."

"Thanks, Cap. I'd hug you, but ..."

"I'd have to thrash you."

"There is that."

Zander patted him on the arm affectionately and dodged a fist aimed for his jaw. He chuckled and jogged away. He heard Cap laughing behind him. That was good. He'd risked his friend coming after him and pummeling him for touching him so casually. So weird how Cap couldn't handle anyone touching him, but he was great, always teasing and keeping things light. More importantly, he was an incredible leader and soldier who never failed at an assignment, was braver than anyone Zander knew, and excelled at combat and marksmanship. The guy had awards dripping from his dress uniform. Recently the Navy Medal of Honor. And he'd unselfishly given up his exemplary career, more advanced trainings and more successful missions than anybody had accomplished to protect the Deltas and their weapon. Cap was somebody Zander always wanted on his team.

Zander's thoughts returned to Jessie. He'd upset her. He hoped he could make that right. But if he was assigned to protect her, he'd get to stay close. Really close. He had to be able to unstick his tongue from the roof of his mouth then. He loved the way this was going and hoped Jessie wouldn't balk at the assignment. He also hoped her mom and dad would allow it.

Every one of the Deltas was ultra-protective of Jessie and that protectiveness had nothing to do with her being the Secret Keeper, as they called it. She was well-loved by each one of them. Zander was playing with fire in so many ways by hoping to get close to her. Even though this assignment would probably be the most important one of his career—and the end of his career—he couldn't get thoughts of Jessie and getting closer to her out of his mind. When he'd touched her jaw earlier, he'd thought he'd found heaven. When he looked in her blue eyes, he was both lost and found.

Now to talk her into being interested in him... or maybe he should keep his mouth shut and just kiss her and see how that went. After the mission was completed, of course.

Right now, he had to focus on the mission of keeping her safe from whatever King Frederick sent their way next. Mercenaries, troops of armed soldiers, elite special ops forces.

And he might have to help her complete her mission and kill King Frederick.

Hooyah.

Chapter Three

It was late Friday afternoon and Jessie had been sent to her room to rest. By her mother. Like a child. She didn't need rest; she needed to figure out if Admiral Gusbane, Chief of Naval Operations, was on their side or a traitor and helping Frederick. She needed to look through that zip drive Papa's coder Thomas had decoded once more and see what additional information she could glean.

The last time she'd had a serious talk with Papa, he'd been concerned about the accuracy and usefulness of the zip drive's information. He'd sent the bank account information on to a trusted associate in the IRS. The man had looked into seizing it, but the account numbers weren't accurate. They could've been changed recently. Who knew what information was correct or who to trust at this point?

During that same conversation, Papa had looked deeply into her eyes and assured her, "Jessica ... I prayed long and hard to *not* make you the Secret Keeper. Colton or Aiden would willingly take this burden and they'd do a fabulous job."

Exactly. They'd do a fabulous job. She wouldn't.

Papa had continued, "Because I adore you so much, I can hardly stand to give you this heavy burden. But I know, I know down deep, and have known for years actually, that you are the Secret Keeper. You are the only one who can be humble, conscientious, and strong enough to take this responsibility and use the weapon at the exact time it is needed. It is a spiritual responsibility unlike anything you'll ever know. But I've trained you, you've always been close to your Savior, and the good Lord will direct you when the time is right."

No pressure. The good Lord would direct her to kill a man. Papa had quoted a scripture she'd never heard, Psalm 37:9-10. "For evildoers will be cut off, But those who wait for the Lord, they will inherit the land. Yet a little while and the wicked man will be no more; And you will look carefully for his place and he will not be there."

Papa had explained that she was the avenging angel, and she had to make the wicked man no more so the good people in Banida, Poland, and Germany could inherit their land once more and many people throughout the world could be protected. King Frederick would not stop, and if the United Nations wouldn't step up and stop him soon, it would be time to use the weapon.

She pushed off her bed and paced her room, annoyed with her mom and Colton for ganging up on her and insisting she take a break and upset at herself for taking it simply to avoid an argument.

The peacemaker in her didn't want to die, no matter if she needed it to.

Die? No, fight to keep working and not rest. Not die. She was too focused on Papa dying. No matter if she didn't want to rest; she was tired from the stress and she hadn't slept well last night. She'd mulled over the intense but awkward conversation with Chief Povey until far too late. He drew her in and completely frustrated her, and she'd admitted to him what she hadn't even told her family. She'd been waiting all day for someone to ask her about firing the weapon. Nothing yet. She hadn't told Zander it was a secret. What if he thought it was common knowledge and he and the SEALs were upset they didn't know?

She chewed at her thumbnail as she paced. Too many questions.

"Jessie?" her dad rapped on her bedroom door.

She hurried across the room to yank the door open. "Hey. Everything okay?" Finally, they needed her again.

"Can you come down to the living area?" His blue eyes studied her thoughtfully. Her dad was protective of her like any dad would be, but he also trusted her. He trusted her because he'd seen how diligently Papa had trained her and had been right there helping her excel.

She could hit the bull's eye of a target with a pistol, rifle, shotgun, A.R., or .50 caliber. She could take down a man twice her size in hand-to-hand combat. She could track, navigate, strategize, and decode. Papa had made sure she excelled in every area. She'd always thought it was because her favorite person in the world loved spending time with her, or because he wanted to make sure she was safe because she was smaller physically than anyone in the family.

Nope. He'd been training her meticulously ... to be Secret Keeper. And more. Papa had trained her to kill. The very thought weighed so heavy on her that she wanted to puke.

She focused on her dad. What was going on that her "rest" had been interrupted? Her mom wouldn't like that. And why was he looking at her as if she'd been scheming something?

"Captain Hendrickson and Chief Povey have an idea they think you'll be interested to hear."

Chief Povey. Zander. She put a hand to her abdomen and hoped her dad didn't see how even the man's name affected her. The fact that he was asking to speak with her, with the Captain nonetheless, and her parents ... he was going to ask about her firing the weapon and upset her parents even more. She knew it.

She'd stayed away from him since last night on the dock. Almost an entire day. Nobody would let her take a stint of protecting the cave. She supposed the reasoning made sense. If a mercenary somehow got through the resistance and to the cave, they'd need her to open it.

She touched the hidden pendant. It was smart to keep her safe and in their little valley where there was so much protection and many eyes watching out for her. Including Zander. Even though he hadn't gotten close enough to talk with her again, she'd felt his gaze on her. And it made her hot clear through every time.

She'd spent the morning training with Colt and Bailey and then she'd worked with her dad and Uncle Keith to respond to condolences from Papa's vast network of military and political friends and associates, cross-referencing with Papa's notes about who had been at Olivet Seamons' party with King Frederick, whose names were listed on the zip drive Admiral Seamons had given to Braden and Maddie, and who Papa had trusted from his experiences. The three of them tried to sort out who was on their side and who was a possible enemy.

In their correspondence, her dad and uncle didn't talk about the Delta weapon to anyone. Interestingly enough, even Admiral Gusbane, who'd sent Zander and the four-man SEAL team to obtain the weapon, didn't ask. So far another special ops team hadn't come after the weapon, but who knew how long they had?

They wanted to keep the Delta weapon from being general knowledge with the military, the government, and especially the public. It seemed King Frederick was doing the same. Though he apparently had a fifteen-million-dollar reward out for the weapon, he didn't seem to want to shout to the world what he was after. It made sense. Someone else stealing it before him would put a cramp in his plans of shooting his nuclear weapons at America while he hid in an unknown location.

Jessie lived every hour in fear that it would be the moment she'd know she had to go use the weapon. At the same time, she wished it was over, King Frederick was gone, the world could have a moment of peace, and she could go back to finishing her master's in speech pathology. What a different life she was living right now. Nobody at school had any clue what she was trained to do or what family emergency had taken her out of the program earlier this fall.

"Are you going to tell me what this idea is?" She cocked her head at her dad.

"They haven't told me. They asked if they could meet with me, you, and Mom."

"Oh." Nerves made her stomach feel twitchy. She wanted to check her makeup and put on some lip gloss, but that was a girly reaction to Zander she couldn't afford to indulge. Not now. Maybe not ever. An elite special ops demolition expert really wasn't a great fit for a speech pathologist.

What was a great fit? She hardly knew Zander, but the thought of him being with any other woman made her body tighten and made her want to fight any woman who'd dare look twice at him. Surely a whole slew of women had. He was irresistible. When he wasn't telling her that "crap happened."

"Okay."

Her dad stepped back as she walked out the door. He followed her through the upstairs hallway and down the stairs. She smoothed her features and tried to look relaxed and nonplussed as she left the entryway and entered the main living area.

Zander and Captain Hendrickson both stood from the couch as they entered. Zander's gaze zeroed in on her with all the power of deep-brown eyes, long lashes, and a connection she needed to ignore.

Jessie pulled her gaze from him with a concerted and she thought heroic effort, nodded to Captain Hendrickson, and walked over to sit by her mom on the opposite couch. Her mom quirked an eyebrow at her, her gaze full of questions and a bit of mischief and matchmaking. Jessie wanted to beg her not to get any ideas. An elite special ops man like Zander Povey, who thought she should just callously get over Papa's death, wasn't the guy Jessie should be falling for.

Her dad came and sat by her mom. The two men settled back down and Jessie wondered if she'd ever noticed how glorious it was to watch a man sit on a couch. Zander's leg muscles flexed as he settled onto the couch and his fit, tall body uncoiled against the cushions, but somehow he looked poised to jump and fight against bad guys at any moment.

"What's going on, Cap?" her dad asked. He wasn't snippy or annoyed, but he didn't have time to waste. Nobody but Jessie really did. Everybody else had assignments at different hours of the night and day and had to fit in sleep and eating and time with their significant other and other family members during those breaks. All she had to do was train, try to help correspond and keep people from coming after the weapon, stay safe, and reconcile in her mind how to kill Frederick and whoever was close to him.

"As I've spoken with different Delta family members, I've become more convinced that keeping Jessica safe and away from the weapon is the most foolproof plan to keep Frederick from obtaining it. Am I correct to assume that only you can access the cave and remove the weapon?" He looked to Jessie, his grayish-blue eyes looking only for a confirmation.

"Yes," she admitted.

Her mom put an arm around her. Jessie knew it was both a show of support and a mother terrified of the responsibility and danger surrounding her youngest child. Her mom was tough but loving. She'd been surrounded by the Delta secret most of her married life and trained her children right along with her husband, but she was still struggling with Jessie being the one to take over the responsibility and danger of the weapon.

Jessie appreciated and loved her mom, but she was still a little perturbed from being forced to go "rest" earlier and she didn't want to look weak in front of either of these men. Especially Chief Petty Officer Zander Povey, EOD. But typical Jessie the peacemaker, she didn't shrug her mom's arm off.

She did boldly meet Zander's gaze and the room seemed to get warm. Very warm. Jessie swallowed hard and hoped no one else saw or felt the temperature spike. She needed to remember the words he'd said that had made her mad last night, but unfortunately she was remembering his fingertips grazing her chin and him telling her he would protect her and she was his mission. His mission to protect, or to hold and kiss?

"Is it also correct you are the only person on earth who can activate or fire the weapon?" the captain continued, yanking her concentration away from Zander and making the entire room feel chilly. So Zander had told him, or he'd overheard.

"Jessie?" her mom and dad both asked at the same time. Her mom's hand on her shoulder trembled. Of course her family had theorized about firing the weapon and why Papa hadn't done it, or maybe he'd done it at some point and never told them. Papa was their hero and their loyalty would be to him, always, but he had been very good at keeping secrets about that weapon.

"Yes, I am," Jessie said, tilting her chin and trying to look brave.

"Jessie." Her mom hugged her tighter but put her other hand to her mouth.

"Why didn't you tell us?" her dad asked.

She looked away from her dad's blue eyes and caught Zander and the captain exchanging a look. Zander nodded to the captain. They'd been worried they were the only ones who didn't know.

Jessie drew in a breath and met her mom's worried eyes and then focused on her dad. "Papa told me a couple weeks ago, the same time he appointed me Secret Keeper." It probably still stung her parents that they hadn't known she was the Keeper. "I wasn't ready to have everybody worry even more than they did at the meeting." The meeting when it had been revealed she was Secret Keeper and her mom had completely flipped out. She wasn't about to admit she didn't know how she would kill Frederick. "Papa also explained," she said before they could ask questions, "that I'd be inspired to know exactly when to kill Frederick, and that it would be soon."

"Oh, Jessie." Her mom pulled her hand away. She knew exactly how tender Jessie's heart was. "How are you going to *kill* someone?"

Jessie heard the captain shift on the couch across from them. She could only imagine what he and Zander were thinking. Would they desert them because of a faulty Secret Keeper? Her doubts and fears tripled.

"I don't really have a choice," Jessie said.

"I'm not sure I understand," her dad said slowly. "Couldn't you open the weapon and let somebody else fire it?"

Jessie shook her head. She and Papa had gone to the cave and he'd somehow transferred the thumb print and voice scan to her. Then he'd explained he knew deeply that she was the only one who could use the weapon at the right time and for the right purpose. If she died, the weapon would die with her. Maybe that wasn't the worst option. Except then Frederick could go on killing and terrorizing the world.

"Papa made certain it can only be me," she said softly. Maybe they could figure out a way to duplicate her voice and thumb print, but when Papa had transferred it to her, she'd known it was her responsibility and destiny. If only she could know she wouldn't fail at it because of her aversion to cold-blooded murder. Sure, Frederick needed to die, even deserved it, but Jessie imagined she could only kill someone to directly defend her family, like Greer had to do for Alivia, Klein, and Emery.

The silence in the room stretched to far past uncomfortable. Luckily, her mom only coddled her with her arm. She didn't go off on how Jessie couldn't, shouldn't, or wouldn't fire the weapon. She was certain her parents and other family members would have more to say about her firing the weapon, but for right now they simply absorbed that fact.

"I fear as soon as Admiral Delta's graveside service is over," the captain redirected and she was grateful to him for it, "or maybe we don't even have that long, we're going to face unprecedented attacks from Frederick's soldiers, armed mercenaries, and probably our own military."

The room felt chilly. It was a gorgeous and unseasonably warm late-September day outside. The maple, cottonwood, and birch trees ringing their beautiful lake were turning orange, yellow, and red. It was a picture-perfect scene as the green pine trees stood straight and tall amidst all that color and the lake and sky were a calm, crystal blue. Would their valley be shattered by attacks and war?

"I agree," her dad said. "We don't have my father's layer of protection any longer. I think his reputation and connections held back people in the American military who might want to seek the secret for the military or personal gain. Plus, the anonymity we had for so many years is disappearing. Secrets are hard to keep once they gain momentum and the weapon is something every military man would like to have for himself or his troops, and politicians would love the power of it."

Everybody nodded. It was unnerving to think of the secret weapon being talked about and leaked around military and political circles. They might not have entire battalions coming after it as no leader would want it to be common knowledge or risk losing it to another branch of the military if they broadcast it, but enough people knew about it now that they were on a slippery slope of exposure, danger, and attacks they hadn't previously seen.

"I feel even Frederick, his people, and other rulers around the world had a fear of my father's power and status," her dad continued. "I've wondered if the man who kidnapped Kelsey and Mo didn't have the assignment to kill Papa after securing the weapon."

It made sense. Frederick would want the well-known and widely respected Admiral Delta out of the picture. It was doubtful he knew that all the Deltas were trained like they were. And he had succeeded in killing Papa. Jessie wrapped her arms around her stomach, and her mom tugged her closer.

"Which brings me back to the reason we've asked to meet with you." The captain looked at Zander and something passed between them. Jessie wondered whose idea it was to meet. It almost seemed like Zander wanted to make the proposition, but he felt Captain Hendrickson sharing it would be received better. Why?

"If we can keep Jessica safe," Hendrickson said, "we can keep Frederick from the weapon, or anyone forcing her to use it. No matter what happens to the rest of us."

That was an awful thought. Would they all be laying down their lives to keep mercenaries, Frederick's men, or even their own soldiers from getting to Jessie? She shivered, not sure she could live with that. Papa had laid down his life for them. She'd wondered if she'd have to do the same, but it was far worse to think about those she loved being killed and her hiding out and staying safe.

Her parents both nodded. Her mom pulled her arm back but stayed pressed into Jessie's side.

"Jessica," Hendrickson said seriously. "Just to be certain. Even if Povey had blown the safe door, which I have complete confidence he could've done, and my SEALs accessed the weapon, we couldn't have removed it or used it? Admiral Delta designed it so only you, and the key I assume you keep on your person," the key around her neck seemed to burn against her skin and she barely kept herself from touching it, "are the only ways to access and either use or remove the weapon. Correct? Can you explain exactly what needs to happen so we can cover all our bases to keep the weapon safe?"

Everybody was staring at her. She should respond, should be able to give these people the details, but Jessie had a sudden unexpected and terrifying thought. What if Hendrickson was a fraud? What if his men were? What if they'd come here at Admiral Gusbane's instructions to get the weapon, no matter what, and when they'd seen all the firepower and resistance from the Deltas they'd changed their game plan? If she gave him explicit details, would he use them against the Deltas?

"Jessie?" her mom questioned.

"Just a moment," she requested. She'd heard about Braden's gift to discern what someone's intentions were and she thought that was incredible. When these men had shown up in the Black-hawk and Zander had told the story of Braden confronting him and begging him not to take the Delta weapon, Zander had said that Braden had reminded him that he "knew him." Braden had seen Zander's goodness. Also, Braden wasn't on Hendrickson's SEAL team, wasn't even a SEAL, and he had already stood up to these men in defense of the Deltas. He could give an unbiased answer.

Jessie looked from Captain Hendrickson to Zander. He met her gaze with his deep-brown eyes, steady and true. She said a prayer in her heart, asking to see clearly. Everyone else in the room disappeared as she and Zander locked gazes. He was impressive. He was loyal. He'd meant it, to his steadfast core, when he'd said he'd protect her last night, that she was his mission. He'd protect her from everyone, even his friend the SEAL captain sitting next to him if he had to.

She felt a pulse of warmth as the truth shot through her. She could trust Zander.

Her dad shifted next to her and took her attention from Zander. She wanted to keep focusing on Zander, but now was not the time for that. She looked at the captain. His gaze was guarded, shut off. His blue eyes were cool, almost a bluish gray, and she had no idea what he was thinking or feeling.

"Jessie?" her mom asked again.

"I can't answer Captain Hendrickson's question right now," she said softly, studying Hendrickson for his reaction.

He cocked an eyebrow at her and she thought he'd make fun of her, but he simply said, "What do you need to answer it?"

She thought about it. She couldn't get through to Captain

Hendrickson's intentions, but she knew who could, and his reaction and assessment would answer the question for her. "Braden."

"You want to know if you can trust me?" Hendrickson asked.

"It's not a matter of want, Captain. I need to know if I can trust you."

"I can respect that." He nodded to her and pulled a walkie-talkie off his belt. None of the SEALs had their cell phones as they'd blown them up in the Blackhawk to support the story of them being killed. Papa had given them each an RT29 walkie-talkie. The preferred military walkie-talkie had excellent transmit signals and the ability to receive weak signals at extreme distances. Hendrickson pushed the button and spoke into it. "We need Moyle at his future in-law's house."

"Copy," a male voice said. She wasn't sure which of the SEALs it was.

Hendrickson clipped the walkie-talkie back on and turned back to her. The silence felt tight, and Jessie was certain she'd offended him. These men had given up everything to transfer to the Deltas' side and now she was questioning his loyalties. It was bold of her, but she had to be certain.

She let her gaze trail back to Zander. He was much easier to look at than the unapproachable too-tough captain.

Those deep-brown eyes were intriguing. His gaze was steady on her, not condemning, not even questioning. She appreciated that. She wanted to get lost in those eyes. Now was the time. Would there ever be a time or would the world end because she'd failed to protect the weapon?

Chapter Four

Resolve tightened her shoulders as Zander seemed to strengthen her with his gaze alone. How much more could he strengthen her with his hand in hers, working side by side? She liked that idea. Too much.

"Jessica." Captain Hendrickson pulled her gaze away from Zander. She wasn't sure what to think of him, but at the moment she was annoyed that he had interrupted her staring. "I have no issue with you sending for Braden to 'read' me. I'm a very closed off person and don't let many people close."

That was kind of him to reassure her he wasn't offended.

"Many people, Cap? How about none?" Zander had the nerve to laugh at the captain.

Hendrickson elbowed him.

Her dad smiled. "My nephews have had brawls and wrestling matches on the carpet if you two want to have a go."

"Don't you dare encourage that," her mom threatened. "I just got that new lamp and you haven't had to redo the sheetrock and paint for almost two weeks."

Zander laughed at that, and Hendrickson's expression softened. Jessie even smiled. She was glad all of them could relax a little.

"Why don't you let people close?" she asked him. It was intriguing and sad. She had all of her family close to her heart and many friends from grade school up through graduate school who still kept in touch. Before she'd left school, she was hiking, biking, or going to lunch or dinner with different friends and dates most days of the week. She missed those easy days.

"If I let people close, then I'd be more likely to answer a question like that, wouldn't I?" He arched an eyebrow.

"If you want me to trust you, answer your specific questions about the weapon, that not even my family know by the way, and consider whatever proposal you have, maybe you should give a little and try to open up," she threw back at him.

"Ooh," Zander teased. "She got you there, Cap." He winked at her, as if they were in cahoots. Jessie felt warm all over. She wanted to be in ... something with him.

No, that was the girlie girl in her trying to get out. She was a responsible Keeper of the biggest secret of the century. She couldn't indulge in girlish fantasies. Not now. Maybe never.

Hendrickson cracked a smile.

Jessie gave him a sassy look that Maddie would've been proud of. "Oh, you actually possess a sense of humor."

Zander laughed loud at that one. She really, really liked him. Was that wrong? Probably with the situation they were in at the moment. Maybe someday, when the weapon was secure. Would that day ever come? Maybe she should let herself get to know Zander. Tell him off for trying to tell her that "crap happens" and she should bury her pain and emotions to get through. Maybe he'd been trying to help her or even impress her with his own mental toughness last night. She wanted to give him another chance, see if they had anything in common, and see if he was as appealing as he seemed right now, or a let-down and source of frustration as he'd been last night.

"Maddie," her mom cautioned.

Jessie looked at her mom, and then she burst out laughing. She looked back at Zander. "I know I'm out of line when she calls me 'Maddie' by mistake."

"Oh, shoot. I did," her mom said.

Her dad chuckled at that. "Jessie's right. Don't tell Maddie."

Zander shared a conspiratorial look with her. "Maddie's the feisty one?"

"Oh, for sure. I'm the angel and the favorite." She put her hands under her chin and blinked rapidly.

Everybody laughed at that.

She'd been Papa's favorite. Everybody knew it, and though they might tease her about it, her parents, uncle and aunt, cousins, and siblings all looked at her just as Papa had—like she was an angel peacemaker who could do no wrong. She'd flourished in her role as the happy, bright light in the family, the one everybody wanted to hug and do something nice for. Because they loved seeing her smile and she had usually done something nice for them first.

The memories were filled with sunshine, fun, love, smiles ... it felt like a different lifetime. Like watching Rapunzel on

Tangled run twirling through the flowers, so sweet and adorable and unaware that men with big knives and Flynn himself were going to hurt her soon—emotionally, physically, and spiritually. Was Zander Jessie's hero? A very different hero from Flynn as he definitely wasn't a thief but a devoted, tough, special ops soldier.

She locked eyes with him as the laughter settled.

Suddenly Hendrickson leaned forward, stealing her focus from Zander again. "Jessie. If I wasn't committed to the Deltas, why would I have given up my military career to be here?"

She eyed him and asked the question that might upset him more. "Did you give it up?"

He shrugged. "I would assume so. Unless this all plays out like a Jack Reacher novel, we save the world, and everything is forgiven in the end." He smirked. "I'm not planning on that."

"I understand what you're saying. I'm not trying to accuse you of having a track phone in your backpack with only Admiral Gusbane's number programmed in it."

"That would stink," Zander said, giving his friend a look as if to make sure he wasn't corresponding with Gusbane. No. He trusted his friend. It was more a look of, sorry she's questioning you.

"I'm just saying I have to trust you completely. Until I do, I can't answer your question, or agree to whatever plan you and Chief Povey have concocted." She congratulated herself on not calling him Zander out loud. "And I'm assuming it's a fabulous plan, because you are some of the most highly trained people in our military. Correct?"

"We are," Hendrickson agreed. There was nothing cocky

about his words, just factual. He tilted his head toward Zander. "Do you trust Chief Povey completely?"

The room went too still again. Jessie focused in on Zander, and as she was coming to see was a troubling thing, she got lost completely in his dark eyes. She nodded and admitted, "I do."

Zander's quick smile curved his lips and made his cheeks crinkle.

"Whoa." Her mom whistled and said in a low tone, "That's an irresistible smile."

"Did you just ..." Her dad broke off and shook his head.

Jessie could only agree, but she wasn't about to voice it. "You see where Maddie gets her sass," she said to Zander instead.

"Maddie ... I mean, Jessie." Her mom sounded exasperated. "You watch it, little girl."

Jessie laughed, but she didn't like being called "little girl" by her mom in front of these men. She needed them to respect her, and she had no desire for Zander to look at her as a little girl.

The front door opened and closed, and rapid footsteps sounded. Braden walked into the room, his gaze quickly sweeping around. He was a handsome blond with teal-blue eyes. Jessie had flirted with him last June when he'd come to their valley and attempted to hike to the secret, having no idea what he was messing with. She'd always been impressed with him, and now knew he was the perfect fit for her sister Maddie. He loved Maddie unconditionally and had helped her to see that her Savior loved her too. He showed her sister she could be a warrior and still be righteous and filled with light from on high.

"You need me?" Braden asked.

"Yes," Hendrickson said evenly. He stood and faced Braden.

"Jessie has a request of you. She needs you to 'read' me and tell her if I can be trusted and if I'm a hundred percent loyal to the Deltas and to protecting the weapon as per Admiral Delta's instructions."

Braden looked to Jessie. He didn't know her well, but he knew she was deeply spiritual and trusted in heaven above. She had to be, or she'd never know when it was the right time to use the weapon. If only it was done and they didn't have to go through all of this. She'd played tennis in high school and had absolutely despised warmups. Once she was in the game she could settle, focus, and succeed, but warmups just made her nervous. She was definitely nervous in this warmup phase they were in, waiting to be attacked or to feel prompted to use the weapon as Papa was so certain she would be. If she could even bring herself to give that final voice command was an even bigger question in her mind.

"You didn't trust what you saw in Captain Hendrickson's eyes?" he asked.

"It wasn't that I didn't trust him," she said slowly, "but he admitted that he's closed off and doesn't let anyone get close. That's more what I felt. He was choosing to shut me out. It scared me that maybe he's hiding more than just his desire to be this tough military guy that nobody can touch emotionally or spiritually."

Braden nodded to her, but Captain Hendrickson's jaw tightened. The captain looked over at Zander and muttered, "I hope this is worth it."

"It is," Zander said evenly. He looked at Jessie, and his dark gaze was warm and liquid. "I promise it is worth it."

Jessie wasn't sure if he was talking to her or his captain.

"Okay." Captain Hendrickson literally gritted his teeth. She heard it. What was his deal? Was he scared of Braden seeing that he was double-crossing them, or was he scared of Braden seeing *him*?

The captain stood straight and tall and faced Braden as if he was facing a Naval Discharge Review Board, or maybe worse than that, as if he were facing a firing squad. No. This tank of a man wouldn't be afraid of dozens of rifles pointed his way. He'd probably call out "Hooyah" and face death with his grayish-blue eyes cool and still unable to reveal any emotion to anyone, even the fear of dying. She was relieved he wasn't the man she was drawn to. The poor girl who fell in love with him.

Braden stared at the captain for a few seconds, then said softly and respectfully, "Captain Hendrickson doesn't want any of us to see what he's feeling. He's very good at hiding his feelings. I respect that, but it's hard to know what he's truly about with how expert he is at hiding behind a mask of toughness and professionalism."

Jessie couldn't live with that. This was life or death, the end of the world if King Frederick had his way. "Captain Hendrickson might need to open up a little so we don't lose the weapon to Frederick and have nuclear weapons obliterate America as we know it."

Zander looked at her, and his gaze was full of respect. Maybe he didn't see her as a little girl but as a woman who could hold her own, even with tough Navy SEALs. She'd show him she could hold her own with him. Could she?

"Do you want me to tell you more about the weapon and listen to yours and Zander's proposal or not?" Jessie realized her mistake instantly. If she corrected to Chief Povey now, it would probably highlight her slip of the tongue even more.

Captain Hendrickson turned to her. His eyebrow lifted, but it wasn't mocking. It looked like her slip of the tongue made him happy. "I do want you to explain about the weapon, and to listen and agree to our proposal," he said. "I'll try to let down my guard so Braden can 'read' me." He turned back to Braden and muttered, "I thought your gift made it so you could read anybody."

"Not anybody. Most people let their guard down at one point or another, especially when emotions are high. You don't."

"Dang straight I don't. I've worked my entire life not to let people see what I'm truly feeling."

"Yet you want me to trust you," Jessie pointed out, even though the captain was focused on Braden, not her. She wasn't trying to be snide, but she couldn't trust him if neither she nor Braden could get a glimpse of what was going on inside, of what his intentions and goals and allegiances were.

"I need you to trust me," Captain Hendrickson admitted quietly, almost humbly, changing want to need like she'd done earlier. She didn't know the guy could be humble. "Okay, let's get this over with." He faced Braden and as they looked on, both men stood straight and stared at each other for several long beats.

Jessie felt like the staring contest or examination of Captain Hendrickson's closed-off heart would never end. She felt almost bad for putting Hendrickson through this. It obviously was hard for him, but she couldn't let her peacemaker tendencies rule her life in these extreme circumstances. Those tendencies could be strengths in regular life, but in her role as Secret Keeper and their current unstable situation, she had to focus on trust, loyalty, and a team that would fight to keep Frederick away from the weapon.

She let her gaze slide to Zander and dang if his dark eyes weren't focused on her. She blew out a breath. It wasn't easy to focus on serious issues when Zander had a slight smile on his appealing lips. Why was he smiling at a time like this? As she studied him, she realized he was smiling for her. To help her relax and know that he was on her team, Captain Hendrickson was a great man, and it would all work out.

It would all work out? She usually had oodles of faith. Some in her church groups at college had expressed envy that their faith didn't come as easy and wasn't as strong.

Not right now. Faith was in short supply when the entire evil sector of the world was breathing down your neck and possibly twisting those who should be on your side to betray and backstab you.

Braden nodded to Captain Hendrickson and the captain's shoulders relaxed slightly. Had he passed? Braden patted the man on the shoulder. Captain Hendrickson immediately stiffened and murmured, "Don't touch me."

The tension in the room amped up as Braden raised questioning eyebrows at him but lifted his hand away.

"Braden is only trying to help," her dad said softly, but with a voice of steel. "I don't appreciate you being short with him for doing what Jessie asked."

Maybe the captain wasn't on their team if he could so easily snarl at Braden.

Zander stood and strode to Captain Hendrickson's side. "Cap isn't trying to be short with him. It's common knowledge with his team. Nobody touches the captain. He's very averse to human touch."

This guy just got colder and colder. Averse to human touch?

"I apologize," Captain Hendrickson said stiffly. "I don't like to draw attention to my issues. It's a holdover from ... childhood."

The room felt stuffy and sad. Captain Hendrickson studied a mirror on the wall above the couch Jessie sat on her with her parents. Braden looked like he wanted to reach out to the captain again, but thought better of it. Zander begged her with those deep-brown eyes of his to not judge the captain too harshly. It was illuminating and brave of Hendrickson to admit that his issues stemmed from childhood. Compassion filled Jessie. She'd seen some cases of abuse in her work of speech pathology with some of the downtown schools in Denver. It infuriated her and broke her heart. How anyone could hurt an innocent child was beyond her.

"So." Captain Hendrickson squared his shoulders and focused back on Braden. "What's the verdict, Lieutenant Moyle? Am I loyal to the Deltas or do I have evil intent?"

Everyone focused on Braden. Jessie had gained a lot of compassion and respect for Captain Hendrickson, but she still needed to have her concerns resolved and the SEAL's loyalty affirmed. Or she couldn't explain how the weapon worked and she certainly wouldn't agree to whatever plan these brilliant military men had concocted. No matter how appealing EOD Zander Povey was.

Chapter Five

Zander prayed diligently that his long-time friend Braden would give a good report on Cap and not be offended by Cap's abruptness and issues.

He wasn't as close to the SEAL captain as Cap's own men were, but he'd served enough missions with him to know that he was a loyal patriot, an unselfish leader, and one of the bravest fighters Zander had ever seen. He was the guy who breached the doors that didn't require Zander's explosives. Cap ran toward the fight when bullets were flying and everybody else wasn't sure they wanted to flirt with death that day. Cap never asked for medals or commendations, but he'd acquired plenty of them anyway.

Zander kept finding his gaze drawn to Jessie. It wasn't just how incredibly beautiful she was or how those blue eyes of hers were like twin sapphires glowing appealingly. She was brave as well. She was carrying a heavy burden and she was the youngest member of this impressive family. She'd been hiding the fact that only she could fire the weapon from even her family.

He had wrongly assumed she would let her parents or oldest brother Colt, the impressive doctor, or her warrior sister Maddie, or any of the other imposing Deltas stand up for her. She didn't. She could speak her mind and she could stand up for herself and she wouldn't back down. Even when it was uncomfortable.

"Captain Hendrickson is loyal to the Deltas," Braden said into the silence. "He will do anything he needs to do, including sacrificing his own life, to keep Jessie and the weapon safe. He's a good man with a warrior's heart."

Zander let out a relieved breath. He'd known all of those things were true, but Jessie needed to hear it from his friend Braden and her future brother-in-law.

"Thank you," Cap said.

"Of course." Braden turned to go.

"Try to stare deeply into my eyes again and I'll pile drive you to the ground," Cap threatened in a low growl. Zander could easily read the hint of humor in his voice, but he didn't know if any of these people could.

He scrambled how to tease off the comment, but Braden grinned widely. "Don't worry. I don't like to stare into other dudes' eyes. I'll save the staring for when it's requested of me, like you just did, and I'll focus on staring into my gorgeous fiancée's eyes."

"Good for you," Cap said. Could anybody else hear the longing in his voice or was Zander imagining it? Cap's own fiancée had dumped him. The captain had finally let his guard down after whatever had happened in his childhood, fallen in love, and gotten burned. Zander doubted Cap would let himself trust a woman that deeply again.

"Do you need anything else?" Braden asked. "Maddie was teaching me some wrestling moves."

They all laughed at that.

"Oh, wow." Joseph shook his head. "It's awkward being the father of gorgeous, grown-up daughters with tough men in love with them, especially when they admit to things I never want to hear about my girls."

Braden pumped his eyebrows at Zander and Zander wondered if someday he'd be privileged to say things that would make Joseph feel awkward. He didn't dare look at Jessie at the moment.

"Sorry, future father-in-law. I was serious. She's teaching me some incredible moves. Have you ever heard of the honeymooner?"

"Just get out of here," Joseph groused.

"It's an actual wrestling move," Cap offered.

"Don't defend him."

Braden grinned and saluted all of them, turning and whistling his way out of the house. Zander loved Braden. Not only had the man saved his life in Afghanistan, but he was an easy-going, hard-working, funny, and dependable friend and comrade.

"Okay." Cap settled back on the couch and Zander sat next to him. "Are you ready to answer my question now?"

Jessie suddenly looked nervous. Zander wished he could be sitting next to her, his arm around her, reassuring her that everybody was on her team, but most of all pledge to never leave her side. He snuck a look at her dad's too-serious blue gaze. He hoped they'd go for his idea.

"The answer is yes," Jessie said, then clarified, "Only I can open the inner part of the cave and retrieve or use the weapon. Papa transferred the capabilities to me, neither can or will be transferred again. Retrieving or firing the weapon require voice and thumbprint activation in an exact sequence. I suppose someone could try to force me to do it, but I would die first."

Her parents both looked sickened by that but as if they knew it was true. Zander took it like a hit to the gut. This woman was incredibly brave and impressive.

"I will only fire the weapon when the Holy Spirit prompts me." She met Zander's gaze and said softly, "No matter what."

No matter what. No matter if someone tortured or killed her or threatened those she loved? No matter if he or someone from the family tried to push her to do it early? No matter if Frederick got sick of waiting to obtain the weapon and shot nuclear weapons at America. He didn't particularly like the "no matter what". Actually he didn't like any of this. It was one thing to have assignments this intense and life-threatening in the military. It was quite another to see the beautiful, innocent woman he was interested in have to assume such a burden.

"I thought so." Cap looked at him, obviously grateful that they hadn't been left out of the loop and Jessie was willing to confide in and trust them, even giving them info her own family didn't have.

Luckily, his friend said nothing about her "Holy Spirit" comment. Cap definitely wasn't religious, seemed to dislike heaven almost as much as human touch, but he didn't stop his men from praying or talking about times the Savior had prompted or helped them. Preach had stopped trying to convert Cap years ago.

Zander hadn't known that about the spirit prompting the Secret Keeper to use the weapon, the thumbprint or voice activation. It explained why Admiral Delta hadn't simply used it yet. Whatever the weapon was. Jessie had said she had to kill King Frederick. That would be nice. If she could do it. Why did she doubt herself? That was alarming, especially if nobody else could fire it for her.

"At the risk of asking too much, how does the weapon work?"

Jessie gave him a look as if he was asking too much. She glanced at her parents quickly then said, "I have hair and follicles from King Frederick that Kylee obtained at her grandmother's party. That DNA is used by the weapon to track King Frederick, anywhere he might be in the world. The weapon can fly to him in about twenty minutes if he's in Europe. It will kill him and everyone within twenty feet of him."

Her parents looked to be ingesting the information just like Zander and Cap were. It was impressive technology and exactly what the world needed with a dictator as twisted and evil as any Zander had encountered. He could understand a little better her reluctance to fire the weapon. She not only would kill Frederick but those close to him. An innocent maid or driver? One of Frederick's many women or children? Zander had heard Frederick's wives were given no choice in marrying him.

"Thank you," he said sincerely. Her trust in him and Cap meant a lot.

She nodded. "None of that is common knowledge. I trust my family explicitly but Papa never shared most of what you know with anybody but me. I feel strongly that it's all right to share it in this circle. Please keep it here."

Zander was again impressed by her spiritual insight and her maturity. She had admitted she didn't know if she could fire the weapon last night on the dock, but he thought she was much stronger and braver than she realized.

"We will take it to our graves," Cap said solemnly.

"Thank you for trusting us," Zander said.

She gave him a flicker of a smile then looked to her parents. They both looked concerned and sick at what they're youngest child had to be responsible for.

"What we'd like to propose," Cap continued, "is that Demo—Chief Povey," he clarified, but they probably caught onto the nickname, "who is highly qualified in not just explosives but defensive strategies, combat, and protection. He has been on many teams in the middle east whose only focus was protection of people or goods and weaponry."

Zander didn't know that he was the only one qualified in this valley to protect Jessie, but he was the most willing and hopefully the most dedicated to protecting her. Maybe that wasn't true. Her loving family members would give their all to protect her, but each of her siblings or cousins had a significant other to protect. Her parents and aunt and uncle needed to be coordinating and working with Admiral Delta's contacts to keep the entire valley and the cave safe. The other SEALs and the competent sheriff's men had better not try to volunteer for his mission. Jessie should be his to protect. And his alone. If she'd agree.

"Demo would be assigned as Jessica's personal bodyguard."

Jessie's eyes widened and her breath popped out. "Um ..."

Cap waited, but when her parents didn't protest and Jessie didn't say more, he continued, "Demo would stay by her side during all hours of the day and night. They will have bags packed with weapons, food, camping gear, whatever they need, to go into hiding at the first sign of trouble. Demo would keep her safe until she is 'inspired' to fire the weapon, or the danger in the valley or surrounding the cave has passed and they can return."

Her dad's brow squiggled at that, and Zander was pretty certain they would get shot down immediately.

"From what I understand, there have been several kidnapping situations already with the Deltas. We can all hope nobody will figure out they should go after Jessica, but every other family member has a significant other right there, watching over them night and day. Jessica doesn't."

"I am Jessie's father. I can watch over her," Joseph said.

Zander's hopes dropped.

Holly reached behind Jessie and touched her husband's shoulder. "Hear them out before you shoot them down. The idea has merit. You can't stick to Jessie like glue all hours of the day and take off if needed. You and Keith have assumed Papa's administrative duties, and it is extremely important you keep talking to any allies and keep any would-be enemies at bay that way."

"I understand that," Joseph said. "And though I like and respect Chief Povey, no man needs to be sleeping in the same room as *my* little girl."

"I'm actually grown up now and the protector of the free world, no matter what Thor wants to think," Jessie said in a semi-teasing voice. "So maybe I could be mature enough to handle Chief Povey." She gave him a challenging look. He couldn't resist smiling, both at her teasing but also because he thought she might be interested in the idea and willing to "handle" him. As a protector. He had to keep his focus on being her protector, but if they had enough time alone, would he relax and be able to chat easily with her, or would he flub it up like last night?

"Thank you, Jessie, for your vote of confidence," Zander teased. She could definitely handle him. She could put him in his place and make him long for her to give him any time or attention. He looked at her dad. "If you aren't okay with me staying in her room, I had another idea. Maddie could stay in her room with her, unless she's assigned to guard duty at night, and those nights I could sleep on her floor to assure she's safe. I promise you I would never take liberties where Jessie is concerned, and her safety will be the focus of my every decision and move. I also hope I can assist and comfort her. She has a heavy responsibility and I would be by her side to support her. If she needs that help."

Jessie raised an impertinent eyebrow at him. Heat filled his body. Maybe he shouldn't have gone to comfort. That gave him all kinds of visions of holding her close. Her safety first. That had to be the focus.

What if she was willing to let him comfort and strengthen her? He could only imagine hugging her, and after his protection detail was done, kissing her. He hoped the desires brewing inside him weren't evident to her mom or dad. More importantly, he had to keep those desires in check and keep her safe.

What if it was months or years before the Delta situation resolved? No, that wasn't possible. Too much was brewing, word was spreading, and either Jessie would be forced to use the weapon or Frederick would somehow obtain it and America would be bombed. That couldn't happen. Which made him even more determined to keep Jessie safe. He'd asked for this assignment because he wanted to be near her, but also because he thought it was the most important assignment of the moment. Yes, he was invested and interested. Could he hide the too-interested, too-drawn to her parts from her? Especially if they were side by side all day?

"I'd be okay with that," her dad admitted. He leaned in front of Jessie to meet his wife's gaze. "What do you think, love?"

Holly studied Zander. He kept his gaze steady and unafraid. He'd faced down insurgents who didn't have the death stare down that well. "You'll keep my girl safe in every possible way?"

Zander knew she meant from himself if need be. He was strong and disciplined. He'd made it through BUD/S training before he'd changed focus and decided to become an EOD. After he achieved EOD he'd pushed himself through other ultra-intense advanced courses to reach the status and training he needed to be a master EOD and assigned to the top SEAL, Navy Ranger, and occasionally Delta Force squads in the world. He had this. Hooyah.

He nodded. "I will. I swear it to you."

She paused and then admitted, "I think it's a good idea. Jessie is extremely tough, brave, resilient, and capable, but two working together is always better than one. Everybody needs a wingman. I also worry some mercenary will try to go after her. Even if they don't find out she's Secret Keeper, she's the smallest and the only one without a partner right now."

"Hey," Jessie protested, flexing her arm, the smooth skin

forming a beautiful layer of muscle. His mouth went dry. "I'm more than 'extremely tough.' Papa taught me to be a weapon."

Zander wondered if what she'd said on that dock had only been frustration. Was she afraid to fire the weapon? Was she only acting tough right now?

Her mom half-laughed and hugged her close again. "I know, love, but you're still my girl and I'm going to do all I can to protect you." She looked at Zander. "And right now, the tough guy with the great smile seems like the best route."

Zander smiled. Might as well use it to his advantage. If Jessie's mom liked his smile, was there any chance her daughter did as well? Oh man, it would be hard to keep his focus on protecting her and not falling for her. He had to keep his head on straight, or he might need to rescind his duty before it even began.

"That's the one," her mom said, winking at Jessie.

Jessie's blue gaze was warm on him.

"Okay, knock the smiling crap off or I'll change my mind," Joseph said.

That wiped the smile off his face.

"Oh, goodness, jealous man," Holly said to her husband.

"Love of my life," Joseph said back, "will you help me find the camping gear and pack the bags of food and supplies for Jessie and Zander in case they have to bug out quick?" He stood, turning his attention back to Zander. "We'll show you where they are in the garage once we get them ready and you can add whatever else you might need." He extended his hand to Holly.

"I'm a comin', I'm a comin'." Holly squeezed Jessie one more time and stood.

Zander and Cap both stood as well.

Jessie's mom zeroed in on Zander and said, "Protected in every way. I'm trusting you, Mr. Chief Demo, Special Ops Expert, Master EOD, whatever your fancy title is."

"You can, ma'am." Zander kept the smile off his face. This wasn't a smiling matter, but he appreciated that Holly liked his smile and was so vocal about it.

Did Jessie like his smile? He met her incredible blue eyes and really hoped all of his honed self control was going to stay in place. She was the most intriguing and desirable woman he'd ever been close to.

The only easy day was yesterday.

The SEAL motto rang in his head. He'd made a mess of things with Jessie yesterday on the dock. Today he had to keep himself from hugging or getting too close to her emotionally. It was going to be rough.

Chapter Six

Joseph turned to walk away but Holly apparently had more to say. She pointed at Cap. "And you ..."

"What did I do?" Cap lifted his hands.

"You're doing a great job, and we're so grateful you and your men are here."

"Thank you, Mrs. Delta."

"But this refusal of human touch is pretty much crap and not healthy." Holly stepped across the room and into Cap's space.

Zander's eyes widened, his gut tightened, and he edged closer to the two of them. Cap would never hurt a woman, but he might strong-arm her and shove her away to keep her from hugging him.

"Don't do it," Holly warned him. "Don't think you're going to avoid me."

Jessie stood and smiled. "Just let her hug you, Captain. It'll go much easier for you."

Cap's body was coiled in the fight-or-flight response. Zander had no idea how his friend would respond, but he doubted it would be positive. "Maybe we should give him some time," he said cautiously.

"Oh, good crap, just hug the boy so we can get stuff done," Joseph said. "Flirting with Zander about his smile, wanting to hug the captain. What's next, love?"

She glared at him. "Don't you tease me."

He chuckled easily, his blue gaze warm on his wife. Zander had suspected Joseph was teasing most of the time, but he appreciated the reassurance that he wasn't upset about Zander smiling at his wife or her being intent on hugging Cap. He really liked this family. His gaze strayed to Jessie as it always wanted to. He *really* liked this family. This assignment would be a great one, being close to Jessie, but it would also be tough to keep his focus on her protection and not her appeal.

Holly moved so fast Zander realized he shouldn't have gotten distracted by Jessie. She had her arms wrapped around his friend's lower back and was in his space before Zander could protect her if need be. He was concerned Cap would react instinctively and break her arm.

Cap didn't, luckily. He lifted his arms as if he was walking through a filthy swamp and didn't want to get them dirty, then stood there like a tough gargoyle who'd been turned to stone.

Holly patted him softly on the back and leaned into him. "It's okay. I won't hurt you. You're welcome here and we all appreciate you and care about you."

Cap blinked at her. Had he ever had a mother figure say such words to him? The captain knew he was accepted, looked up to, and probably cared about as his squad was loyal to each other, but not like this. There was nothing like a mom hug, and suddenly Zander missed his mom with a sharp ache. He prayed his parents and brothers and their wives were all doing well. He didn't see them often, but he loved them.

The room was full of anticipation. Everybody seemed to expect Cap to return the hug. Zander wanted to tell them not to hold their breath.

Cap suddenly leaned in and then awkwardly put his arms around Holly's back, clasping his own hands together as if afraid to relax or touch her too much.

"Good job," Holly said, easing in even closer.

As Zander watched in amazement, Holly smiled up at Cap and patted his back. "Good job. I don't want to push you too hard, but we'll try this at least once a day."

"Once a day?" Cap croaked out, concern filling his face and his voice, still pressed against her with his hands clasped together.

"Yep. The world might be ending, but mama hugs are still important medicine. You can try to evade me, but I will find you." She patted him on the cheek like he was a little boy. Cap didn't flinch, which shocked Zander.

Cap looked down at her and he sort of smiled. "I believe you would." He released his clasp around her back and stepped away, clearing his throat and not focusing on anyone. "Thank you for your time, everyone. I think this will be a great solution. Zander is the perfect soldier for this job." He turned and strode out of the house.

"I think that went well," Holly said after the front door shut.

"If you knew Cap ... that was amazing. I was prepared to stop him from breaking your arm or knocking you to the floor."

"He wouldn't dare," Joseph protested.

"Cap would never hurt a woman," Zander explained, "but his natural reaction to touch is not good. You're extremely brave."

"Of course I am. I'm married to this guy." Holly winked at her husband.

Joseph laughed.

She turned and gave Zander a hug, which surprised him. He missed his own mom back in Indiana even more and Holly was right: mama hugs were definitely a necessity. He looked at Jessie over her mom's head. A hug from Jessie would be even better. Would that fit in his protection detail duties, or did he need to keep his hands off? If they were in a safe spot, he supposed he could let his guard down. Would that make it easier to let his guard down when they weren't in a safe spot, or would that make him more invested and an even better protection? He couldn't riddle that one out. Probably smarter to keep an emotional distance, at least. If he could at this point.

Holly released him and patted his cheek. "Keep her safe."

"Always." He nodded.

She leaned in. "And use that smile on her. It's fabulous."

"Mom," Jessie protested.

"Holly," Joseph joined in.

"Okay, okay, we're going." Holly strode to her husband's side, took his hand, and he teased her about flirting with boys as she teased him about being a jealous old man. They headed to the front entry and down to the basement.

Just like that, he was alone with Jessie. His nerves ramped up. He had to calm down. He would be alone with her often now; it was what he wanted, what he'd asked for. Now he had to figure out how to balance his probably obvious feelings for her with staying somewhat aloof and focused on her protection.

"So." She looked at him and then away.

"So." He gave her his smile, hoping it would work some magic.

She laughed. "Is that going to be your solution every time you're uncomfortable?"

"The Joker-worthy smile? For sure." He waited, but she didn't give him any indication that she was faltering under his smile. "Your mom seemed to like it."

"She is *easily* impressed."

He laughed at that. "Well, she impressed me, getting Cap to hug her. I've seen him maim men for less contact than that."

"Was he abused as a child?" Her blue eyes turned somber.

He shrugged. "What he said earlier ... that's the most I've ever heard him admit." He didn't know if he should share about the fiancée dumping his friend. It was probably Cap's story to share.

"That's awful. I hate abuse and hate that he feels he can't confide in anyone."

He nodded.

"Well, um, why don't we line up the food and snacks we want going in those backpacks? If not, my mom will have us eating no sugar, no flour, or something equally disturbing."

She gave a little fake shudder, and he smiled. She was super cute, and sexy, and appealing, and apparently the protector of the free world. And he was her protector. What a stimulating yet difficult job he'd volunteered for.

"Maybe be careful wielding the power of that smile," she teased and smiled back, so he hoped she wasn't serious. He was in a serious profession, but the guys liked to joke and he smiled often. Not smiling at her would be even harder than not saying anything wrong like he had last night and not touching her.

"I'll try."

She turned to the kitchen, but he stopped her with his hand on her arm. She had nicely smooth and toned arms. He liked touching them. A whole lot. And he'd forgotten he shouldn't touch her really quick.

Focus, dude.

She looked down at his hand, then back up at him. "Yes?" The tip of her tongue moistened her lips.

He had no idea what he had been planning to say. He just stared at her, awestruck. There was something huge happening to him, something bigger than risking his career, his reputation, prison, and maybe never seeing his family again to trust Braden and the Deltas and fight for them. He loved the sensation of being close to her and anticipating what she would say or do next. Could he ever have the privilege of kissing those enticing lips? Would that be completely out of line? Cap had given him permission. Cap was the captain, after all. But Joseph and Keith were in charge in this valley. Should he ask her dad for permission to kiss her?

"Are you okay?" she asked him softly.

"I don't know." He released his hold on her and nervously pushed his hand through his hair. He was stirred up and doubting if this protection detail was going to work. "You make me a little ... nervous."

"*I* make *you* nervous?" she asked. "Tough military expert who's traveled the world is intimidated by a speech pathologist?"

"Well, you are the protector of the free world, so there is that." He smiled to ease the tension building inside him.

She returned it, and her beautiful smile didn't calm his nerves. At all.

"Speech pathologist?" he asked. That fit her. "I didn't know that. Impressive."

"Not as impressive as your highly decorated military career."

"It is," he insisted. "Very impressive."

"Thanks."

He nodded and rushed on, "I'm sorry about last night. I was awkward and said ... a lot of things. I just wanted to help. Let you know that we're all there for you."

"So did you mean all the stuff about 'crap happens' and push past the emotional junk and the devil didn't get Papa's soul?" She stared at him, folding her arms across her trim chest.

Dang. Were they going to be back to her yelling at him and storming away?

"I didn't mean to offend or upset you," he tried.

She arched her eyebrows. "But you meant the words. You just didn't want me upset?"

"Well." He pushed a hand at his hair, but then he gestured back to where her mom had that crazy interaction with hugging Cap. "You understand I'm usually talking to people with the emotional capacity of Cap, right?"

"So do I need to remind you regularly that I'm a woman?"

"No." He stared at her. "Nope. I need no reminders that you are a gorgeous, irresistible, and inspiring woman." He was far too aware of all of that and hoped it wouldn't be his downfall.

Her blue eyes darkened to a smolder that made heat pulse

through him. He eased a step closer without realizing he was even moving. "Thank you," she said in a husky voice.

Did she realize how attractive she was to him? The power she had over him? She seemed so innocent.

"I meant emotionally," she said. "Do I need to remind you to be careful with my emotions?"

His hand went to her waist of its own volition. They were in a safe spot right now, but was letting down his guard smart? Emotionally? That wasn't something he worried about often.

She blinked up at him, but thankfully she didn't draw away. A whiff of sweet peaches and cream tantalized his senses. She smelled incredible. He could bet she would taste even better. He gently tugged her closer as he took another step in. Her hands landed on his chest, and he'd never been so grateful for twice-daily workouts as he was when she blushed, gasped, and said, "Oh my. Those pectoral muscles are almost as great as your smile."

He might've been the one blushing now. He bent closer and whispered, "I'll be careful with your emotions, Jess. I've promised to protect you in every single way."

"Jess?"

"Is that okay?" He'd given her a nickname, not a huge one, but she'd noticed.

"I'll think about it."

He smiled.

Her eyelashes fluttered against her cheek as she blinked, and then she focused the full force of the trademark Delta blue eyes on him. He'd noticed the other family members had them, but none were as entrancing as Jess's.

He couldn't resist her. Not right now. Nobody would expect

him to. He circled his arms around her and pulled her in tight to his chest. Her hands wound around his neck and she threaded her fingers into his hair, making good tingles work their way across his scalp and down his body.

"What if you have to protect me from you?" she asked.

Zander was trying to reason out if that was a tease or if he needed to back off and prove he'd keep her safe from him. Prove it to her and to himself. But all he wanted was one sweet kiss. Was that infringing on her safety or not being careful with her emotions? He didn't like that thought, but kissing her if he planned to leave once this mission was done could definitely be toying with emotions. What were his intentions? He was intrigued by and invested in her, but he hardly knew her. He should take a step back and slow down.

But who knew what tomorrow would bring? Frederick might decide to rain down nuclear warfare without obtaining the weapon. He or Jess might be killed defending it. Could he justify that he'd protect her better than ever after one sweet taste of her lips? Just one. The kiss would be a motivator and hone his focus. He leaned closer and pushed any worries far, far away.

Her beautiful blue eyes warmed with anticipation and she arched up toward him.

Footfalls came up the stairs and voices floated to them from the entryway.

Jess jerked away from him and hurried into the kitchen, opening the pantry. "What's your favorite kind of jerky?"

"I've survived on MREs," he said, following her and wondering if his voice sounded shaky to her or just to him. "Any kind of jerky is amazing."

74

She tossed him a grateful smile as her parents entered the kitchen. Was she grateful he hadn't kissed her, grateful for him watching over her, or grateful her parents hadn't caught them?

He didn't know. He spent most of his days with men. He could pretend he was in control with Jess, but what did he know about women's emotions or taking care of them?

He'd been driven to spend more with Jess and he'd give up his M4A1 for a taste of those lips.

He pushed a hand at his hair and tried to respond to her queries and her mom and dad showing him what they'd packed in the two decent-sized backpacks.

Focus. That's what he needed. Focus on protecting her and not on how much he liked her.

Focus might be hard to come by with a beautiful woman like Jess Delta as his assignment. But if he couldn't figure it out, he'd have to let Cap assign Chaos, Preach, or Wolf to protection detail. The thought of his SEAL friends staying close to Jess and touching her like Zander longed to hardened his resolve.

Focus.

Please help me focus, he prayed. Prayer had gotten him through some tough things both safety-wise and when he was discouraged or alone. He hoped heaven could get him through this one. He'd be walking a tightrope with Jess Delta.

She smiled shyly at him. Falling off the tightrope would be worth it to be close to her and make sure nobody hurt her.

Chapter Seven

Jessie stayed busy the next day and a half, and Zander was her constant shadow, or companion; she couldn't decide which. He was great to have around, helpful, had great insight and ideas about Papa's associates as she met with her dad and uncle to work through the emails, texts, and phone calls. They spent time with Thor, Greer, and Alivia going over maps and doing bird's-eye reconnaissance of every section of forest between them and the cave, a couple abandoned cabins they could hide in, where the fresh-water streams were, caves to avoid that housed bears and mountain lions, and on and on.

The full truth about the weapon was kept secret, but Jessie's dad asked if he could reveal that Jessie alone could fire the weapon so everyone would know they had to keep her far from the cave until the right moment. She agreed. None of her family members or the SEALs treated her differently or acted like she couldn't do it, but she got some concerned looks that seemed to back up her own insecurities—would she do it? Would she kill Frederick and whatever innocent or not innocent people were near him? She prayed hard for the inspiration to know when to fire, and the ability to complete the task.

Zander stole her attention quite often, and she didn't mind that at all. He was smart, great to be around, fun to talk to, tease with, and look at.

Unfortunately, he also had impressive self-control. He hadn't touched her since the kitchen, besides incidental brushes or taking her elbow to escort her, and he hadn't gotten anywhere close to kissing her again. She'd been pretty certain he was going to kiss her in her parents' kitchen before they had interrupted.

No matter how she longed for him to hold her and kiss her, it was for the best that he hadn't. When she'd asked if he would protect her from himself, she'd meant breaking her heart, not that she thought he'd do anything untoward.

She appreciated him thinking her career was great, but his accomplishments and achievements were lightyears beyond anything she'd done. She'd heard Braden praising Zander like he was the most impressive soldier in the United States Armed Forces. It should've reassured her that she had the best protection possible. Instead, it highlighted her insecurities. She had Papa Delta's training, but she'd never completed a real-life mission.

Zander didn't seem like was toying with her. The look in his dark eyes felt very sincere and very warm. It simply didn't seem plausible that a relationship would ever work between them. She was rushing ahead worrying about a relationship when they didn't know each other that well and hadn't even kissed, but she couldn't help herself.

A man like Zander would be on his way back to glory, honor, and military service as soon as this mission was accomplished. She could bet on it. Aiden had been very reluctant to commit to Melene because of the failed marriages and relationships he'd seen on his own SEAL team. He'd told Jessie the divorce rate was eighty percent for special ops forces and it had scared him.

It scared her. And she also realized it was ludicrous to even worry about relationships or divorce rates. The world could end tomorrow. One or both of them could be killed. He might not have a career to go back to when everything exploded, unless it was proven that the Deltas had done the right thing in keeping the weapon secured here and using it at their discretion, not the Commander-in-Chief's. It was terrifying to think of the repercussions now that more people were finding out about the weapon and Papa wasn't here to insulate them with his status, reputation, and connections. Zander and his friends could be stripped of everything they'd earned and possibly thrown in prison for directly disobeying orders and blowing up a Blackhawk helicopter. Whatever one of those things cost, it probably wasn't something their commanding officer could excuse without repercussions.

Saturday night, the family members who weren't on duty had gotten together for dinner. She and Zander weren't a couple, but it was easy to pretend they were and it certainly felt that way. He stayed close by her side and he was great to be around. Everybody else in her family had their significant other right there, so it felt like they fit right in.

They hadn't talked more about his callous comments from that night by the lake or how he would keep her and her emotions safe. She got the impression he was trying to focus on protecting her, not falling for her. She wanted to tempt him into falling. It seemed silly to even think about it as there was so much going on and so much demanding their time, but if they were going to die tomorrow, maybe they should forget the future worries, and sneak in some kissing time.

Two separate teams of mercenaries had tried to get around the cave's security earlier today. They'd been distracted by the fog, caught, and were currently in the sheriff's jail cells, but that wasn't a long-term solution. The FBI had been great working with Papa to take the criminals off their hands. Most of them already had a rap sheet internationally. But without Papa here, they hadn't contacted the FBI yet. They could use Papa's recent death to guilt them into working with them, but Papa had been an expert on redirecting or evading questions. Her dad and Uncle Keith both worried about letting something slip. They wanted her to advise them on correspondence because of all the time she'd spent with Papa while he was doing it and the fact that she was the responsible Secret Keeper now. Being worried about when and if to fire the weapon was enough responsibility.

It was chilly and dark outside when she and Zander walked from Papa's house toward her parents'. She wanted to ask him to walk down by the lake or up into the woods, but even with Zander as her constant shadow and armed as he was right now, it was best to stay close to the nucleus of family protecting her. More mercenaries were probably coming and who knew if they'd try to attack the cave, the family, or kidnap somebody else? What if their own military, Frederick's, or some other country launched a full-scale attack? Jessie shivered at the thought.

"Are you cold?" Zander asked.

"No. Just thinking what we'll do if an entire platoon of SEALs shows up."

"You and I will disappear, and I'll keep you safe."

He said the words simply, as if there was no worry, but she wasn't just worried about herself. What if they disappeared and her entire family got killed protecting her and the cave? It was a horrifying thought, and she had to push it away or she'd run to the cave right now and activate the weapon to ensure her family's safety. She couldn't do that or she'd be as self-serving as the people Papa had protected the weapon from all these years. People who thought they would use it for the greater good but ultimately would make the wrong decision because it benefitted them or someone they cared about.

"Is Maddie staying with you tonight?" Zander asked as they approached the back door, pulling her from her stewing.

"Yes. She should be here soon." Jessie wondered what would happen when Maddie had patrol duty at night. It was bound to happen, unless her dad and mom were making sure it didn't so Zander wouldn't have to sleep on her floor. Warmth pulsed through her simply imagining Zander in her room throughout the night. He was an honorable man and wouldn't try anything, but what if he simply held her close for emotional support? Maybe they could share a few long, tantalizing kisses as well. Her face heated.

"Okay. I'll walk you to your door." He opened the back door and gave her that smile of his.

"Your smile is like a weapon, you know," she tried to tease as her knees felt weak and her throat parched.

He chuckled at that, and they walked through the living area.

Her parents were already in bed and Maddie had been saying goodbye to Braden, who was leaving to patrol the cave for the next six hours. Zander had slept in the bedroom next to hers last night. Alivia's old room. It was comforting to have him and Maddie so close and her parents downstairs. She also knew all the cameras and sensors they had set up throughout the valley, mountains, around the cave, and even in the main area of the homes would alert them to trouble. She didn't know how someone would find out she was the Secret Keeper, how that would leak, but the protection was nice and she could sleep soundly.

"I don't mean to use the smile as a weapon," he said. "I just hope it will disarm you and make me irresistible."

They reached the entryway and the stairs. She had visions of him pinning her against the railing and kissing her long and slow.

"Who says you're not irresistible?" she tried to tease, but her voice quavered. Any worry about secrets, Frederick, and the world ending was far away right now as she stared into those deep-brown eyes. They seemed to see into her very soul. She was falling for him. It wasn't smart and the timing was horrible, but who could blame her?

His smile was so big she wanted to take a picture and never forget it or the sparkle in his dark eyes or how he made her feel all lit up inside.

She leaned against the railing and he leaned in, resting his hand on the railing next to her, his eyes darkening and the meaningful and smitten look in those eyes shooting fire through her body. He smelled clean and fresh and irresistible. Was this tough, highly decorated, elite soldier really taken with her? He'd said she made him nervous yesterday afternoon before he almost kissed her, and she loved that she could affect him like that. Unless she had no idea what an interested man looked like, Zander Povey was very, very interested in her.

What about the future and him leaving her?

He edged closer and used his free hand to cup her jaw.

Who cared about the future? He was here now.

"I know it's not smart, but I want to be irresistible to you."

"Why isn't it smart?" she asked, leaning into his palm.

"I'm assigned to protect you. I want to make sure I stay focused and don't risk your safety." His dark eyes seemed to fill with regret, and she was afraid he'd pull away.

"I think you can let your guard down for this moment," she said. "We're surrounded by protection with my family, your SEAL buddies, and the sheriff's department. We have all kinds of sensors set up that will let us know if anyone's approaching. We're safe inside this house." Was she begging him to fall for her, to kiss her? Yes, she was.

He kept his hand on her face, but a battle raged in his dark gaze.

"Unless you aren't interested in me or willing to take a chance on me." She took a deep breath and rushed to say, "Personally, I've never met a man as appealing and impressive as you. I've never been around a man I want to keep spending every minute with."

There. She'd done it. She'd admitted how interested she was, and now it was his turn. She wished she could give him a challenging, sassy look like Maddie would, but she wasn't Maddie, so she simply begged him with her eyes to forget about protecting her, for this moment, and take a chance on loving her.

Zander took a long breath and then admitted in a quiet voice that pulsed through her, "I didn't know it was possible for a frogman to appeal to an incredible, accomplished beauty like the speech pathologist, expert at hand-to-hand combat and weaponry, and protector of the free world Jess Delta." His thumb trailed along her cheek. "I shouldn't admit this, but ... I'd give up every weapon I own if I had a chance with you."

Her body quivered, anticipation of him kissing her and the sweetness of his words making her happier than she could remember being in a long time. She loved his compliments, but she knew how military men ticked. Giving up their weapons was like taking away everything they'd worked for and loved. This ultra-impressive warrior was gone over her.

"That means a lot," she told him.

"I shouldn't have admitted that. I need to be focused on your protection." He was trying to remind himself. He held eye contact, but he backed away.

Jessie wasn't giving up that easily. Her world was falling down around her, she'd lost her Papa, and she had a responsibility on her shoulders that no twenty-three-year-old should ever carry. This man with his strength, experience, and incredible smile was a reprieve, safety, and excitement she hadn't ever planned on. She needed him in her life, not just as her protector but as the man she was falling too quickly for.

She rested her hands on his waist and tugged him closer, hoping she could tease him into kissing her. Would a kiss change everything like she was hoping? Bind them together and make him realize he could protect her and care deeply for her at the same time?

"So if you're a frogman," she started with, "I suppose I must give you a kiss and see if you'll turn into a handsome prince." It was such a silly tease, as there'd never been a more handsome or princely man in her life than Zander Povey.

He grinned, and she held on to him so she wouldn't fall over from the effects of that smile. If they somehow miraculously ended up together, and spent sixty years loving each other, would she ever be immune to the effects of that smile? She hoped not. And she was rushing way ahead of herself.

Despite how deeply she felt about him and the sweet words he'd said to her, they weren't a couple and she worried he'd leave as soon as this assignment was completed. They hadn't even kissed. Though she thought her chances of getting a kiss were looking pretty great at the moment.

"I don't know what your kiss would do to me, but I imagine it would be life-changing." He pressed ever closer to her and her body lit up with heat and anticipation, feelings that were much safer here in the entryway of the house than they would be outside where he'd be looking around to make certain she was safe. "If anybody has the power to turn a lowly frogman into a handsome prince, it would be you, beautiful Jess."

Jessie didn't have any idea how to protect her heart any longer. All day, her previously overwrought emotions had settled with him by her side. He'd silently strengthened her by helping and encouraging her any chance he got. Him shortening her name had made her feel special to him. She'd probably be a mess again at Papa's graveside service tomorrow and even more so when she had to fire that weapon, but at this moment she had Zander on her side and she was in his arms. Nothing else mattered.

She pushed all the worries behind her and arched up closer to him, running her fingers through his hair and loving that he quivered under her touch. This strong, amazing man could be weak for her.

"There's nothing lowly about you, Zander Povey," she said, moving so close that their lips were only a fraction of an inch apart. "And you're already too handsome for your own good, so maybe it's better if I don't kiss you and you stay a frogman." She hoped to tempt and tease him.

He ran his hand along her jaw and into her hair, gently massaging her scalp. It felt incredible and made her tingle with pleasure. No wonder he'd quivered as she did the same.

"Don't leave me as a lowly frogman, beautiful princess. I'll drown without your kiss."

She laughed at his silly words. Was this what love felt like? She'd dated a lot, but she'd never been on fire from simple touches, looks, and smiles. This man had the power to captivate her body and soul. She wanted to commit everything to him. And she hardly knew him.

"I can't let you drown," she said.

He chuckled. Then he said against her lips, every word brushing her lips with his warm, sweet breath, "I pride myself on my patience and self-control. I told myself I wouldn't get close to you until I was done protecting you, but I can't resist you. I have no pride around you. I'm a humble frogman at your mercy, beautiful princess. Can I kiss you, Jess?"

"Yes," she cried out.

He wasted no time covering the negligible distance and capturing her mouth with his. Rapture and light and warmth filled her. She returned the kiss with all the longing and appreciation she had for him. She wanted him in her life, near her side, kissing her every chance they got. Why hadn't they been doing this every spare minute since he arrived last week?

She clung to him, and he wrapped her up tight and lifted her off her feet. The kisses grew in intensity and she wanted to scream that she loved him and she would never let him go, no matter what. But she wasn't screaming right now. She was kissing him until the sun rose tomorrow.

"Whoa!" Maddie's voice came from much too close. "I guess the bodyguard has new duties?"

Jessie did not want to let him go. She refused to. She clung to Zander as he released her from the kiss and slowly lowered her to her feet. He kept her within the circle of his arms as they both looked at Maddie standing in the foyer and staring at the two of them.

"Um, I hate to interrupt this ... beautifully passionate display," Maddie said, but her voice was cool and she obviously thought it was her duty to interrupt, "but Jessie and I need to get some rest. Tomorrow is going to be a very big and busy day."

Jessie adored her sister. She'd looked up to and wanted to be like Maddie for as long as she could remember. But right now, she wanted to punch her. The sisters didn't get in wrestling matches like their crazy boy cousins. Tonight they might. And no matter that Maddie was the experienced warrior and a lethal weapon, Jessie would win.

"I will be up in a minute," Jessie said firmly, giving her sister the stink eye.

Maddie raised her hands and backed up the steps. "Don't let big sis get in the way of your mac-daddying."

"I won't," she shot back at her.

Maddie gave her a look that said she was going to get an ear full. It ticked Jessie off. She was a full-grown woman and could kiss who she wanted. Zander was the most incredible man she'd ever kissed, and it wasn't like Jessie gave Maddie crap about her and Braden kissing all the time.

"Goodnight," Maddie said.

"'Night," they both murmured.

She walked up the stairs. Neither of them said anything until the door shut.

Zander looked down at her, and his grip softened. He gently tucked her hair behind her ear and said, "I'm sorry."

"Why are you sorry? She's the one who's acting like a controlling snot." Jessie tried to talk positive about everyone, especially her family, but Maddie had just treated Jessie like a child and Zander as if he was in the wrong and shouldn't be kissing her.

Zander cleared his throat, released her, and stepped back.

"What are you doing?" she demanded, transferring her anger from her sister to him.

His gaze trailed over her face, and he didn't give her that incredible smile. "She's right. I should never have let my control slip like this. I got caught up in the teasing, how incredible you are, and my out-of-control desire for you, but I'm your bodyguard, Jess. That means I need to keep my head on straight. I have to be focused on any dangers approaching you and how to keep you safe, not on how I can get you alone and kiss you some more." He pushed a hand through his hair.

She glared up at him. "Well, if you're my bodyguard, that means I get to order you around, and I'm ordering you to stop being stupid and on some higher plane and kiss me anytime you want to."

His gaze got intense and warm, and she loved it. He was going to kiss her again, and she could hardly wait. "I would absolutely love to kiss you anytime I wanted." His voice dropped to a husky whisper. "Now that I've had a taste of your lips, I don't know how I'll ever get enough. But that would mean all we did all day, every day, was kiss each other."

Heat filled her, and she eased closer again. "Now that's a plan we can live with."

He shook his head and let out a low groan that seemed to rip through her. "Jess ..."

She loved that he called her Jess and not Jessie like everyone else. It felt like he saw her as an adult, not a little girl. An equal. A woman he could fall in love with. Zander was down-to-earth, fun, and she was comfortable around him, but he still seemed like a superhero warrior to her. She was fascinated by him and already falling for him.

He moved in quickly, framed her face with his hands, and rested his forehead against hers. Her breath came in quick pants. She moistened her lips and his gaze sharpened on her as his strong body overshadowed hers.

"I care about you far too much, Jess," he said in a low rumble that she felt as much as heard.

"I care about you, too."

"We have to slow this down," he said, regret lacing his voice. His thumbs gently caressed her cheeks, and she prayed he'd reconsider.

"Why?"

"This isn't just about you and me right now. Your safety has to be the focus. I won't be able to protect you if I'm distracted by all the desires to kiss and hold you, flirt with you, and stare into your beautiful blue eyes for hours on end."

He was staring into her eyes and touching her so tenderly, and she loved it. Would he really make himself stop? His self-control was a million times stronger than hers.

"From what you explained being Secret Keeper involves a lot of prayer and specific insight. You need to focus on that and I need to focus on my job of protecting you."

She hated his words, but she hated even more that he was right. She didn't want to admit to it or even think about pulling away.

"Once this is all over, maybe we'll have a chance—"

She jerked away from his touch and straightened. He straightened as well, looking down at her with concern in his dark eyes.

"Don't patronize me, Zander."

"What do you mean?"

"We both know once this is over, you'll be back on some mission saving a democracy or taking out a dictator. You won't settle down in Colorado and date a speech pathologist." She stared at him, willing him to tell her she was wrong.

He didn't. His jaw worked and he pushed his hand through his hair, but he said nothing.

She nodded, despair coursing through her. "Lie to yourself and say that you need to focus on protecting me and I need to focus on the being Keeper and that's why we can't grow closer. But don't lie to me and claim you're going to stick around, because we both know you won't." She stepped up closer to him, but she didn't touch him. "My Papa's funeral is tomorrow. He's one of the best men I've ever known. He spent the past thirty years protecting this secret weapon, ready at any time to use it but luckily never having to. But he always, always put his family first. If you can't put me first, fine, but own up to it and please don't claim we can have a future later. With King Frederick still alive, moments like tonight might be the only future we have."

She pushed past him and raced up the stairs before he could stop her. As she got to the top, she realized he hadn't even tried. She looked back down from the second-story balcony. Zander stared up at her. He looked desperately sad, but he wasn't willing to do anything about it. He would protect her, but he wouldn't love her. He wouldn't chase after her.

His loss.

And sadly, hers too.

Her parents' bedroom door opened and her dad hurried out. Jessie could see him and Zander from the balcony. Zander turned to face him.

"Jessie?" her dad demanded.

"Up here," Jessie said as Zander pointed up. She met Zander's gaze, longing and regret mixed in his dark eyes.

"Jessie, you've got to see this," her dad urged.

She hurried back down the stairs. Her dad held up an iPad. A paused video filled the screen. She recognized the swarthy face, dark beard and eyes of King Frederick. Her stomach churned.

"What?" she asked.

"Let me show you first," he said.

Zander eased in close to her and her dad as her dad pushed

play. She could feel Zander's strong presence reassuring her, but his delicious scent made her want to kiss him all over again.

As soon as the vile Frederick started talking, all other concerns were pushed away. "Greetings, Delta family." His smile was sickening and patronizing. "I've tried to be patient and wait for someone to succeed and bring me the famed Delta weapon, but I'm through waiting. As a demonstration of my power, a small island country will be annihilated by a nuclear weapon in twenty-six hours. I liked the idea of death at midnight. Twenty-six hours from now will be midnight on mountain standard time. Isn't that your time zone?" He smiled again as if he were giving them some gift. "No, there is nothing you can do to prevent this. It is retribution for keeping the weapon from me for too long."

Jessie's heart raced out of control. Some island country would be decimated tomorrow night and there was nothing they could do? She met Zander's gaze and she could see exactly what he was thinking. There was something she could do. She could go fire the weapon and stop this now.

But Papa had been adamant that she could only fire it when she felt inspired from above.

Please inspire me, Father, she begged.

Would she do it? Would she kill Frederick and those closest to him to protect an entire country? Her stomach churned and her pulse raced. She had to. There was no choice of if she could or would.

"After those innocent lives are obliterated, I feel you'll be ready to bring the weapon to me. If you don't, I'll keep taking out increasingly larger countries, one each day, until you're prepared to be reasonable. Don't worry. I have a large supply of nuclear warheads. I won't run out before you give up the weapon. *Auf wiederershen.*"

The video paused on his ugly face.

Jessie leaned against Zander. He wrapped his arm around her waist and held her up. She was trembling and sweating.

"He'll really ..." She couldn't even put voice to it. How many more would die before that monster was stopped? She had the power to stop him. Her reluctance to kill could not factor into the equation any longer.

Her dad's gaze went from her to Zander and back again. He didn't comment on her leaning into Zander instead of him. His jaw was tight and his blue eyes flickered to the screen in his hands before focusing on her again. "He will kill those people, Jessie. Unless ..."

He didn't have to say it. Unless she was inspired to engage the weapon. She could envision herself going through the correct motions, just as Papa had taught her. She could do it. She had to do it.

She searched in her heart, begged heaven silently. Nothing. She shook her head slowly.

He nodded his understanding, though he obviously had wanted a better answer. Zander said nothing, but his silent support meant a lot.

"We've got until tomorrow evening. I'm going to meet with Keith and we'll get Admiral Seamons and some other contacts we trust on the phone. Maybe this will be the push we need for the military to send in elite special ops."

He studied them. Zander still had his arm around her. Jessie knew normally her dad would hug her to comfort her, but he only said to Zander, "You've got her?"

"Yes, sir," Zander said.

"Try to rest, love," he said to Jessie. "Tomorrow is going to be rough. It will all work out ... somehow." He hurried back to his bedroom.

Tomorrow would be rough. That was an understatement. They were burying Papa, and if she didn't get the impression to fire the weapon or some elite team didn't get the go-ahead and complete the mission, King Frederick would kill innocent people.

Zander turned her to him and simply held her. Jessie leaned into him. She was too stressed to even cry.

"What do you need, Jess?" he whispered in her ear.

She needed inspiration from above, the assurance she could fire the weapon when she needed, and ... him.

"Just hold me," she begged.

"I can do that."

He held her close, and his strength was the only thing keeping her from falling apart.

If she didn't fire the weapon soon, King Frederick would nuke an entire country. They didn't even know which one to warn them.

Chapter Eight

Zander spent a miserable night trying to rest but thinking about Jess in his arms nonstop but Frederick's nuclear threat lingered as well. He knew he should've stayed in control of himself. He should never have kissed her. Now those earth-shattering kisses were all he could think about and all he wanted to spend his time and energy on.

With King Frederick promising to nuke a small island country, Zander needed to be even more focused on protecting Jess and not distracting her from the inspiration she needed to fire that weapon. The elite special ops teams going after Frederick would be a great option. If they could find him and contain the threat before he fired that nuclear warhead.

Despite the dire situation of the nuclear threat and Frederick, he couldn't stop thinking about Jess. Not as the Secret Keeper, but as the woman he wanted to be with. He'd hated the sadness in her eyes as she said that he could lie to himself but asked him not to lie to her. He wasn't trying to lie to her. Maybe they could have a future, if Frederick was ever taken care of, even though it would be difficult and would require sacrifice on both their parts.

Did she think the only way they could have a future was if he gave up his career? Did she expect him to not go back to being an EOD? Did she have any idea how many different specialty trainings he'd gone through? How many missions he'd accomplished? How many times he'd made a mission successful? How many times he'd risked his life? Being an EOD and working with these elite SEAL teams was what he was made for.

Or was it? What if he had been trained and worked so hard throughout his career so he could be prepared to protect Jess and help the Delta family save the world? What if he'd been created ultimately to find her and this valley, to love the unreal and irresistible Jessica Delta?

He should be more upset with himself for letting his self-control go and kissing her, especially now that King Frederick's direct threat hung over their heads, but he couldn't dredge that up. Not when he'd loved every minute of their interactions and was struggling not to go experience it all over again. Her firm body pressed against him. Her looking at him with those blue eyes. Her teasing and flirting with him about becoming her handsome prince. Her delicious lips lighting up his world.

He groaned and rolled over in bed again, praying for strength and for some of his control to reappear. He knew he had to be strong right now and focus on keeping her safe. He couldn't worry about the future because, like she said, they might not have one.

His assignment was to be Jess's bodyguard, not her kissing

partner. Dang, that sucked, but he had to focus from here on out. Frederick was pushing the conflict into overdrive, and Jess would be at the center of it. This was no time to let down his guard. He'd be by her side to protect her. He'd keep her safe and she would hopefully soon be ready to fire the weapon. Love and soft kisses couldn't be on the mission docket right now.

Help me be strong, he prayed again.

The sky finally lightened.

Jess and Maddie were both a little standoffish with him and with each other at breakfast. He wondered if they'd fought last night or if Jess was just mad at anybody saying they shouldn't be together. He loved that fire in her. A fire for him. He could match and surpass that fire. Someday.

You can lie to yourself ... but don't lie to me.

All the conflict boiling within him was threatening to burst out. He wanted to throw back his chair, rush around the table, drop to his knees, and declare his devotion to her. Not as the Secret Keeper. As the man who loved Jess Delta.

And he shouldn't even be thinking about that with King Frederick ready to kill thousands of innocent people.

He pushed at his hair. It was all a mess. He was a mess.

He met her dad's gaze over his veggie and bacon omelet and could imagine her father would agree that he should keep his lips off her until everything was settled. If her dad had anything to say about it, he'd probably want Zander's lips off her permanently. Jess was the type of angelic perfection whose family, and especially her dad, would think no one was good enough for. They were right. Zander wanted to prove he could be. That meant shelving the kissing desire. Did Joseph know he'd kissed her? His neck heated, and he took a long drink of orange juice.

Joseph and Holly finished their breakfast quickly and headed out. Joseph was going to meet with Keith and Cap and see what Admiral Seamons and their other contacts had to say about taking out Frederick. He'd asked quietly before breakfast if Jess had felt any impressions yet. She'd only shaken her head no. It was a disappointment, to be sure. Was there a point where Frederick killing an entire island nation took precedence over spiritual insight on when to fire the weapon?

Zander didn't want to second guess Jess or her spiritual intuitiveness. The clock was ticking, though, and the threat was ugly.

He forced his focus back to what was happening right now. Holly was going to deal with final touches for the church service and the graveside service immediately following. The pastor who'd married Hudson and Kelsey had agreed to come up and do a service for the family a little after eleven, then the graveside service about noon, and then they'd have lunch at one.

The family usually went down to church service at ten at Summit Valley, but they wanted everyone to stay close today. Zander hadn't been to church in a while. Once they'd gotten here, they couldn't reveal they were alive by showing up at church. He was often on assignments that had him working on Sundays as if it was any other day of the week. He didn't like it, but there was no way to change it.

Unless he gave it all up to never leave Jess again.

Stop, please, he begged his own mind.

Zander was a soldier. It had always been his dream and his purpose in life. He couldn't be getting distracted and let down his focus and guard on the most important mission of his life for a simple kiss.

But that had *not* been a simple kiss. Jess Delta could easily become his world.

He, Maddie, and Jess cleaned up breakfast together, none of them saying much. As they finished loading the dishwasher, Jess put the soap in and started it as Maddie wiped down the counter. Zander stacked the rest of the leftovers in the fridge, then turned back to stare at Jess as she straightened. Simply looking at her made him light up inside. No woman stirred and drew him in like she did. No woman inspired him like she did. He wanted to be there for her and lift her.

Maddie tossed the rag into the sink and faced both of them. "Look," she said. "I'm sorry that I embarrassed and berated you two, but what is happening right now is much bigger than all of us. You know that, right?"

Jess just glared at her. "If I told you to stay away from Braden, would you think that was reasonable because 'this is bigger than all of us'?"

"I would," she came right back with. "If I was the Secret Keeper and it was Braden's job to keep me safe, I personally would want his head on straight to do that. King Frederick is going to kill innocent people if you don't fire that weapon when you're inspired to. Is anything more important at this moment than you being safe, protecting those people, and ending Frederick's reign of terror?"

"No." Jess shook her head. "You're right." She gnawed at her lip. "But what if I don't get my answer and Frederick kills them and keeps on killing?"

Jess was focused on the inspiration to fire the weapon. As she should be.

"You will," Maddie reassured. "You'll know."

"I don't know anything right now," Jess burst out with. Zander thought she was referring to firing the weapon, but she could be referring to their relationship as well. Jess looked at him, and the despair in her blue eyes ripped at his heart. "I'm a complete mess."

Jess brushed past him, hurried from the room and up the stairs, slamming a door.

Maddie looked at Zander. "I am sorry," she said, and though she was feisty as a rule, it looked like she meant it.

"Me too," he admitted. "But you're right." He nodded, strengthening his own resolve. He had to protect Jess and strengthen her to know that she would get that inspiration and she'd fire the weapon at the right time. "I will focus on her protection. She means the world to me, and even though the world doesn't know it, she has the key to protect everyone."

Maddie nodded. "So you agree this is bigger than all of us? Bigger than your desire for my adorable and sweet sister?"

"I do." If only it didn't hurt so much.

"Thank you." Maddie gave him a watery smile. "She means the world to all of us and Braden promises me you'll protect her with your expert skills and your life, if necessary."

"I will."

She looked him over, and then she abruptly turned and walked through the living room and out the back door.

Zander didn't like that the sisters were fighting on this important day. Because of him. Admiral Delta's graveside service should take precedence for the family. He and the SEALs would protect them while they grieved. Frederick's horrific threat hung over the valley like a black cloud. He hoped the Delta family could focus on their beloved Papa and their grief. They deserved at least a brief reprieve from the heavy burden they all carried.

Zander went up to the room he was staying in. Each of the SEALs had a duffel bag with them when they came to the valley, but he didn't have any church clothes in it, so he simply used the other bathroom upstairs to wash his face, brush his teeth, and try to style his wavy hair. Then he dressed in a black T-shirt and black pants, strapping on his hip holster and his Sauer P226 and ensuring his knives and utility tools were in his pockets. He worried somebody would try to attack at the graveside and wanted to strap on some heavy weaponry, but his place was next to Jess right now and he didn't want to detract from the service. Cap and the other SEALs would monitor the valley and the entire Sheriff's department was up monitoring the cave. Kelsey's mom Lori had been trained on the cameras and sensors in Admiral Delta's basement. She would monitor them and keep Granny Klein with her during the church service and graveside service. Everything would be fine, until Frederick attacked that island tonight, but Zander was still itching to pick up an A.R.

He left his bedroom and paced in front of the bathroom that Jess had sequestered herself in. It was ten-fifty and they should probably get going before somebody came for them.

The bathroom door clicked and his anticipation immediately amped up. He wondered how he was going to keep his distance when the mere thought of seeing her affected him more than kissing other women had done.

Jess pulled the door open and walked out of the bathroom. She stopped and stared at him, her mouth slightly open as if he looked good to her. That was a laugh compared to how she looked to him.

She was absolutely gorgeous in a black fitted dress that showed off her perfect curves. Her dark hair was curled down her back, her makeup done to perfection, highlighting those gorgeous blue eyes and those lips ... oh man, he couldn't let himself look at her lips.

He pushed his hand through his hair, messing up the attempt he'd made at styling it.

"Oh, Jess," he said in a far too husky and telling voice. "You are the most beautiful woman I've ever seen."

Her eyes lit up. She looked him over and said, "You're pretty handsome, for a frogman."

He smiled at that, and she bit at her lip. Dang, that wasn't good; it drew his attention there. Sadly, he was still a frogman, not her handsome prince. That was good. Focus on being a frogman. Focus on being a soldier. Focus on being her protector.

His gaze traveled over her face again. What would she do if he pinned her against the wall and kissed her until somebody came to separate them?

Please somebody help me focus, he begged heaven. He was sure the good Lord and all His angels were trying, but he had to put forth a little effort himself.

He pushed out a breath, ran his fingers through his hair again, and then managed, "We'd better go before Maddie comes for us."

She lifted her eyebrows, her mouth drawing into a pretty bow of disdain. "My bossy sis. I have to love her, or I'll get kicked out of the family."

He laughed at that. "I doubt you're at any risk of getting booted."

She smiled, and it made him so happy. He eased in closer without realizing he was doing it.

"Jess," he groaned, longing and desire battling with his need to keep his distance and keep his head.

She blinked up at him, so beautiful, so appealing. He shouldn't kiss her, he definitely shouldn't let himself lose control like that right now, but couldn't he hold her like he had last night after they'd seen that horrific video? She would bury her grandfather today and she could probably use the comfort a hug could give. He'd heard Holly had tracked Cap down yesterday afternoon and given him a hug. It had made him smile, but right now, he wasn't smiling. He was longing to touch his Jess.

A door opened downstairs and they both startled. Footsteps moved through the main level.

Jess gave him a smile that wasn't convincing at all. It looked longing and sad.

He stepped back and she walked in front of him to the stairs. He followed, focused on protecting her.

Protection. Jess safe. The Delta weapon. Secret Keeper. Stopping Frederick.

He repeated those words like a mantra as he trailed behind Jess, greeted her brother Colton downstairs, and walked across the lawn on a bright, chilly late-September morning to the church service being held in the pavilion.

He stayed by her side and tried to pretend everything was okay and he wasn't a stirred-up mess inside. Jess was his focus and his mission. It was easy to focus on her, but focusing on any threat coming her way was a little tougher as that meant he had to look away often from her gorgeous, captivating face and body in that fitted black dress.

She shivered and he instinctively wanted to wrap her up tight. Just to keep her warm. He held his ground. Barely.

Pastor Sam talked about the Savior living, atoning for our sins, giving His life on the cross, and then picking it back up for each one of them. He promised that because the Savior lived, Papa Delta would rise again as well.

It was a beautiful sermon. Zander was proud of himself for registering any of the words. Jess's arm brushed against his and he was lost for a few delicious seconds.

The church service was almost over and they were singing Amazing Grace when every Delta family member's phone lit up. Joseph grabbed his phone and stood, striding away from the gathering. Keith rushed after him.

Zander saw the Navy SEAL team converging on them.

The other Deltas pulled their phones out but stayed seated. Pastor Sam looked confused but he kept singing. A few others sang as well, but most dropped off. Jess held her phone where Zander could see.

Unidentified Lexus ES coming up canyon.

He leaned in closer and whispered, "Let's make our way to your parents' house, just in case."

It was only a single car and might be some friend of the family intent on disregarding the request to let the family have a private service today, but he wasn't taking any chances. Not with Frederick escalating everything last night and the unsettled feelings churning in his gut.

Jess should change out of her beautiful dress and heels into something she could move easily in and stay warm in. He should grab some extra weapons and the backpacks prepared for them to hide out as long as they needed. He'd added some C4 and detonators to his backpack last night. He wasn't sure what he'd need them for but he wanted to be prepared for anything.

She nodded, and they both stood.

The song stopped abruptly as Joseph and Keith strode back to the gathering. The SEALs spread out again and clutched their A.R.s.

"Forgive us, Pastor Sam," Joseph said easily, but his mouth was tight and his blue eyes worried. "Can you say a quick benediction and then Bailey will escort you to Papa's house and your ride will get ready to take you to the grave? We'll be ready for the graveside service in a few minutes. We just have an unexpected guest coming to say hello." His gaze traveled around the group. Everyone knew their assignments. 'Unexpected guest' meant it wasn't a vehicle from town.

"Um, sure." Pastor Sam probably had a lot of questions tracing through his mind. "Would you like to ... sit for the prayer?"

Keith shook his head and reiterated, "Brief, please."

"Oh." The pastor bowed his head and said a very brief prayer for peace to be on the family and Papa's memory to live on in them.

The amen had barely been pronounced when the Delta family members scattered. Zander took Jess's arm and they speed-walked across the grass. He heard some running footsteps and then motors starting. Some of the family would go intercept the uninvited guest and some would take up defensive positions, while others would probably head for the cave to reinforce the Sheriff's men.

Jess's heels sank in the grass with each step, slowing them down. He wanted to sweep her into his arms and run. Would that be out of line? No. It would keep her safe.

"Jess." Zander tugged her to a stop, then bent down and plucked her off the ground and easily secured her alluring, perfect, irresistible body against his chest and in his arms. The breath whooshed out of him.

Protection. Jess safe. The Delta weapon. Secret Keeper. Stopping Frederick.

He tried to repeat his mantra, but he was far too distracted right now.

She clung to him, her blue eyes lighting up with a desire that he felt reflected inside him.

"Demo, go!" Aiden commanded from behind him.

The barking command was exactly what he needed. He took off at a fast jog, eating up the distance to her parents' house.

They reached the back door and he forced himself to set her on her feet, release her, and yank open the door. She hurried inside. He glanced over his shoulder and could see across the distance the silver Lexus with trucks and SUVs blocking its way into the valley. Who was it? What did this mean for them? It was only a single vehicle, but no matter how small or big the threat, he wasn't taking chances with Jess.

He had to focus on his mission. Protect Jess. It disturbed him that he'd lost concentration so easily. Picking her up had to be off the docket.

Jess hurried through the main area ahead of him. Zander shut the door and took off after her. He would strap on a couple of A.R.s, in case Jess needed one too at some point, and a weapon belt, then he'd grab the backpacks. The backpacks had handguns and extra bullets, plus his explosives.

His walkie-talkie buzzed as he reached the top landing. He could hear Jess's phone ring as well. He pushed the button. "Povey."

"Keith is asking that you and Jess come to the graveside service not to arouse suspicion," Cap said.

"Who's here?" he demanded.

"Admiral Seamons."

Zander's gut turned over. Admiral Seamons. One of Davidson Delta's close friends, their top ally right now, and a two-star Admiral based out of Great Lakes Naval Station. The threat dissipated. But what was he doing here? He was Kylee's grandfather and his wife had hosted King Frederick in their home. He'd taken two bullets, one to protect Kylee and one to protect Braden and Maddie, and he'd given them the zip drive. That screamed loyalty, but there were red flags with him showing up right now. It felt like a premonition of bad things coming their way. It would be interesting to see how he reacted to the elite SEAL team who'd been proclaimed MIA after their Blackhawk "crashed" in a meadow up by the cave being alive, heavily armed, and patrolling the valley.

Zander looked through his open bedroom door and out the window that overlooked the lake and forest beyond. He searched the sky, but it was bright blue and clear. No Blackhawks descending. Yet.

"He's alone," Cap's voice said on the radio.

That made no sense. No bodyguard? Seamons was a target just like the rest of them.

"Out," Cap added.

Zander pocketed the walkie talkie and waited outside Jess's closed bedroom door. He could hear her talking. She sounded upset.

"Papa trusted him," she insisted.

A pause.

"Braden promises he's good."

Another pause.

"Okay. I'll meet you at the graveside."

There was silence. He rested his shoulder against the wall and waited impatiently. Was Jess okay? It was a stressful emotional roller coaster. From the abrupt instructions to get out of here to everyone asking them to stay. He agreed it would be suspicious if Jess wasn't at the graveside service. But if he felt one premonition of danger from Admiral Seamons, or if the sensors or cameras were tripped again with anyone else approaching, he would take Jess and they would disappear. Even if he had to carry her and somehow keep a clear head.

His mind wandered briefly to holding her in his arms last night. The intensity of her kiss. The love he felt for her.

Love? Was he seriously thinking that word?

Her door opened and just like earlier today, he lost every sane thought and could only focus on the woman standing there. Love? Heck yeah, he could love her for the rest of his days and never complain.

Luckily for her own protection, her eyes were clear and

focused. She didn't appear to be wandering back to sweet kisses like he was struggling with. "You heard it was Seamons?"

"Yeah. They want us to stay and not arouse suspicion."

She nodded.

"But Jess ... if anybody else comes, we're gone."

"Okay." She straightened her shoulders and looked as brave, classy, and strong as any woman he'd ever seen.

"You trust Admiral Seamons?" he asked, referring to her phone conversation that he'd overheard.

"I do," she said. "What do you think of him?"

"I've only rarely interacted with him over the years, but I've always been impressed with him. Braden trusts him and for me, that's enough."

"Papa trusted him, and for me, that's enough."

"All right. Let's head back out, then."

She strode past him. He wished they could be alone and talk more, but there were too many pressing issues at the moment. He hoped those who trusted Admiral Seamons, including him and Jess, were correct. He hoped Frederick could be stopped before he set off a nuclear weapon at midnight tonight. He hoped he could keep Jess safe.

Protection. Jess safe. The Delta weapon. Secret Keeper. Stopping Frederick.

That was what mattered right now. But the whiff of sweet peaches and cream that he got as he followed Jess and held the exterior door for her, and the beautiful smile she gave him before they walked out, were powerful. This woman could easily distract him and have every power over him. If she was safe and the world wasn't in mortal peril, he'd be happy to give her that power and be distracted by her every moment of the day.

Right now, it was time for the most important mission of his life.

Protection. Jess safe. The Delta weapon. Secret Keeper. Stopping Frederick.

Hooyah.

Chapter Nine

Jessie attempted to climb into the back of Greer's Razor as Zander held the door for her. It was more than a little awkward in the fitted dress and three-inch heels. It might be impossible without ripping her dress.

Zander pushed his hip against the door, swept her off her feet, and lifted her into the seat. Luckily he didn't pull her tight against his chest like he had earlier today, robbing her of all conscious thought and filling her with a sweet ache that only he could satiate.

Their gazes met and got tangled and she willed him to lean down and just give her one soft kiss. There was so much pressure, angst, and sadness surrounding her. She wanted to escape into his arms for a minute and forget it all. His dark gaze was full of the longing and conflict she felt tugging at her insides.

Is this what forbidden love felt like? That seemed far too dramatic, but Jessie's entire life was far too dramatic at the moment. The only thing that felt safe, real, solid, and at the same time deliciously enticing, was Zander.

"Ready?" Greer asked from the driver's seat. Emery was already strapped into the five-point harness.

"Yep." Zander released her, shut the door, and hurried around to climb in.

She fumbled to secure the too-tight seatbelt that went over her chest and lap. It seemed overkill anyway. They were just going around the lake and up into the meadow where Granny was buried, not on some fun off-road adventure. Fun wasn't part of life right now. Except for when Zander teased with her or touched her. No mountain bike ride, ski slope, or Razor off-roading adventure could compare to that high.

Zander climbed in and then his hands were suddenly on hers. She caught her breath. He wasn't looking at her, which helped her not throw good sense into the forest and kiss him. As he loosened the straps and then secured them over her shoulders and buckled the upper straps into the lower at her waist, his fingers brushed against her several times. Despite the thickness of her black velvet dress, she could feel his touch and got warm all over.

Greer started the engine and moved into the line of the funeral procession. Everyone was either in side-by-sides like the Razor or on dirt bikes. Hudson, Kelsey, and Mo were all on Papa's Honda 450 CR dirt bike. It was adorable with Mo sitting in front of Hudson and Kelsey hugging Hudson from the back. Papa's casket was at the front in a cool glass-covered trailer attached to the back of Uncle Keith's silver and white Can-Am Maverick. Her parents were in the backseat. That sight wasn't happy like Hudson's little family.

Jessie drew in a breath and could finally shift her focus from her too-prevalent thoughts of Zander and her worries over the weapon and Frederick's evil threats to her Papa.

It stunk that everything was in such upheaval they hadn't really mourned Papa. She felt a sting of guilt that she'd been so obsessed with Zander. She hadn't focused on her Papa, his life and legacy and all the wonderful memories and love she had for him. The weight of the world had settled on her shoulders in the past week since he'd died. Papa had shouldered it for decades, all the while worrying about his growing family and how to teach and protect each of them.

No one spoke as they motored with the funeral procession along the east bank of the lake and then up a mountain trail.

She knew two of the SEALs were staying in the valley to patrol, but the other two were at the back of the line in Thor's new two-person Yamaha Wolverine. A wedding present for himself, he'd joked.

The beauty of the thick forest was lost on her. Some of the leaves had fallen, but there was still a lot of red, orange, and yellow amongst the green of the pines.

They reached the clearing and everyone slowly found a place to park and disembarked. Greer and Zander both hurried around, opened their doors, and lifted Emery and Jessie out of the vehicle. These vehicles were not built for formalwear. Jessie did all she could not to get distracted by Zander's warm, strong touch or his clean, masculine scent.

He looked down at her, and she was amazed by him. He was the perfect hero in her mind. Gently setting her feet on the ground, he kept one arm around her and escorted her over the uneven forest floor toward the gravesite. She appreciated his strength and support and did all she could to not get lost in his touch and shock the entire family, and tick off Maddie again, by turning into him and kissing him.

They approached the site and then Zander released her. She tottered on her heels but steadied herself. He stood respectfully by her side.

She looked over the headstone Papa had made when Granny passed. It was a beautiful gray marble that sparkled in the dappled sunlight coming through the trees. It had both of their names on it, Granny's on her side, Rachel Bradford Delta, and Papa's on his side, Admiral Davidson Delta. Birth dates and death dates and their wedding date.

Papa's death date wasn't burned in professionally like the rest of the dates. Someone had come up here and chiseled it in by hand. Jessie wondered who. She loved it. It was raw and imperfect and spoke of deep love and devotion.

Granny's burial spot was covered with thick, wild grass. Papa's yawned wide open. That hurt. She wasn't ready to have her Papa settled into the dirt. But he was gone, and there was nothing she could do about it.

Jessie looked around at her family, so many people she loved and who loved her back. She was thankful for them, even more so now that Papa was gone. Any of these people could be gone tomorrow, especially with the danger surrounding their family right now.

Pastor Sam walked up next to the grave as her dad, Uncle Keith, Colt, and her male cousins easily lifted the casket and carried it over to the stand next to the grave. Today's service would be simple. They all hoped that when they did the public memorial service, they could have the honors of a fly-by the military had offered and the presenting of the flag to her dad and Uncle Keith, but for today Aiden would perform the three-volley salute and it was enough that the family was all here.

Admiral Seamons stood by Kylee and Chandler. He was in his black Admiral uniform with his right arm in a sling and crutches resting against the tree behind him. He'd gone through a lot lately.

He noticed her and gave her a very solemn look and a nod. It was right that he was here, even if it had caused some stress. If Papa trusted him and Braden trusted him and it looked like Kylee had reconciled with him, Jessie would trust him and be grateful he was here for them at such a time.

None of the family or SEALs would reveal she was Secret Keeper. Even though she trusted the Admiral, she'd keep her distance while he was here to avoid something slipping out in any conversation with her family or him.

"Joseph and Keith have requested that the casket be opened so you can each say your final goodbyes," Pastor Sam began. "Then I will close the casket and Joseph will say a prayer on behalf of the family, after which I will say a few words. Holly and Myrna will sing *The Wind Beneath my Wings*, and Keith will then dedicate the grave."

He stepped over and lifted the front of the casket's lid. Jessie felt ... unsteady. She hadn't seen Papa since he'd passed that awful morning. She knew the body had been prepared and the casket had waited at Uncle Keith and Aunt Myrna's. She imagined most of her family members had gone to have a private moment, but she hadn't. She could justify that she'd been busy, but truthfully, she hadn't been ready.

Other members of the family approached the casket, said their quiet goodbyes, and moved over for someone else. The only one she saw who didn't walk away with tears streaming down their face was Greer. She smiled at that. Greer was so tough he'd probably never cried in his life.

It was solemn in the clearing. Only the twittering of birds, shuffling footsteps, and sniffles broke the silence. She realized that almost everyone had said their goodbyes. Zander moved closer and touched her elbow. "Jess? Do you want me to come with you?"

She looked up at him, his blue gaze full of concern for her, and nodded her acceptance and appreciation of his offer.

He wrapped his arm around her waist and slowly escorted her across the small clearing. He released her as she hugged her uncle and aunt, then her mom and dad. Then her dad kept his arm around her and directed her toward the casket.

Her breath caught as she stared down at Papa. He looked good, but weird. Not himself yet exactly like himself. His skin was taut and his eyes closed, his hands resting over his abdomen. He was in his dress whites, medals decorating the chest of his uniform, crisp and clean and regal and so Papa.

Jessie stared at him. Tears wet her cheeks, and she bit at her lip to stay in control. What was there to say? How could she say goodbye to the man who'd loved, protected, and taught her all her life? She'd always appreciated and looked up to him, but now more than ever she knew what he'd gone through for all of them and to protect a weapon he'd agreed to protect with his life. Like her, he hadn't asked for it.

"I love you, Papa," she managed to get out. Her dad hugged her tighter, but she focused on her grandfather's beloved face. "Thank you. Thank you for teaching me, seeing the best in me, challenging me, loving me..." A sob wrenched out of her throat and she could say no more.

Her dad turned her into him and held her. She clung to him, wet his suit coat with tears, and wondered how she'd get through this pain.

A warmth washed over her. Her dad's hug, or her Papa watching over her like he'd promised, or the love of all her family members being around her and praying for her and lifting her? It was probably a combination of all of the above.

She lifted her head and gave her dad a kiss on the cheek.

"Love you, my girl," he said.

"I love you."

She pulled back and let her gaze sweep around the family. So many blue eyes, and a few brown and green. All loving her, supporting her, looking to her.

The first shall be the last and the last shall be the first.

The scripture that Colt had quoted when the family had found out she was Secret Keeper came so clearly to her mind that she startled, but then she focused on Zander. His deep-brown eyes told her she had this and he would stand by her side. She could lead the family, even though she was the least of them.

Power surged through her. Power from on high. Soon she'd have the impression to fire the weapon. She'd been afraid, uncertain if she could kill Frederick and others, but she knew now that Papa was right. Better to kill Frederick than to let thousands or possibly millions of innocent people be murdered. She didn't want to kill, but she could. She was strong enough. She was brave enough. She had Zander to protect, lift, and comfort her. She had her family all praying for her, fighting for her, and watching her back.

A warm wind swept through the trees, and it seemed to propel her back to Zander. He reached out his hand and she clasped hers in it. The strength of his hand and the warmth of his palm against hers gave her support and steadied her.

They slowly walked back to their spot as her uncle, aunt, dad, and mom each said their goodbyes. The pastor solemnly closed the casket and her dad gave a touching and simple prayer, a prayer of gratitude and love for Papa, for their Savior, and for this family.

The amens rang throughout the clearing.

Jessie prayed no one would dare interrupt this sacred moment.

Her mom and Aunt Myrna stepped forward and sang the haunting but beautiful *Wind Beneath my Wings*. Tears traced down their beautiful faces, and they wrapped an arm around each other's backs as if to steady and support, but Jessie saw it also as a unity. Her mom and aunt were incredible women. They hadn't known what they were getting into when they married a handsome Delta man, but they'd risen to the occasion and could fight alongside their men and had raised their children to be tough, righteous, hard-working, and filled with faith and love. Papa had adored his daughters-in-law and treated them as his own. And they were. These women were Deltas.

Jessie looked around at the group. All the in-laws and future in-laws were Deltas all the way through. They'd each added strength, variety, and love to the family and the Protection Detail.

They'd each give anything and everything to protect her, the weapon, and the family.

Zander squeezed her hand, and she couldn't resist looking at his handsome face. He and the SEAL team had sacrificed deeply to support their family. Could he be a Delta? Her cheeks heated, and she looked away.

The song finished with the touching, "Thank God for you, the wind beneath my wings."

There wasn't a dry cheek amongst the Deltas. Jessie even caught Greer knocking his fists against the corner of his eyes.

It was a fitting song. Papa had been the wind beneath their wings, and now he would be from the other side. With Zander close and Papa lifting her, Jessie would do whatever needed to be done. A soft and warm wind passed over the group.

The pastor's words were filled with faith and hope. Jessie would need a lot of both to get through whatever was coming. She both dreaded and welcomed it. She was ready to be in the fight, sweating and working hard and focused on winning. Not a win for herself but for all mankind.

Uncle Keith said a benediction and then Aiden shot off the three-volley salute with Papa's favorite Winchester 1895. She clung to Zander's hand, and a current went through her. She looked over at him. He was staring steadily at her as if she'd made the warm current happen and he'd felt it as well.

"You okay?" he mouthed.

She could only shrug. Was she okay? Not really. But at least she didn't want to run screaming and hide under her bed. She was strong. Strong enough to stop Frederick and do what needed to be done.

Zander had his hand covering hers. Her family had her back. Papa was watching from heaven. She would stop Frederick from killing those people.

Now she just needed that inspiration from heaven that it was time to head for the cave. Papa had been adamant she couldn't fire the weapon until she felt it.

Please help me feel it soon.

She couldn't let those people die.

Chapter Ten

Zander had felt something spark between him and Jess at the end of the funeral service. It had traced through their hands. He'd mouthed if she was okay and she'd only shrugged, but there was something different in her eyes. He'd seen it in the eyes of soldiers going into battle. Soldiers who were prepared and determined. They would succeed or die trying. It scared him to see that in Jess's blue gaze. Was the battle coming? What if she was killed? He would not allow that to happen. The only way Jess was dying was a nuclear explosion or some other bomb that took them both out, or if there was no breath left in his body to fight. He tightened his resolve and his grip on her hand. He wanted to love her, but he would protect her and see her through this first.

Protection. Jess safe. The Delta weapon. Secret Keeper. Stopping Frederick.

They solemnly left the gravesite and rode back to the valley. He was relieved nothing had happened and nobody had tried to attack during the service. The Delta family deserved at least that much of a reprieve. Actually, they deserved much more. This family should be given the Navy Cross, if not the Medal of Honor. Selfless service with no thought of reward was deeply embedded in each of them.

He glanced over at Jess as they walked hand in hand to the lunch at Papa's house. She'd wrenched his heart and impressed him at the graveside service. She was a strong woman. He didn't think she even knew how strong. He planned to protect, help, and support her, but he knew she could and would accomplish whatever was required of her, with or without him.

The lunch after the service was delicious, and the family seemed to relax and resorted to some of their former humor and jokes. Thor and Aiden kept everyone laughing, reciting Papa's favorite jokes and taking shots at each other. Admiral Seamons seemed comfortable with the family, happy to be close to Kylee and Chandler, and everyone appeared to welcome him.

The dinner was over and everyone pitched in to clean up when Admiral Seamons approached Jess and Zander, lumbering forward on his crutches.

"Jessie," he said, steadying himself on one crutch and opening his other arm to her.

Jess gave him a quick hug, then stepped back to Zander. Zander automatically put his arm around her, hoping to support her or give her whatever else she needed.

The admiral was generally serious, but he gave Jess a smile like a loving uncle. "Davidson was always so proud of you."

"Thank you." She tilted her chin up. "I was proud of him, too."

"As you should be. One of the best men I've ever known." He looked properly solemn.

There was a pause and then Seamons leaned in a little closer. "If you need anything, Jessie, anything, I'm here to help."

She studied him.

"I have the connections and the power to protect the weapon, stop King Frederick, and whatever else the Delta family needs."

"I'm sure my dad and Uncle Keith will be happy to have the support," she said smoothly.

Zander tensed. His neck prickled. Her words were spot on. Why was the admiral offering help to Jess, the youngest in the family? Did he somehow know she was Secret Keeper? Would Chandler or Kylee have entrusted him with that secret? They all claimed to trust Admiral Seamons, but everyone was so protective of Jess he didn't know that even the Sheriff's men, who had been admirably committed to the protection detail and the family, knew Jess was the Secret Keeper.

"Of course. I've already told them the same, and most of your siblings and cousins. I just wanted to make sure you knew as well." It was a good cover. Was it a cover? Zander was being overly protective of Jess, and Frederick's ticking time bomb was hanging over their heads, so everything and everyone outside the immediate trusted circle raised suspicion for him.

"Thank you, Admiral. It means a lot that you're here."

"There's nowhere else in the world I'd want to be." His dark eyes looked sincere, but Zander had some concerns.

"Who knows you're here?" Zander heard himself demand.

Admiral Seamons finally looked at him. "Chief Petty Officer Zander Povey, Master EOD." He listed out Zander's full title like a proud uncle. "It's wonderful to see you alive, son. You and your SEAL team accomplices have caused quite a stir."

Zander studied him, weighing his words before responding, "As you can see, sir, Admiral Delta's mission and his family's protection is where our allegiance lies."

Seamons looked from Jessie to him and arched an eyebrow. "I *can* see that."

He was obviously thinking Zander was overstepping bounds. Zander didn't need his approval, and he wanted to make sure the man knew, "And we would all prefer we stayed dead for the time being."

He offered a partial smile. "I can imagine. Your secret's safe with me, son."

"Thank you." Zander bobbed his head. He should probably salute, but it didn't seem like Seamons cared.

"And to answer your question, no one knows I'm here, Chief Povey. I've got a friend masquerading as me at the Chicago Retreat Center. All that stress surrounding my wife's betrayal and arrest and being shot twice finally got to me." He winked and stood tall despite the crutches.

Zander had to admit ... he was impressed. And he prayed, like everyone else, that Seamons was on their side. The man had taken two bullets to prove it. "Thank you, sir," he said, and he did salute.

"None of that, son. We're all friends here."

"Thank you, Admiral," Jess said, and it sounded like she trusted Seamons fully as well.

"Excuse me," he said, lumbering over to talk to Braden and Maddie.

Braden's face lit up as his admiral approached. It was another vote for Seamons in Zander's mind. He'd never known Braden to be wrong about a person's true intentions.

He looked at Jess.

"We're trusting the admiral," she said firmly.

"I'm with you."

"That's what I need." She smiled at him and he wanted to be all she needed. Her beautiful face looked drained and her eyes were red-rimmed.

"Did you sleep last night?" he asked, checking to see if this was emotional exhaustion or more.

"Not really." She grimaced. "You try sleeping with a nuclear threat hanging over you, in a bed with your sister who's mad at you, and after an unreal kiss that you'll *never* get out of your head."

His stomach swirled with heat at the mention of their kiss. Someday. Oh, how he hoped someday.

"Let's go back to your house. You need to take a nap."

"Really? You're commanding me around now, Mr. Bodyguard?"

He smiled, liking her sass coming out. "Yes, I am. I have to protect you from everything and everyone, including lack of sleep." He didn't add that she needed peace and quiet to feel the promptings of the spirit telling her to head to the cave. It had to be soon. It just had to. Zander had dedicated his life to fighting for and protecting the innocent. He couldn't handle the thought of Frederick blowing up an entire nation island.

"I need to help clean up," she said.

"Really?" He gestured around at the family who was making short work of any leftovers, dishes, and already had the temporary tables and plastic chairs cleared out of the large living room. "Let's go."

He didn't give her a chance to protest. He took her hand and she let him lead her through the living room and toward the front entry.

Her mom stood in the entry talking quietly with Emery and Greer. "There's my beauty," she said when she saw Jess, and enfolded her daughter in her arms. "How are you holding up, love?"

"I'm okay. How are you, beautiful Mama?"

Her mom shrugged, lowered her voice, and asked, "Is it time?"

Jess shook her head. Zander felt the disappointment that was reflected in her mom's face. If she didn't feel the prompting soon, they'd need to at least head closer to the cave so when she felt it they could move quick and stop all of those people being killed.

Zander released her hand and turned to Emery and Greer as Jess and her mom quietly conversed.

Greer offered his hand, and Zander shook it. "Thanks," he grunted out.

"For?" Zander cocked his head to the side, appraising the large cowboy. He had to be over six-five and he was fit. Zander could hold his own with any man, but this guy might be a challenge.

Greer's wife, Emery, laughed. "He's the strong, silent type. He's thanking you for giving up your life, your family, and all your hard-earned military advancements to be here for all of us, and especially for Jessie. We honor, admire, respect, exalt, commend, applaud, praise, and revere you for your service to the Deltas, your country, and the Navy, Chief Petty Officer Povey."

"Thank you," he said, humbled by her quick speech. What was with all the synonyms?

"All of that," Greer said, grinning down at his wife as if she were the most perfect human on the planet.

Zander couldn't help but smile at the two of them. "You really don't like to talk?" he asked Greer, intrigued by the cowboy and his adorable wife. He'd heard they had quite the story of him killing her only brother to protect Alivia and Klein and then somehow falling in love when Emery came to avenge her brother's death.

"Nope," Greer said.

Emery cuddled into his side and he wrapped her up tight. She was tiny compared to him. They looked great together. He found himself wondering how he and Jess looked together. Then remembered he shouldn't be thinking about that right now.

"It all works out perfectly," Emery said. "Because I can talk the hind leg off a mule, plus I'm an expert on the English language and know more synonyms than anyone you've ever met. In addition I like, love, revere, respect, and adore this tough, silent, perfect cowboy of mine."

Greer leaned down to kiss her and Zander thought he should probably give them some space. He edged closer to Jess.

Her mom released her as soon as she noticed Zander. "Oh, come on, handsome, give me that smile of yours. I could use one about now."

Zander smiled, and he hoped he made it a good one.

Holly grinned back and then tears formed in her eyes and she hugged him fiercely around the middle. Zander patted her on the back, hoping she was okay. This was a rough day for a family this committed to each other and to a higher cause. Losing their patriarch and the awful threat from Frederick. Everybody had to step up and lead out, yet somehow stay unified and not mess up anybody's else role. They worked well together, but he knew the challenges were only going to get more fierce. In the heat of battle, could they all stay true to their purpose and not let the enemy through when they loved each other so much they might get distracted by that? There was the reason, once again, he needed to be in control of himself around Jess. But this family would probably astonish him in battle because they were selflessly fighting for each other and for their country. It was something to think about.

"Take care of her," she whispered into his neck, her voice filled with emotion.

"I will." He looked down at her mom. "I promise you, Mama Delta. I will give my life for her. Nothing will happen to Jess unless my body is scattered in pieces across the valley."

Her eyes widened and he heard Jess say, "That was a little extreme."

He looked over at her, hoping she could read his sincerity. "And it's true."

Jess's blue eyes were solemn. He wasn't sure if she appreciated his declaration, if it worried her, or if she was going to tell him off and kiss him soon. The latter sounded great.

Her mom hugged him tighter, and he returned it. Then she released him and wiped at her eyes.

"We're going to rest," Jess told her. "Pray for me to know."

"All of us will," her mom assured them. She started crying again. Zander had no idea how hard it would be to let your innocent daughter have this kind of responsibility thrust upon her.

Holly Delta was tough, but this had to be overwhelming. She shooed them with her hands as she seemed unable to talk anymore.

Zander waved to Greer and Emery, who were thankfully done kissing, and then put his hand on Jess's back and escorted her out the tall front door.

They walked quietly across the porch and along the sidewalk that connected Papa's house with Joseph and Holly's. It was probably much easier walking for Jessie with her heels on the concrete, but it didn't give him any opportunity to pick her up and carry her. Oh, wait. He wasn't supposed to do that any longer, so the sidewalk was a good thing. Not very fun though.

"Wait up, Jess, Demo," Aiden's voice carried from Papa's house.

They both spun and watched as the tough SEAL ran to them. Zander liked that Aiden had adopted his nickname. His blue eyes were ultra-serious right now. He got in close, real close, and stared at Jess.

"I just got word from my CO and Seamons has confirmed it ... SEAL Team 6 and Delta Force were deployed to find Frederick and his top leaders after Admiral Seamons was able to pull some string and the President watched the video threat from Frederick."

Zander's eyes widened. That was fabulous news. SEAL Team 6 and Delta Force were unarguably the most elite, well-trained, and battle-tested warriors on earth. He'd worked with both teams and had been blown away by their precision, skill, focus, and trust in each other. Finally, the President had decided to take action. What a relief.

He looked at Jess. Her blue eyes lit up and he could see the burden being lifted. She threw her arms around her cousin's neck. "Aiden, that's absolutely wonderful! How long do you think until we know he's been apprehended and won't kill all the people on that island?"

Aiden didn't return her happiness or her smile. He gently pulled her back and focused in on her. "Jessie. It's not good news. SEAL Team 6 reports that they cannot find Frederick or his leaders anywhere they are supposed to be. Falsified information and reports from what should be secure sources."

Zander's stomach took a nosedive and Jess's beautiful mouth turned down.

"Even worse, they fear Delta Force is lost. They haven't reported in since early this morning. Hopefully just ... out of service or needing radio silence ..." He shrugged, obviously fearing the worst.

The hit of disappointment made Zander's gut churn and his body feel weak. He saw worse reflected in Jess's blue eyes. If Frederick was taken out, they could hopefully root out the traitors and not have his mercenaries or their own military after the weapon. The Deltas could be safe, and Zander and Jess could have a chance to be together.

"I'm sorry, Jessie." Aiden gave her a quick hug. "Dad thought you needed to know ... Jessie, we can consider other alternatives. There's still time—"

"No, there isn't," Jess cut him off, standing tall even though Zander and Aiden both towered over her. "I will be inspired when to fire the weapon, Zander will be by my side to help me all he can, and Frederick will be stopped."

Aiden's blue eyes filled with respect and hope. "Then you've felt ..." Aiden wanted her to go fire the weapon right now. Zander could relate. It was almost a two-hour ride on dirt bikes or in a side-by-side to the cave. Well before nine p.m., they would have to head that direction and pray that the inspiration came to her. Those people couldn't die when Jess could stop them. Heaven wouldn't let that happen. Right?

"Not yet." She shook her head. "Pray for me."

"Always."

Aiden's blue eyes were disappointed but still determined. He nodded to them and then turned and jogged back to Papa's.

They stood there for a few seconds. "You okay?" Zander asked.

"I doubt I'll sleep, but I need to change and maybe just lay down and pray and think for a bit," she said, forcing a small smile.

He nodded. "Anything you need, Jess ... I'm here."

Their gazes met and got tangled. She didn't say anything, but he could see the instant her thoughts turned from worrying about when to fire the weapon and the weight of the world and protection of some unknown island on her shoulders to a deep desire to be in his arms and kiss him and forget this nightmare for a few wonderful minutes.

His stomach flip-flopped and his chest grew warm. He wanted her kiss and the connection with her with a burning need, but they had to get through tonight first. He needed to get her inside and lying down, and he needed to do some meditation or something. Where was Preach? Zander could beg him to give him a sermon about self-control, higher purposes, and trusting in heaven's timing.

Zander took her elbow and escorted her up the stairs and across the porch. She didn't say anything.

Entering her parents' house, they walked through the foyer and up the grand staircase. He stopped outside her bedroom door. "Why don't you change, then I'll come watch over you." He hated to have her take off that soft, fitted black dress, but she needed to be comfortable and they both needed to be prepared. Even if she didn't get the prompting, they needed to be close to the cave well before midnight.

Her eyebrows rose. "You're going to watch me ... sleep?"

"It worked for Edward and Bella."

"Excuse me?" Her brow wrinkled. "Did you just reference *Twilight*?"

"Well, it was a very desolate base. And there was only one book anywhere in camp." He should've been embarrassed to admit he'd read that, but it had been a fun distraction and he could admit anything to her. Anything but how much he wanted to hold and kiss her right now.

She laughed. It was great to hear her laugh. "My tough military stud. Reading *Twilight*. When I tell Cap ..."

"Oh, no!" He laughed but a dart of concern raced through him. "If you tell Cap, I'll ..." He couldn't think of a threat. He never wanted to threaten her, but he had to follow through with the tease, and he really didn't want Cap knowing he'd read that. "I'll dunk you in that ice cold lake."

"You're coming in with me," she teased.

"That actually sounds kind of fun."

She shivered, still grinning, but then her blue eyes deepened. "So now you're going to just ... watch me rest?"

"Oh yeah." He was embarrassed by how husky his voice got. "I can't imagine anything I'd like better." He'd like kissing her better, but that had to wait. Right? The second he was alone with her and she focused those blue eyes on him, all his lofty ideals slipped quick.

He'd always been black and white—do things right and stay loyal and true no matter what. He supposed kissing the irresistible Jess didn't constitute as a moral failure, but he wanted to stay in control and keep her safe, no matter how it strained him.

"It was awkward reading about Edward watching Bella sleep." She winked. "Let's not go there. Maybe you should lay down and rest too."

"I don't know about that." Lying down anywhere close to her would not let him rest for a second.

"Did you sleep last night?" She folded her arms across her chest and gave him an impertinent look.

"Not really," he admitted. He shouldn't have done it, but he stepped closer and trailed his fingers along her smooth neck, brushing her long hair back. She trembled under his touch and gazed up at him. "I was too stirred up thinking about a kiss with the most incredible woman I've ever met."

The warmth and appeal in her blue eyes about took his legs out from under him. He stayed steady and luckily didn't fall to his knees and beg for her to have mercy on his heart. But he did find himself bending down low and softly kissing the thrumming pulse point in her neck.

She moaned, wrapped her arms around his neck, and tilted her head, giving him access to that smooth, lovely neck and all the way up to her face. Self-control? He didn't need to be in control every minute. They were safe here, all the Deltas watching over them, as well as his favorite SEAL team, and sensors and cameras placed all over the valley and in the main areas of each home.

What did it matter if he kissed his way up her neck, across her jawline, her cheek, and then captured those perfect lips with his? Who needed rest? Kissing her would energize him and make him even more committed to her safety. They could kiss the hours away until someone interrupted them, she said it was time to head to the cave, nine o'clock came, the Delta alarm engaged on her phone, or Cap screeched through his walkie-talkie at him.

He slowly kissed her neck, trailing his way up inch by inch, wrapping his hands around her lower back and pulling her body flush to his. She moaned again, threaded her fingers into his hair and massaged his scalp. Tingles pulsed through his head and Jess was the only person who existed in his world. He knew he was lost and in deep, deep trouble. He'd never felt this way. It was incredible, exhilarating, mind-blowing.

He reached her jawline and then her cheek. He edged his way toward her lips, anticipation and hunger filling him. Just a brief sample of her lips and he'd let her rest. Only a taste.

Right before their lips connected, he raised his eyes to hers. What he saw there hit him like a Halligan bar breaching a door. Complete and utter trust. The purest trust he'd ever seen in his life. Jess trusted him to protect her, love her, do the right thing for her and for the rest of the world.

He felt weak, weaker than he ever had in his life. Kissing her might not be wrong, but it could *not* consume him right now. If he let this go any longer, he'd be consumed and might damage her trust.

He wanted to fully earn the trust that she already seemed to have in him, and he had to keep his own promises to stay strong and protect her. If he kissed her right now with all the passion coursing through him, he might take things too far, ruin her beautiful innocence and trust in him, and he'd never forgive himself.

Straightening, he had to slowly release each finger from his grip on her. She swayed on her heels and suddenly looked confused, lost, and much younger than she ever had. She was so innocent and good. He had to be careful not to lose his head around her. Especially because she needed heaven's inspiration so desperately right now. Maddie was sadly right. This was so much bigger than his selfish need to kiss Jess and grow closer to his dream woman.

He gave her a smile that he didn't feel at all and said softly, "Go change, Jess. You need to rest."

She swallowed, and he barely held himself back from kissing that enticing neck again. Had anything been so hard as this? He'd go through BUD/S training again rather than keep denying himself meeting her lips.

"What just happened, Zander?"

He drew in a breath. He could try to play it off as she was tired, he was tired, but she trusted him and he wanted to be straight with her. She'd told him not to lie to her.

"You are so incredibly appealing to me," he said in a gravelly voice that hurt his throat. "If I kiss you right now, I don't know how I'll ever stop." He looked her over and the blood started roaring in his ears again. Never stopping sounded just about right.

"You have to focus on my protection, not on me." Her voice was sad and hurt him almost as much as pulling away had.

"Yes, but I also have to keep you pure and show my respect and devotion to you. I can't do anything that would damage your ability to know when to fire the weapon or your trust in me."

As he said the words, he felt strengthened. He could do this. It would be torture, but he could keep her safe and stay strong. Heaven above would help him.

She studied him and then she nodded. Turning, she walked toward the closet.

He hurried to step back and shut the door, leaning against the wall and trying not to listen to her changing her clothes. He clenched his fists and prayed for help.

Her soft foot treads approached the door, and she opened it. She looked just as appealing in a fitted, long-sleeved running shirt and pants as she had in that incredible dress.

"Come on in and ... watch me, Edward. I won't make you use the window."

Zander's breath rushed out. He wanted to do a lot more than watch her. "I like scaling walls," he teased, grinning and winking at her, hoping his unsteady voice didn't betray him.

She half-laughed and then lifted her hands as if in surrender. "I wish you'd rest too, but I don't think I can bend your will on that any more than I can force you to kiss me again."

His eyes widened. Did she have to go there? He'd been doing ... well, not good, but semi-okay being strong. "Don't try to push a frogman around, ma'am. It will end badly for you."

"My frogman won't be pushed, no matter how badly his princess wants to keep kissing him and turn him into her prince." She fluttered her eyelashes, and he knew she was only teasing, but every time she brought up kissing, his stomach heated and his entire body tightened in response.

"Princes are overrated." He pumped his eyebrows cockily. "A frogman can protect you much better."

"Maybe this princess can protect herself and only wants her prince to stand by her side."

"I'm sure the princess could protect herself. But she might realize that a frogman standing next to her could be the support she needs."

"You're probably right." She smiled sadly at him. Turning, she sauntered to the bed, beguiling him with every step she took. She lay down on top of the covers, closing her eyes and stretching her arms above her head and moving her beautiful body around on the bed as if she didn't even know he was there.

Zander groaned audibly. She opened her eyes and gave him a flirtatious smile.

"Sorry. I didn't want to make it easy on you to resist me. 'The only easy day was yesterday.' Right?"

He almost smiled at her quoting a SEAL mantra, but he was too stirred up inside. The quote was actually perfect. Yesterday had been easy compared to today. Yesterday, he'd let down his guard and kissed her. That memory filled him with heat. He wanted to create that memory again.

Stepping into the room, he shut the door behind him and then leaned against the wall. He didn't need sleep. He didn't need to kiss her. He was just fine.

"Go to sleep, Jess. I'm watching over you."

"I'm counting on it, frogman."

Him *watching* her or him watching *over* her? She was innocent and beautiful and had no idea how tempting she was to him. He ached to show her through some delicious kisses, but knew it was wrong on so many levels to even think about devouring her mouth right now.

Protection. Jess safe. The Delta weapon. Secret Keeper. Stopping Frederick.

He had to be strong until the threat was over. He'd been strong a lot longer than that on many missions. But he'd never had to be strong around the likes of Jess Delta.

Chapter Eleven

Jessie was feeling regret for stretching out on the bed and trying to tempt Zander to come hold her and kiss her. She knew it was wrong to try to seduce a handsome man, and she knew she needed the spirit more than ever right now. She'd done it partially to tease him, but also because she was reeling from him pulling away from their almost-kiss. She'd been melting in his arms as he trailed his lips closer to hers, making her skin tingle in the wake of his lips.

How could he stop himself that close to a kiss they both knew would be insanely wonderful? She knew Zander was impressively strong physically, but she'd never met anyone with that kind of iron self control. Or maybe she wasn't as tempting to him as he was to her.

All kinds of ideas swirled through her head about how to entice him. Then she thought of everything riding on her shoulders right now. She sighed and forced herself to say a prayer.

Forgive me for my wayward thoughts. Help me to be strong like

Zander. Help me to respect him and to know what he needs, not be consumed with what I want. Help me to be in touch and inspired to know when to go for the weapon.

It had to be tonight. She couldn't stand the thought of those people dying.

She kept her eyes closed as she finished the prayer, and peace and warmth enveloped her. It had been an exhausting few days. Her Father above would forgive her for being too invested and passionate for Zander and He'd help her just as He always had. Papa was watching over her as well. She knew it as surely as she knew she was lying in this bed.

She didn't know if she could sleep, but resting would help settle her down and clear her mind. Zander was wise and focused on her and what she needed. She wanted him to stand by her side, be her frogman and her prince, but she also wanted to help and lift him in return.

Opening her eyes, she looked at him leaning against the wall. His eyes had been closed when she'd closed hers, but now they were wide open and focused intently on her. She loved his deep-brown eyes. She loved him. Remorse sprang up inside her again at trying to tease or force him into kissing her.

"I'm sorry," she said. Earlier she'd apologized, but she'd been taunting him, trying to get him to bend to her will and come to her.

"It's okay." He nodded to her. "You don't have to make it easy on me, but resisting kissing you is complete torture."

Her breath shortened. She never wanted to torture him, but him admitting to the same feeling made her appreciate and love him all the more.

"I don't have to make it hard on you, either. You're as tired as I am," she said softly. She picked up the alarm clock on the nightstand and set it for seven. That would give them plenty of time to get to the cave. "Please come lie down."

His gaze instantly got wary, and he shook his head.

"I'll turn away and put a pillow between us if you need. But we're safe here and have lots of eyes and elite fighters watching over us. If I don't feel the impression before nine, we'll need to head to the cave so we're close, and pray I feel it before midnight." She bit at her lip. She couldn't let those people down. If only Delta Force or SEAL Team 6 would find Frederick. Aiden hadn't been very hopeful.

He nodded. "That's exactly what I've been thinking."

"I've set the alarm for seven. We can rest for a couple of hours and then get ready. You have to be ready to protect me. Despite my teasing, I need you and I want you ... protecting me." She added the last part, but she needed and wanted him for a whole lot more than that.

Heat flared in his gaze, but he schooled it.

"Please come rest."

He drew in a breath and then he finally nodded. He walked over to the bed, staring down at her. Her pulse sped up, despite her trying to remind herself she wouldn't make a move on him.

"You said you'd roll over and put a pillow between us," he reminded her.

"Oh, goodness, I did." She wanted him to hold her close, despite how un-smart that was. She'd lost her Papa and was facing the biggest challenge of her life. Was it too much to ask for him to simply hold her like he had last night after they'd seen that awful video? Maybe. Him holding her while they were lying in this bed would be playing with fire for sure.

She lifted one of the long decorative pillows to the middle of the bed, gave him one more perusal to remember how handsome he was, as if she'd forget that, and then she rolled over and faced the wall.

She could hear his breath coming in quicker pants and then his weight lowered onto the bed, shifting the mattress. Her heart raced at that simple move.

"Just for the record," he said, his voice rough and unsteady. "This was not my idea."

"The princess forced the tough frogman to do what she wanted?" she asked, smiling and wishing she could roll over and look at him.

"Exactly. The princess is so irresistible, the frogman has no idea how to say no to her."

That got her to roll over. He was right there, facing her, with only the decorative pillow between them.

"Please don't," he begged.

She rolled back over, wanting to honor him and not make this harder than it already was. There was silence between them and despite how tired she'd been earlier, she had no idea how she would fall asleep with him right there, within reach, and all the tension swirling around in this room.

Long minutes ticked by with neither of them saying anything or so much as moving a pinky finger. Neither of them seemed able to regulate their breathing, either.

"This won't work," he said, finally breaking the silence. "I'll never fall asleep like this."

"You said the frogman can't say no to the princess." She bit at her lip, praying he'd just give a little.

"It's a serious character flaw he has."

She wanted to roll over so badly, but feared he'd jump off the bed if she did. "I think it's a beautiful facet of his personality."

"You would."

She laughed.

Silence fell again. She was amazed none of her family had come back to the house yet. It was barely four in the afternoon, too late for a nap, but they both knew what was coming tonight. She was now fully committed to kill Frederick and protect those people and knew it would take all of her physical and emotional strength. She was grateful for this time alone with Zander. If only she could have him just a little closer.

"Zander?"

"Jess?"

She smiled. "First of all, I love that you call me Jess."

"Nobody else does?"

"Nope. Only you, Zander." She waited, feeling so connected to him. "Do you know what your name means?"

"Defender of man," he answered quickly.

She liked that. His name fit him. "Or in this case, defender of woman."

"The best assignment ever."

Her chest filled with warmth. "I'm your best assignment?"

"Definitely."

"Even if I tempt and tease you?"

He chuckled. "I've already admitted it's torture to not kiss you or hold you close, but I shouldn't admit that I love that you tempt and tease me."

"Oh, good, because I love doing it."

"Can you please wait until my protection detail is finished before torturing me again? That stretching on the bed thing. Whew." He blew out a breath.

Jessie was so gone over him. She wanted to stretch out on the bed and see that look in his eyes again.

"Don't," he warned, as if knowing exactly what she was thinking about.

"Just close your eyes," she teased.

"I should ... but I won't."

Jessie didn't move, but it was fun teasing him. "I'd say I'm sorry."

"But you're not."

"Not really."

He chuckled and then he said in a fierce tone that pierced her to the core, "You are exactly the woman I've hoped to find all my life."

As soon as the words were out, the room seemed to freeze. Or maybe not, because it was very warm. Incredibly warm.

"You are exactly the man I hoped to find all my life too," she admitted.

They were both back to breathing much too fast. She could hardly believe she affected a man like Zander. A couple of weeks ago, he'd seemed like an unapproachable superhero—too tough, far too impressive and accomplished, and definitely out of her reach, but somehow he'd fallen for her just as she'd fallen for him.

If they could only get through this nightmare by firing the

Delta weapon tonight and stopping Frederick. She didn't want to stress about a future that might never happen, but she wanted Zander in it.

"What does your name mean?" he asked.

She didn't love the change of subject, but it was probably necessary. "God beholds, or to see before," she told him.

"I like that."

"Thanks. Hopefully I can see, or know, and fire that weapon before Frederick fires his nuke at that island."

"You will."

She appreciated the reassurance but hadn't felt the prompting yet.

A few beats passed and she shouldn't have, but she asked anyway, "Zander, if I scoot back against that pillow and promise not to look at you, would you just put your arm over me? I just need you close right now." She didn't want to bellyache about all the fears of being enough and doing the right thing with the weapon, the stress over all those people dying, one of her family members being hurt, how awful it had been to lose Papa, and on and on, but she was sure just a simple touch from him would settle her, comfort her, and help her sleep.

He said nothing except to maybe breathe a little faster.

"If that's asking too much ..."

"It is." He drew in a breath. "But I think I'm strong enough."

She laughed at that. "You're incredibly strong. I've felt those pec muscles, remember?"

"I remember." There was no teasing in his voice and suddenly she remembered, too. She would love to touch him whenever she wanted.

"Okay," he said. "Scoot back slowly, and no looking."

She smiled and eased back until her backside hit the cushion. She waited, anticipation thrumming through her. Just a simple touch, Zander's touch. That was all she needed.

He scooted closer. The pillow kept them apart a little, but his legs still pressed against hers and his warm breath brushed her ear. She was breathing far too fast and not settled at all. His arm came over her side, and then his hand ran along her abdomen and his palm rested there.

Jessie was going to have heart failure. His hand on her abdomen was intimate and beautiful and she could feel him behind her. It took every bit of strength she didn't know she had to not spin around and kiss him. She wanted to get lost in him and forget all the evil that seemed to be surging toward their valley.

"How's that?" he asked hoarsely.

"It's incredible," she admitted. "I didn't realize how ... perfect that would feel."

"Yeah," he agreed. "Can you rest?"

"No. Can you?"

He let out a short laugh. "I highly doubt it."

She smiled. She wished she could gush about everything he did for her—protection, strength, excitement, love, laughter. She should be sobbing from losing her Papa and horrified about what she had to do tonight, but this man took her attention and somehow assuaged the pain and the worries.

"Can you please at least close your eyes and try?" he asked. "I don't want you worn out tonight."

That sobered her. In hours, it should be done. Unless she never got the impression to fire the weapon. Papa had been so insistent that she couldn't fire it without heaven's help. She'd have to kill Frederick and whoever was close to him tonight. If she didn't, an entire island nation would be obliterated and then Frederick would keep killing. They'd go through this same stress and angst tomorrow. She wanted it all behind them. So she could be free to love Zander but more importantly so Frederick couldn't hurt, torture, manipulate, or kill anyone else.

She shuddered. It was heavy and awful, but at least Zander was here.

Papa, please watch over all of us. Please keep our family all safe and help me do the right thing at the right time.

She cuddled back against Zander, closed her eyes, and knew this man would stand by her side and heaven was watching over them. That was all she needed to know right now. Somehow, the rest would work itself out.

Or maybe not. But then they'd be in heaven with Papa. That didn't sound too bad, as long as Zander was there.

Chapter Twelve

Zander heard movement and was instantly awake. Jess was cuddled close to his chest, the separation pillow all but flattened between them. Nothing had ever felt so right as her in his arms, but he instantly worried he'd endangered her by sleeping so deeply.

He didn't move, listening to see what had woken him. The light in the room was dim, the sun was behind the mountains, but not yet set. He heard footsteps walking away and realized what had awakened him was just a family member walking along the upstairs balcony. The alarm clock said six-twenty. Not that late, but it got dark early at the end of September, especially this high in the mountains.

He should release Jess and slowly move away. Hopefully she could keep sleeping, at least until the seven o'clock alarm. With all the stress she was facing, she needed every bit of rest she could get.

Jess sighed and cuddled in tighter to him. Her hand rested

over the top of his and her hair was like silk against his neck. He breathed in the sweet scent of peaches and cream. Jess's lips far surpassed the taste of any peaches and cream he'd ever sampled.

He wondered why Maddie hadn't burst in here and pulled them apart. As upset as she'd been last night finding them kissing, she'd be livid about them cuddling like this as they slept. Zander would take the cuss-out. It would be worth it for these stolen moments with Jess, and he was cussing himself out for having such a hard time resisting her. He knew she didn't understand the power she had over him. Jess was too sweet to ever try to wield that power to hurt him, but she was more intriguing and desirable than anything in the world to him.

His other arm was trapped under his body. He shifted slightly and laid it up above her head on the pillow. More silky tendrils of hair ran through his fingertips. Ah, Jess. Was there anything about her that didn't appeal to him?

Would this mess with Frederick and the weapon be over tonight? Could he and Jess have a chance at a normal life then? With him doing covert ops all over the world and her here in Colorado? He groaned aloud at the thought of leaving her.

Jess shifted on the bed and he realized his mistake. "Zander?"

"Hey."

She rolled over, tossed the pillow out of the way, and cuddled against him. He was shocked and absolutely loved having her so close.

"You okay?" he managed to get out.

"I had a horrible dream earlier," she said quietly. "I can't believe I didn't wake you. I must've finally fallen back to sleep."

"I'm so sorry." How could he have been so exhausted he slept through her having a nightmare? "Do you want to tell me about it?"

"You were gone, and I thought you'd left me ..." Her voice caught and he realized she was crying.

"Ah, Jess." He cradled her against him and tenderly kissed her forehead. "I wouldn't leave you." Was that true? He was committed to be with her right now. Would he leave her for missions someday soon?

"Then I realized you were dead."

His eyebrows lifted as she clung to him. Her tears wet his neck and her worries pressed down on him. He wouldn't die. He was too tough to die. She was probably simply terrified because of all the unknowns, what might come their way, and losing her grandfather so tragically and recently.

He let her cry until she seemed to calm down, and then he whispered against her hairline, "You probably needed that release, to just let it all out and cry."

She grabbed his shirt in her hand and fisted it. Obviously she hadn't calmed down at all. He could barely see her face in the murky darkness, but he could feel and hear the intensity. "Promise me you won't die."

"Jess." Her name came out as a stunned sort of laughter. Nobody could promise that. Especially somebody in his line of work.

"Don't laugh at me." She grabbed his shoulder and tried to shake him. "Don't die, Zander. Please promise me you won't die."

"Jess." He stroked his palm up and down her back. "I promise I'll do everything in my power to stay alive. It'll be okay. It's all going to be okay."

She turned her tear-stained face up toward him and somebody must've turned on a light outside the house because he could suddenly see her face more clearly.

"How do you know?" she asked. "I'm afraid nothing will ever be okay or normal or happy again."

He studied her beautiful face. "Jess. I promise you I will do everything in my power to keep you safe, bring you back to a normal life, and make you happy. I swear it."

"That includes you not leaving me, ever."

He wanted to kiss her so badly. He kissed her soft cheek and murmured in her ear, "I'll do everything I can to not leave you ... ever."

She let out a half-sob that sounded relieved, worried, and almost happy. She turned her face slightly, and he knew she was going to kiss him. How could he possibly resist her if she initiated the contact? How could he not lose his mind if they kissed cuddled up on this bed?

Her phone buzzed loudly and his walkie-talkie beeped.

Disappointment raced through him, but also concern. They both scrambled off the bed. She lifted her phone as he grabbed the walkie-talkie.

"Zander," she rushed out, reading aloud. "Troops have just entered Summit Valley and are headed this way." She looked up at him with horror in her eyes. "Troops?"

Zander had been on so many missions that he prided himself on being almost immune to fear, but he felt fear at that moment. "Troops?" He pushed the button on the walkie-talkie. "Cap, talk to me."

"Get her out of here," Cap demanded. "We've got birds

incoming. Multiple."

"We're leaving and I'm going silent." He turned off the walkie-talkie and put it in one of his cargo-pants pockets. It would vibrate if they needed to contact him.

Blackhawks descending on the valley? Special ops teams or more troop movement? Which branch of the military? Who'd ordered it? Was it a mission for America to get the weapon to use against Frederick, or was it a ploy from Frederick and some admiral on the take like they feared Admiral Gusbane might be? Somebody using the military to secure the weapon for Frederick?

It didn't matter. It did, but not for him or his mission at the moment. All that mattered was getting Jess close to the weapon so when she felt prompted they could use it to end this nightmare. Unfortunately, with troops and helicopters approaching, they couldn't risk a motorized vehicle. The hike to the cave was just under four hours. They had five and a half. As long as special ops teams weren't waiting up there to intercept them. Admiral Gusbane had known to send Zander and the SEALs to that clearing by the cave. How many Blackhawks were headed there?

Jess was tying her shoes. She stood and pocketed her phone. He grabbed her hand and rushed out of her room and into the one he'd been staying in. He strapped the A.R.s and weapon belt across his chest and then they ran down the stairs and for the backpacks in the garage. Her mom raced into the garage from the side door as they were strapping their backpacks on and putting night vision goggles on their heads.

She hugged Zander and begged him, "Protect her."

"With my life," he vowed.

"Thank you." She turned to Jess and immediately started

crying.

"Oh, Mama. It's okay. It's okay."

They hugged and Zander checked weapons and pockets in the backpack and tried not to intrude on their private moment.

"Father above, keep my girl and Zander safe," Holly said in prayer, and he closed his eyes and stopped moving. "Strengthen Jessie in her duties and inspire her and Zander your guiding light. Amen."

"Amen," they both echoed.

Zander heard the low thrum of helicopters. Many helicopters. They needed to move.

"I love you, baby girl."

"I love you."

Her mom kissed her cheek, then it looked like she had to pry herself away. "I'll be praying. I'll see you both soon."

"We'll pray for you too." Jessie blew her a kiss and then Zander tugged at her hand and pulled her out of the garage.

It wasn't a moment too soon. He could see the glows of the Blackhawks swooping over the mountains and closing in on their location. Even though it wasn't full-on dark, the helicopters switched their search lights on as they reached the other side of the lake. They were coming in hot. They weren't afraid of the Deltas shooting them down, which he knew the Deltas wouldn't do, but the way they were coming in felt far too aggressive. It was an offensive mission, which he'd been on the other end of far too many times.

He and Jess pivoted the other direction, running behind the houses and into the nearest trees. It got darker surrounded by thick trees. They switched on their night vision. He could hear the

Deltas and the SEALs calling to each other and running. They'd be lining up with their own weapons, just as they had when he and his SEAL buddies had arrived. Was that two weeks ago now? How his life had changed.

He clung to Jess's hand as they found the trail behind Alivia's house and pounded up it at a quick jog. Who knew if the invaders would send trackers after them or how long it would take before they knew they were missing. There would be Deltas and SEALs patrolling the cave and reinforcements headed immediately that way. He'd heard talk after dinner of the next group already headed up to relieve the Sheriff's men who'd been there all day so the Deltas could be at the funeral.

So many thoughts ran through his head as they ran. Practical thoughts morphed into frenzied worry. Their own military wouldn't fire upon American citizens. They'd get boots on the ground and investigate. Right? Unless someone had fed them lies and claimed the Deltas had committed treason and were threatening to fire a weapon of mass destruction to hurt Americans or something far-fetched like that.

Please don't let any of them get hurt, he begged heaven above.

If he was this worried with all his experience and it not being his immediate family, he could only imagine what was going through Jess's mind. At the same time, she'd never seen special ops forces take out a village or a camp or whatever target they'd been assigned. They tried not to kill women and children, but anyone armed like the Deltas would be neutralized. An armed rebel had to be taken down.

He pictured Holly standing next to Jess the day he'd arrived, both of them holding those .50-caliber machine guns. He could picture so many of the Deltas standing tall and ready to defend their homes, and more importantly the weapon and Jess.

Ah, no. His stomach clenched, and he prayed harder. Frederick was ready to fire a nuclear weapon on an unknown island in five and a half hours. Troops were moving through the lower valley and heading for their homes. Multiple Blackhawks had probably already landed. Maybe special ops teams were headed for the cave. How much resistance did they think the Deltas would put up?

He strained to listen over his and Jess's pounding footsteps and quick breaths. She seemed to be in incredible shape, and he was grateful for that. They had to get to the cave as quick as possible, not flirt with that midnight deadline. If Gusbane, who had sent him and his team on their mission, had organized this attack, they would know the cave's location and that meadow his men had destroyed the Blackhawk in. All the other soldiers coming into the valley could be a distraction to draw attention away from the real teams heading for the cave and the weapon. But at least that would mean they wouldn't gun down the Deltas. He couldn't hear the helicopters any longer, but he hadn't heard any gunshots. That was good. That was great.

When they were far enough away, he slowed his steps and then stopped. Turning to Jess, he said quietly, "There were no gunshots."

She nodded. "That's good."

"For sure." He pulled out a water bottle and offered it to her. She took a quick swallow, then handed it to him. He took a longer drink, savoring the cool liquid running down his parched throat. The fear and worrying made him thirstier than even the running.

It was cool in the mountains, which was nice for running or hiking. It wouldn't be quite so great when they stopped, but they had plenty of supplies to keep them warm in their backpacks.

He handed the water bottle back, and she took a longer drink. He shoved it back in the backpack's pocket and then focused on her. It was weird to see her with the night vision goggles on, but they sure helped in this dark forest.

"You okay?" he asked.

"Not really."

"Sorry, stupid question." He ran his palm up and down her back, trying to reassure her. "Admiral Seamons is there. That's good. He'll vouch for your family and help them negotiate and work this out. That's really good."

"You're right." She took a long breath, then nodded. "Good things. No shots fired yet. Admiral Seamons is there."

He wondered, though, if Seamons, Keith, or Joseph had the talent that Admiral Delta had. That cool under pressure, you will listen to and respect me, but everybody is my friend kind of guy. It would be hard for most people not to trust or at least listen to Admiral Delta. And he was gone.

"Okay. Do we head straight for the cave?" He wanted to be there well before midnight and before special ops teams beat them there. He had to keep reminding himself nobody else could use or retrieve the weapon without her. But if they had a hope of saving those people, they couldn't risk a detour.

"Give me a second." She seemed to be thinking, then she grabbed his arm and begged, "Pray with me, Zander. I'm so upset that I'm getting no impressions or feelings at all except for the overwhelming fear for my family."

"Nobody could blame you for that."

"But it's essential I know when to go to the cave. Papa said I can only fire the weapon with inspiration. I need to know what to do. Help me."

He'd help her with anything. He extended his hands and she grasped them. Bringing her closer, he rested their clasped hands against his chest and bowed his head over her. "Father ... we need your help. Please protect the Delta family, the SEALs, and everyone in the valley. Please help them to talk things out peacefully. At this time, we need to protect the weapon and keep anyone but Jess from using it." Maybe it wasn't possible for anyone else to access it, but he was concerned the impressive special ops teams he'd served with could somehow make it happen. At least SEAL Team 6 and Delta Force were pursuing Frederick. If only they could find and kill him. "Please help us. We desperately need your guidance, inspiration, and light. Guide our steps, keep us safe, and help Jess to know the exact moment she needs to head to the cave and the exact moment she needs to fire the weapon. Help us save those innocent people in danger. Amen."

"Amen," Jess echoed.

Neither of them moved. He waited, praying silently for her inspiration. He wished he could help her more, but she was the key and the Keeper. It was hard to push away his usual tendencies to lead the way. He prayed silently for humility and to trust heaven and Jess. He had faith, but that ticking clock was hanging over their heads.

As they stood there, he instinctively wanted to rub his thumbs along the soft backs of her hands in his grip or raise her hands to his lips and kiss her knuckles. He stayed any movement and focused on listening to the night sounds of the surrounding forest, trying to pick up on any sounds that were out of place.

Reassured that no one was following them for the moment, he returned to praying silently for Jess and staring at her beautiful face in the soft light.

She opened her eyes and squeezed his hands. "Let's go to the cabin that is closest to the cave but still hidden well. We might be able to contact whoever is guarding the cave, but also we'll be ready and close by when the time is right."

"Okay. But the time isn't right now?"

"No."

He could hear the disappointment in her voice and felt it course through him. It would be much better to head straight for the cave, use the weapon, and have it done. Then they could go back and diffuse the situation in the valley. Frederick would be dead and hopefully his evil regime more easily stopped. Admiral Seamons would advise the troops to leave. Everything would be good. He and Jess could kiss for a long time and then see how to navigate their future. A tantalizing future that felt even further out of reach at the moment.

Not right now.

He felt his own impression, and it was strong. The time wasn't right. Would it be right before midnight to protect those people? He didn't know. It chafed at him not to go take care of the problem. Zander was a man of action. Patience was far from his strong suit. Unless he was wiring explosives or building a bomb, he rarely sat still.

But he'd prayed hard for Jess's inspiration. She was confident

that Papa had created to distract and confuse anyone coming would be activated round the clock. She and her family had goggles to get through it. What if the military did as well? Those mercenaries who had failed to get the secret could've shared intel about the fog if someone smart from the military had questioned them in prison.

She couldn't let her worries affect her decision. Her family and the SEALs would protect the valley and the cave. The weapon should be safe. She wanted to go to her family, but she knew Zander would agree. He was hyper-focused on keeping her safe. If the Secret Keeper wasn't near the cave, the mercenaries couldn't get into the inner section or retrieve the weapon or fire it. She appreciated Zander keeping her safe as the Keeper, but it seemed his obsession was more personal. She loved that, but sadly neither of them could be worried about their growing relationship when her entire world was imploding and possibly *the* entire world would explode. She had to get that confirmation to stop Frederick. Soon. It reassured her that she'd heard the voice so strongly to come to this cabin. At least she was getting inspiration. But what if she didn't get it in time to save that island?

She couldn't think like that.

A small clearing appeared and then a small wood cabin. Jessie let out a breath of relief. At least they could hunker down for a little bit. She kept praying for instruction. She wasn't looking forward to killing anyone, but she wanted it done. The sooner they went, the better. To protect those people and stop Frederick and stop whoever had sent the troops after the weapon. It wouldn't be long before they were sending soldiers to secure it.

What would they do to coerce her family into leading them there? Her gut churned, and she said another prayer for their safety.

Zander led the way and then held up a hand. He lifted the latch on the cabin door and swung it open. Jess stepped forward and held the door as he checked the interior. Papa and her dad and uncle had cleaned out and reinforced the small hunting cabins in these woods years ago. This one was an open room with a small wooden table and two chairs, a double bed with a thin mattress pressed against one wall, and a short counter with some cabinets above and below it. There were cobwebs and lots of dust. Jess wondered if they wouldn't do better staying outside. At the same time, she knew these mountains and the dangers. She'd never had a scary encounter with a bear, moose, or mountain lion, but some had, including her sister Alivia and Klein. It was better to be in a structure rather than risk an animal stumbling onto them. What if a human stumbled onto the cabin, though?

"It's ... not clean but clean, you know?" Zander grinned. With her night vision goggles on and not traipsing through the woods, she got the full force of that grin. She'd missed it.

"You're using that smile to your benefit, aren't you?"

"Oh, yes ma'am." He smiled bigger. "Let me put up some perimeter security and clean the cobwebs out, and then we can have a snack and hunker down until you're ready to move."

She didn't realize he had perimeter security. That was good, and of course he would. He was smart and prepared and she would be lost without him. She could also hear in his voice and felt it clear through: *please don't let it be too long until you're ready to move.* She did not want to flirt with that midnight deadline.

Papa had explained that the weapon would take about twenty to thirty minutes to reach its destination, so really eleven-thirty had to be her deadline.

"I can clean cobwebs," she offered.

"You sure?"

"I'm a tough chick."

"I know that."

She smiled and he returned it, but now was definitely not the time to have a moment. He set his backpack on the ground and started pulling stuff out of it. She also set her backpack on the ground outside the cabin. It felt nice to have the pressure relieved from her shoulder blades.

Walking into the small cabin, she grabbed the broom by the door and started going after the cobwebs. When she was satisfied, she set the broom down outside in case spiders were on it. She picked up her backpack and pulled out a couple of water bottles she'd emptied and then grabbed the empty water bottles from Zander's backpack.

He was out in the trees. She approached him slowly.

"Hey." He stood and walked around a tree. "Armed and ready to alert us to any intruders." He smiled and took the water bottles. "I'll go fill these." He'd studied the maps, so he knew exactly where the spring was. It was close, but she didn't like the idea of him being out of her sight.

"Can I come with you?"

"Sure."

He pivoted and they navigated through the undergrowth and trees to the spring, filled the water bottles, took some long drinks, and then filled them again. It seemed so peaceful in the quiet woods, untouched by the ugliness of Frederick's killing and threats. Were mercenaries or special ops nearby? They were about half an hour's hike from the cave here. What if somebody chanced upon them? Her nerves grew, but then Zander smiled at her and gestured for her to walk back to the cabin. Zander was here and she'd felt strongly that they should come here. She had to trust in that.

They made it back to the cabin, carried their backpacks in, sat on the chairs by the table, and pulled out a small lantern and some food. It was a relief to take off the night vision goggles. Jessie was surprised that she was hungry. They'd missed dinner with their nap. She liked reflecting on that nap, teasing and luring Zander in and feeling so safe, comfortable, and happy.

Immediately she remembered how desperately she'd wanted to kiss him.

She looked at his mouth. It was dim in the cabin with only the glow of the small camp light Zander had put on the table, but she could see his irresistible lips. She could see him. He was perfect. Could they let down their guard for just a minute and kiss and hold each other? Kissing Zander would strengthen her to do what needed to be done. It was interesting that a few days ago she hadn't known if she'd be able to fire the weapon, or how perfectly incredible Zander was. She felt stronger, braver, and more in love than she'd ever imagined she could.

She forced herself to chew and slow, knowing she'd need the energy. She ate the jerky, protein bar, nuts, and dried fruit, chasing it all down with lots of water. On their hike she'd had to stop and pee, so she luckily didn't have to right now. Zander had taken her needing to pee in stride and been great about it and respectful of her, just as he was with everything.

They didn't talk as they ate. It wasn't uncomfortable. She liked that. Zander stored the wrappers in an inner pocket of her backpack and then pulled something out and grinned. Ah, his smile could light up any dark night. She'd needed to see that smile.

"Mint?" he asked, pulling out a sleeve of mint Mentos.

"Yes, please." The only thing better would be a toothbrush. A clean mouth shouldn't matter at all right now, but it would sure feel nice.

Zander opened the pack and held it out to her. She pulled a circular Mento out and put it in her mouth, chewing on it and appreciating the fresh taste of mint. Zander slid his own mint in and then stowed the rest in the backpack. He still had the weapons strapped to his back and the weapons belt on. She loved the way it made him look so tough and brave, outlining his chest muscles. But he could relax a bit here with their perimeter security armed. Right?

"Do you want to take those A.R.s off?" she asked him.

He shook his head. "I want to be prepared if anyone comes or when you decide it's time to go."

She nodded and appreciated his trust in her. *She* had to decide. He'd support her, even if she horrifically missed that deadline. She supposed that could be the Lord's will, there were times in the scriptures when innocent people died. She sure hoped tonight wasn't one of those times.

She closed her eyes and prayed for inspiration. Nothing came. Dang. Opening her eyes, she focused on Zander sitting next to her in the dimly lit room.

"Yes?" he asked, sounding like a hopeful little boy.

She smiled at that, but shook her head. "No. Not yet."

"Okay." He smiled at her—trying to reassure her or because he knew how much she loved his smile? She wasn't sure.

A few beats passed as they studied each other. His smile turned into a more serious look. An intense, longing look that made her heart rate pick up. Their one kiss was never far from her mind. There was so much in her mind, she wondered how she had room for the kiss, but it was easily recalled and at the forefront right now. What would he do if she stood, sat on his lap, wrapped her arms around his neck, and kissed him for a good, long time?

Zander jumped to his feet and pushed a hand through his hair. It was almost as if he'd read her mind and was afraid she'd act on her idea.

The rejection and sting of disappointment hit her in the chest. She didn't move as he paced the small cabin.

Finally, she stood. He stopped his pacing and looked at her warily.

"You're not very good at waiting, are you?" she asked.

He chuckled and pushed his hand through his hair. "I should be. In the military it's wait and then hurry up and why weren't you here faster?"

She smiled. "I can't imagine."

"I hope you can't." He turned slightly away from her, clenching his fists at his side and making his arm muscles more pronounced.

She walked up to him. "Are the missions horrible?"

He swallowed and met her gaze. "Sometimes." He nodded. "A lot of times. But it's what I signed up for, what I train so hard for.

The targets that special ops teams take out are definitely people that need to be removed from this world. But I'm not the guy who wants to kill just to kill. So it makes it hard sometimes."

She really couldn't imagine. She was grateful men like Zander not only existed but were willing to give their life to protect and serve. He was incredible. But even in the dim light, she could see the killing, as well as seeing his comrades be killed, had taken a toll. It still hurt him.

"You know how my mom forced Captain Hendrickson to hug her?"

"Poor Cap." He smiled. "It was good for him."

"Would it be good for you?" She eased closer.

Zander's breath came out in a rush. "I need to focus on the mission, on keeping you safe."

"I know that. But you've got the sensors armed and until it's time to go to the cave we're just here, the two of us, together."

He swallowed hard and pushed at his hair again.

"Would a hug be good for you?" she asked again. She didn't want to force him, but he'd admitted back in her bedroom that she was the woman he'd always been looking for. She wanted to be the woman he needed. The woman who could help, love, and heal him.

"Probably," he admitted, though his dark eyes looked wary, as if he knew a hug wasn't all she was after.

She stepped in and snaked her arms around his lower back. Zander released a heavy breath and wrapped her up tight. She leaned into his chest, resting her head in the crook of his neck. They simply held each other. He would protect her and she would strengthen him. They were a perfect fit.

"This is a good way to pass the time, right?" she asked softly, not wanting to disturb this peace. At the moment, she wasn't even worried. With Zander by her side, she could do what needed to be done and her family would do what they needed to do.

"Oh yeah." He smiled down at her.

She tilted her head up and their mouths were almost aligned. If she arched up or he bent down ...

His dark eyes filled with longing for her, and only her.

"Zander." She loved his name on her lips. "Defender of woman. Have you ever been in love?"

He stared at her as if weighing his answer. "I used to think I had, but now I know I've never truly loved someone ... not before."

"Before?" she asked.

"Before you."

Her eyes widened, but she didn't have time to respond in kind or process it too deeply before his lips came down on hers. The kiss started intense and full of desperate longing. She followed his lead and clung to him as they kissed and tried to satiate the need for each other and the fact one or both of them could be killed soon and they may never kiss again.

Then Zander slowed the kiss and it changed to an exchange of devotion, love, and patience. He'd promised her he would do everything in his power to protect her and to stay alive. This kiss confirmed that. He loved her. He was wholly committed to her. They didn't need to rush ahead or take what wasn't there for them yet. But this kiss was a kiss of promise, hope, and a beautiful future.

He pulled back, ushered her head to his chest, and held her.

He held her gently but firmly. He was her man, the defender of his woman, and he would care for her. He trusted her and was humble enough to let her lead when she needed and to stand by her side. He was patient and good and true and loyal. Zander was her everything.

They held each other in the dark cabin and she savored the kisses they'd exchanged and the warm, peaceful feeling surrounding them. This was love, not some passionate spark that would burn them or burn out. They'd be there for each other. No matter what.

Suddenly, she knew. Her mind and heart and soul filled with the knowledge. It was terrifying and exciting and ... it was time.

"Zander!" She pulled back. "We've got to go."

"Now?"

"Right now."

She released him and ran for the table, sweeping up her backpack by the straps, pulling on her night vision goggles, and heading for the door. Zander was right on her heels.

They burst out of the cabin and into the dark night. She paused and let Zander lead the way. He took her hand and squeezed it, stopping as they entered the trees. She didn't think they had time to stop, but he pulled her closer and said, "Lord, we're putting ourselves and the safety of millions of others in your hands. Protect, guide, and make us more than we are. Make up what we lack. Amen."

"Amen." Jessie loved his prayer. She squeezed his hand and looked up at the sky. A star seemed to twinkle above the exact spot the cave was. Papa Delta watching over them? The twinkle filled her, and she was confident in her inspiration. It was time. She had to protect those innocent people and take out Frederick.

God willing ... they'd succeed.

They took off at a run and she started praying desperately in her heart.

Chapter Fourteen

Zander was grateful he'd studied and memorized the maps and landmarks and that he instinctively excelled with navigation. They ran through the night. He had to release Jess's hand as they were on no kind of trail. He also listened intently. What if they ran right into a special ops team? He couldn't let Jess fall into anyone's hands. It was rough to think of fighting against his own, but for Jess he would do anything. And he also knew that this Delta weapon was meant to be in their hands—actually, in Jess's hands. He was relieved she'd finally felt the prompting to go to the cave.

He thought he heard something. He stopped, tugged Jess behind a tall poplar tree, and listened.

There it was again. Footsteps. Approaching. He could hear Jess's panting breaths behind him and the sound of it energized and strengthened him. *This We'll Defend* was an Army theme, and he was a Navy guy, but he'd worked with the Army Rangers enough to hear it often and right now he knew he would defend Jess to the death.

He slowly pulled one of his A.R.s off his back, checked the safety, and aimed in the direction the footsteps were coming.

Two people. A man and a woman was his best guess. They walked slowly, obviously looking for something. They had weapons out and weren't messing around.

Suddenly, Jess stepped to the side and away from the protection of the tree.

He held the gun with his left hand and grabbed her with his right.

"It's okay," she said softly. "Maddie?"

"Jessie!" Maddie's voice was a hushed whisper filled with relief.

Zander let out a breath he hadn't known he was holding and hurried after Jessie as she rushed to her sister. The women hugged.

Zander couldn't help himself. He hugged Braden. Then he remembered Braden was not touch-phobic like Cap. That was a relief. Seeing friendly faces instead of those intent on capturing Jess was a bigger relief.

"Hey, man. What's happening?" Zander needed to know any information he could get to keep Jess safe as they went to the cave.

"Aiden, Thor, and all the SEALs are here patrolling. We've seen some special ops teams searching for the cave, but so far the fog has distracted them. I don't think any of them have the thermal-imaging goggles, all night vision so far. That's a relief. They haven't gotten close, and we haven't had to take anyone out."

Zander knew his friend would have as hard a time engaging their own men as he would. "Any word from the valley?"

"Not since the initial alarm and then the SEALs showing up

here a couple hours later. They bugged out quick and ran double-time to get here, but they said no shots were fired initially, so that's encouraging."

"We didn't hear any either."

"Is it time?" Maddie asked, looking at her sister.

"Yes." Jess stood straight and nodded.

"Thank heavens. Take that loser out, sis, and protect that island."

"Zander and I will head directly for the cave." Jessie radiated confidence. "If you see anyone else, please ask them to keep the soldiers as far away as they can."

He loved that she was taking charge. Stepping up like her grandfather had known she would. She had this. Zander was support staff, and that was all right. Better than all right. He was Jess's support staff. Most important job in the world, and not because she was Secret Keeper, but because she was Jess. His Jess. He was ready. Ready to be in the action and to end this. Then he'd kiss Jess as long as he wanted with no worries about it endangering her or the mission.

"We've got it ... and you've got this." Maddie squeezed Jess and then looked at him with those eerily similar blue eyes. "Protect her."

"With my life," he told her, just as he had her mom.

She squeezed his arm and then they eased off into the darkness.

Zander kept his A.R. out. "Let's take it a little slower," he cautioned Jess. Though maybe not too much slower. He needed to keep an eye on the time. "Stay behind me."

"All right."

They found a semi-broken trail and progressed along it, but every chirp of a chipmunk, twig broken by a small animal, or owl hooting made him jumpy. He was more keyed up than he'd ever been on a mission. But usually on missions, everyone with him was highly trained and qualified, and though he cared deeply about them, he wasn't in love with them or hoping his future was contingent on their survival.

Jess touched his back. He stopped and glanced over his shoulder at her. She held up a pair of goggles. "For the fog," she whispered.

"Thanks."

She traded out hers and put the night vision ones in the backpack, and he did the same. The world changed from green hues to shades of white and gray. It was harder going without the night vision, but it was smart to have these on as he knew they were getting close.

"Hey." She leaned in close to his ear and whispered, "I know you're worried, but I can fight, remember?"

How had she read his mind like that? He did know she could fight. He just didn't want her to have to.

Movement sounded behind them. Pounding footsteps.

No words were needed as he maneuvered Jess in front of him and they both broke into a run. If anybody was getting shot in the back, it was him.

"Stop!" a male voice commanded. "Now!"

Zander and Jess ran faster. Their eyes had adjusted to the thermal imaging goggles, but they didn't light up the trail like night-vision goggles would. It was disconcerting to be sprinting that fast when the trail wasn't clear below their feet.

Were the men gaining on them? How many? Was there any possibility he knew them and he could talk them into switching sides like he and his men had? It wasn't worth the risk and they didn't have the time. But what if they shot and hit Jess? That wasn't worth the risk either.

"Stand down ... or we will fire," the voice called.

His head pounded with the stress of protecting Jess and the sprint they were maintaining along the semi-broken trail in the dark. Should they stop? Should they keep running? Would they really fire?

Shots hit the branches above him and bits of wood stung his head. Jess dropped and he followed her. She army-crawled forward. He was forced to strap the gun onto his back and follow her. It was smart to stay low and keep moving, but the men's footsteps were pounding along the trail behind them. They definitely had night vision goggles on, and they'd easily catch them.

He needed to get Jess off the trail, take up a defensive position, and take these men out.

They were almost upon them.

"Jess," he hissed. "Hide."

"No. The fog." She pointed ahead of them, and he could see the misty fog swirling over the trail. The thermal-imaging goggles they had on would cut through it, but not eliminate the fog completely.

But there was no way they would make it army crawling.

"We've got to run," he said.

She popped up and ran. Zander leaped to his feet and went after her. Shots fired again, splintering the branches above them.

Clearly, the men didn't want to kill the Deltas any more than Zander wanted to kill them. But they would.

"Stop or we shoot lower," the voice said, exactly as he feared.

The fog was right there. Twenty feet and they wouldn't be safe from the bullets, but the men with their night vision goggles wouldn't be able to see them. At least they'd be harder targets.

From behind, he heard a grunt and then something heavy rammed into a tree. Or somebody? Something else slammed into the ground. Or someone? He didn't dare look back as he sprinted right behind Jess.

Low commands were issued, but there were also sounds of confusion and what sounded like a wrestling match or a fist fight. Had someone come to their rescue?

They were so close to the fog now. A couple more steps and Jess would be obscured from their vision.

He chanced a glance back and could see a rainbow of human figures duking it out in hand-to-hand fighting. Yes! The SEALs and Deltas had come through! He focused back ahead, knowing they all could hold their own, and fist-fighting was much better than bullets flying. He prayed if he and Jess could use the weapon like she planned to, they could then settle the battle and explain what had happened.

Jess reached the fog. She took her first step in and relief made his steps slow.

Until a large man sprang from the trees and tackled her.

"No!" Zander yelled, flying at them.

Jess elbowed the guy and blood spurted from his nose. Zander grabbed him around the shoulders and ripped him off her.

"Go," he yelled.

She didn't look like she wanted to, but she rushed into the fog.

The man slammed his fist into Zander's gut. He doubled over but refused to go down. Jess needed him and he wouldn't fail her.

He grabbed the man around the waist and twisted as hard and fast as he could, like throwing a massive discus in the track and field event. The man's head knocked into a tree branch, and he went down. Zander didn't stop to see if he was down for the count or if he had buddies nearby.

He pulled in a shaky breath. Holding his abdomen, he sprinted into the fog where Jess had disappeared. A few steps in and he had to slow his pace. The goggles made it possible to see, but it wasn't crystal clear. He wanted to call for Jess, but he couldn't give away her position. He prayed he could find her and protect her. He hated the thought of her being alone, unprotected, and facing this insanely epic moment with the Delta weapon and stopping Frederick by herself.

The farther he went, the denser the fog felt, surrounding him like a living thing. An icy cold living thing. The sounds of the fight behind him and any forest noise dampened and then disappeared. It was eerie, and he really wanted to find Jess. Had somebody else gone after her? Was she okay? What if he wandered around and never found her? What if the men out there found her first?

A hand on his arm made him jump. He instinctively threw a punch, but the small person ducked out of his way.

"Zander!"

"Oh, Jess." He grabbed her and hugged her tight, wishing these goggles cleared the fog a little better, grateful he hadn't hit her on accident, and grateful she'd waited for him. "You're okay?"

"Yes. Stay close. We don't have much time." He didn't think

she knew the exact time, but her spiritual instincts seemed to be spot on.

She pulled from him, turned, and jogged up the thin ribbon of a trail. He worried about the trail. It was skinny, but it was well-broken. If someone was smart, they could drop to the ground and crawl along it. If one of the men fighting his SEALs stole the thermal imaging goggles, they could follow as well.

They hurried together and he got more used to the unsettling fog, the heavy darkness, the abnormal silence, and the deep chill. He actually welcomed the cold after the heat of the run and the fight.

Jess was with him, and that was all that mattered right now. She could do this, and he'd never leave her side.

She stopped. "This way," she said. She turned and went through a thick part of the forest that was barely passable.

A granite cliff appeared a few dozen feet later. Zander's nerves ramped up. They'd made it. Right? From everything he'd studied, the cave door was in this granite wall.

Jess eased along, studying it as if searching for something. A few seconds later, she pressed her hand to the wall. A door creaked open and Zander's heart thumped quicker. Surreal. Almost like he was in *National Treasure*.

Jess looked back at him. He could barely see her, but he could sense her angst, her fears. They'd made it and she was prepared, but now she had to use the weapon and kill Frederick. He wished he could do it for her, but that wasn't his role.

Support. Protection. Loving Jess. Helping her kill Frederick.

He'd changed his mantra slightly.

Jess stepped into the cave, and he slowly followed her.

"Can I shut the door?" he asked.

"No. The weapon needs a flight path."

That made him nervous, but it made sense.

He eased into the cave, not seeing anyone approaching, which helped settle his nerves. Slightly.

This was it. No turning back now.

Chapter Fifteen

Jessie's heart raced out of control and her palms were sweaty as they entered the cave, but inside she was steadier than she'd ever been. Zander was right behind her. He wouldn't leave her side. He'd protect her. That lifted and reassured her more than anything. She didn't like that he'd told her mom and Maddie that he'd protect her with his life. He had to live. That was the most important thing to her.

But first she had to complete the mission Papa had trained her throughout her life to complete, and then she and Zander could get out of here, hopefully dispel the tensions in the valley, and then ... who knew?

As she lifted her goggles onto her forehead, the cave suddenly lit up. Zander had pulled out a light bar headlamp, and the glow helped a lot.

She walked across the outer cave lined with gold bars. Zander gave a low whistle. She hardly noticed the gold on her way to the inner door. She pulled her necklace out and fit the small pendant into the door, pressed her thumbprint into the slot, and spoke clearly, "Jessica Delta, Secret Keeper."

It slid open.

She tried to slow down her breathing, but her heart was racing too fast. She just wanted to get it over with at this point. Tightening her jaw, she walked to where the weapon rested in its case. It was similar to a large black gun case. Zander stayed right by her, not saying anything.

She hadn't asked for this job or to kill Frederick, but he would shoot a nuclear weapon at that island and keep on killing until he was stopped. She knew it was time and she would do what she had to do. As Secret Keeper. As a Delta. As Admiral Davidson Delta's descendent. Heaven had inspired her this far, and she was trusting that light wouldn't leave her now.

She kneeled and pressed her thumbprint into the spot on the handle of the case. It clicked, and she flipped it open. The weapon was exactly how she remembered it. A long, white glider plane with a wingspan slightly longer than her forearm. For all the drama that surrounded it, the weapon wasn't much to look at.

She yanked off her backpack. Pulling Frederick's hair and follicles out of an inner pocket, she inserted them into the slot Papa had shown her. Then she took the special solution that activated the DNA. She filled the slot with exactly five drops and stored the solution back in the backpack. Would the weapon be used again after this? Would *she* have to use it again? She wasn't sure about that, but she'd keep the solution in case.

She closed the panel and then took her necklace and fit it into position in a slot above the cockpit. It hit her how steady her hands were. Now that she was here, there was no hesitation. She needed to press her thumbprint in, turn the pendant a hundred and eighty degrees, push the button, speak the command, and this plane would take off, zeroed in on its target. King Frederick and those closest to him would be dead in half an hour.

She opened the panel for her thumbprint and pressed down. The weapon lit up with a red glow. Red like blood. The blood of Frederick and those near him would be on her hands. What if someone innocent was near him?

Her stomach turned over and suddenly her hands weren't so steady.

It was awful, but she had to weigh the costs. Time was ticking quickly by, and she knew Frederick wasn't bluffing. He would kill everyone on whatever island he'd picked to annihilate first. If one or two innocent people near Frederick died, it was better than thousands dying on the island.

Zander was standing behind her, pointing his A.R. out the open inner door, but he must've somehow sensed she was struggling. He eased back toward her, gripped the gun with his right hand, and rested his left on her shoulder.

"You've got this, Jess. You felt it was time. You know it's right. Finish this and let's bug out."

His words were confident, to the point, and exactly what she needed.

She held her thumb in place and grasped the pendant to turn it.

Footsteps pounded into the cave. Jessie didn't know if they were friend or foe, but her hand was slick with sweat and she couldn't keep hold of the small pendant. She wiped her fingers on her pants.

"Stop!" a loud, male voice commanded.

"No, you stop," Zander said in a cold, military voice she'd never heard from him.

Should she just push the button, say her name and title, and be done with it?

"Remove your hands from the weapon," the guy instructed, pointing his huge gun straight at Zander. How did he know threatening Zander was the key to stopping her?

He had the same goggles on that Zander and Jess had. Had he hurt one of her family members to get the goggles? No! Her stomach churned in horror. She had to fire this weapon, kill Frederick, and stop him from killing many others. Hopefully they could then end the Deltas fighting with their own military.

She had to finish this. Her mind scrambled instead of becoming clearer with her purpose. She tried to spiritually reach out for her family. Could she sense if they'd been hurt? What if somebody she loved was dead or injured and bleeding to death?

"Do it!" the man yelled. "Or I kill him."

Zander held his own gun level. "Fire it, Jess. I've got the shot and I will take it before he can fire."

"Who are you?" the man demanded.

"Chief Petty Officer Zander Povey, Master EOD. Who are you?"

Jess could not believe how calm and brave Zander was. She'd lifted her trembling hands up to show the guy she wouldn't fire the weapon. She couldn't risk him hurting Zander.

"But you're dead," he said, staring at Zander with a mixture of shock and respect.

"Obviously not. I came here two weeks ago to secure the weapon on a mission, just as I assume you're doing. Admiral Davidson Delta showed me and the elite SEAL team I accompanied that the Delta family are the right people to be responsible for the Delta weapon. They are the *only* people on earth who will wield it responsibly and unselfishly. You can't trust whoever instructed you to come here."

Beads of sweat were popping on the man's forehead. "But I can't let you kill the President," the man said.

"Kill the President?" Jessie and Zander both said at the same time.

"You've got misinformation, my friend," Zander said evenly. "We would never harm the President. This weapon is being used to take out King Frederick before he shoots a nuclear weapon at a defenseless island of innocent people." He tilted his head to Jessie. "This woman is the only one who can fire the weapon, and she has been waiting for the exact moment to do so. Stand down so we can rid the world of the dictator that neither SEAL Team 6 nor Delta Force have been able to capture. We've only got a few minutes before an entire island nation die. Do you want that on your head?"

The man's A.R. shook in his hands. "I don't know if I can afford to trust you. Let's talk with Admiral Seamons. He's on his way. You can wait long enough to talk it out with him. If he confirms your story and orders the hit on Frederick, I'll stand down."

"Admiral Seamons is who ordered you here?" Zander looked

back at Jessie, his eyes full of questions. "What about Admiral Gusbane?"

"Seamons," the man insisted.

Maddie and Braden appeared behind the man. Maddie cocked a pistol and pushed it into his neck. "Drop it, dude. If you interfere with this mission to stop Frederick from killing thousands of innocent people, you are betraying your country and everything you fight for."

For some reason that Jessie couldn't understand, the cold metal of the wrong end of a pistol ready to end his life and Maddie's words calmed the man. He stopped shaking, and he said calmly, "I would never betray my country and I have never failed at a mission."

"Tell us what Admiral Seamons' instructions were," Zander commanded.

"To secure the Delta weapon and bring it to him."

Braden's face twisted in surprise. "Why would he ..."

"We were informed the Delta family will assassinate the President with the weapon and then the Deltas will hand the weapon over to King Frederick."

Maddie barked out a disbelieving laugh. "That's insane. We would never collude with Frederick or harm the President in any way. Do you even know who our grandfather was, dude?"

"Yes, I do. But when he died, the Delta family decided to use the fabled weapon and go a different direction with it."

"Why would we do that?"

"Money. That's what Admiral Seamons explained."

"I can't believe it ... You mean Gusbane, not Seamons," Braden insisted.

"Seamons," the guy said, shaking his head as if they were all slow or hard of hearing.

"Not Seamons." Braden's muscles were bunched, and he was obviously disturbed. No, disturbed probably wasn't strong enough for the angst in Braden's aqua blue eyes.

"Is it possible you read him wrong?" Maddie asked him quietly.

"It's possible. But he'd have to be a master at hiding his true feelings. Trained to do it, actually."

"I'm sorry, love, but we'll have to deal with Seamons later. We're wasting time. Jessie needs to fire the weapon and stop Frederick. Then we need to call off these special ops teams, get back to the valley, and force Seamons to disband his troops."

"Maddie, Braden." Aiden's voice came from behind them. It was getting very, very crowded and stuffy in this cave. Jessie wiped her sweaty hands on her pants again. They needed to clear out so the weapon would have a path or it could hurt one of them as fast as it would move once she engaged it. She was running out of precious time.

"My CO Jake Pitcher is here," Aiden said. "He'll help us talk down the other special ops teams. He said Seamons is the traitor."

"No," Braden groaned.

Jessie felt bad for him. He'd trusted Seamons when almost nobody else had, and he'd convinced the rest of the family to trust him as well. Maddie was right. They'd have to deal with Seamons later. She'd felt the prompting earlier to run for the weapon. She needed to act and fire the weapon. Now. She wasn't sure the exact time, but she knew she had next to not time left to stop Frederick.

"Ollie," Jake barked from behind. "Stand down."

"Yes, sir." The man lowered his weapon.

Maddie removed the pistol from his neck and Zander lowered his gun.

"Everybody out," Aiden instructed. "Zander, stay with Jess. She's got to finish this, then we can contain the situation up here and in the valley."

"Is everyone okay back home?" Jess asked.

"I haven't heard anything yet. I'm sure they're okay." He gave her an encouraging smile. "You got this, Jessie."

"Thanks. Make sure the cave and the entrance are clear."

"Sure thing."

She tried to smile, but her lip was trembling and so were her hands. Her head felt too big for her body, and she had hot and cold chills running through her. Could she do this? She knew she could. Now was the time. It seemed as if Aiden and his SEAL commander had cleared the way for her to complete her mission.

Jake's radio started buzzing on his hip, spouting out words that were broken up. He must have a high-frequency military radio that received transmissions from satellites, but in the cave the signal would struggle to get through. She wondered if it was Seamons checking if they'd secured the weapon.

Aiden ushered everyone out. Maddie gave her a reassuring smile as they left. Braden looked too upset about Seamons tricking him and being a traitor to be thinking about much else.

Zander set his gun down and hurried to her side, kneeling next to her. He wrapped an arm around her waist and she leaned into him. Her entire body shook.

"Jess?" His voice was full of concern.

"I think I ... Zander, I was so convinced it was time, but I don't feel right." She was confused, her head ached, and she had cold chills all over her body. What was going on?

"What?" Zander supported her. "Is the weapon hurting you? Let's get you out of here."

"No. I have to do this, Zander. I have to kill him." Nausea rose in her throat. King Frederick was the most evil man on the planet and he was going to blow up an island if she didn't fire this weapon. She was a Delta and had been raised for this.

She didn't know if she *should* do it. But that made no sense. She was protecting innocent people by taking out one horrific dictator and his staff.

Please help me, she begged everyone in heaven who cared.

"Okay. I've got you. Let's do this, then get you home." She could read the fear in Zander's eyes and felt it reflected in her own. Papa had taught her how to fire the weapon but really hadn't given her all the information she needed, telling her to have faith and it would all work out.

What if the weapon required her to give her life or something insane like that? What if it took out Zander too? She wanted to tell him to leave, but she could barely hold herself upright. Is that why Papa had never fired it? She couldn't imagine her Papa would make her Secret Keeper if that was true. He would've told her. Right? But then it made terrifying sense in a way—Papa having such a hard time appointing another Keeper and putting it off until he was certain he was going to die. It almost seemed like he was hoping he'd be killed before passing it on, assuring the weapon could never be used. But if Papa knew he was going to die, he would've used the weapon and sacrificed himself to protect her.

Her mind was scrambling for solutions as her head pounded

and the certainty she'd felt minutes ago disappeared. The confusion scared her. Confusion wasn't from God, peace was. Should she fire the weapon or not?

"Help me, Zander," she begged.

She lifted her thumb toward the right spot. Zander guided her trembling hand and secured her thumb. Then she took her other hand and tried to twist the pendant into place. That was all she had to do, then she could speak the command as they pressed the button to fire it.

Zander helped her twist the pendant. It was awkward with both of their hands and hers shaking so badly. Finally, finally, it clicked into place. The room swam before her. She leaned heavily into Zander, afraid she would pass out. She just had to push the other button and speak the command.

Keeping her thumb on the right spot, she lifted her left hand toward the button. Zander's hand guided hers.

"Almost there, Jess. You've got this."

She had to push the button and say her name and title. Then it would be done. All those people would be safe. King Frederick's reign of horror would be finished.

And suddenly her head cleared, and she knew. She knew it clear through.

She should not fire the weapon.

Yanking her thumb from the spot, she twisted and pulled out the pendant.

"What are you doing?" Zander asked. "Jess, we haven't got time. Those people on the island will die if you don't fire."

She looked into his dark gaze. He trusted her, but he didn't understand.

"I'm not supposed to fire it," she said confidently, meeting his eyes and hoping he could see that she was doing the right thing. Even if it seemed insane at this moment.

"Are you sure?" He looked at the weapon, then back at her. Their gazes held and he nodded. "Okay, Jess. Okay." He gathered her close and held her.

She knew it was right not to fire it, but would all those people die because she hadn't? Would their deaths be on her head?

A loud cheer from multiple people sounded outside the cave. She and Zander pulled apart. "What are they cheering about?"

Footsteps pounded into the cave. Zander sprang to his feet and pointed his A.R. at the opening. Jessie climbed up behind him. Her legs were weak, but she knew she'd done the right thing and that gave her faith and strength to face whatever was coming.

"Frederick is dead," Aiden yelled, running into the small room. "Delta Force got him and have captured all the men who were with him. The rest of his leaders are bugging out. He didn't fire any of his nukes. Jake just got the message." He beamed and then he looked at Jessie and the weapon about ready to fire. "Jessie?"

Jessie let out a shuddering breath. Zander lowered his weapon and reached for her. She collapsed against him.

"Jess?" Zander asked.

"I'm okay," she said. She lifted the pendant and hung it around her neck. "Do you realize if I would've fired, I would've killed whoever was next to Frederick's body? Probably a large contingent of the Delta Force taking his body back to their COs to prove he's dead." She pushed out a breath, not shaky any longer, but kind of shaky at what had been averted. "That's why I was told not to fire. Heaven was staying my hand."

Zander stared at her. "And that's why you weren't inspired to come straight to the weapon and fire it. You would've hurt the Delta Force team who probably found him at about that same time."

She cuddled into Zander. "No wonder Papa was so insistent about only firing it with the right inspiration."

Zander's dark gaze was wide. "And now you feel okay?"

"Perfect." She leaned in. "And I'd really like to secure this weapon and kiss you for a long time."

His lips curved up. "We can definitely arrange that."

Aiden cleared his throat. "All right. You two good to secure the weapon and lock up the cave? Jake is sharing the news and bringing the special ops forces to a rendezvous point a little bit from here. We'll leave a team patrolling, but we'll head back to the valley and figure out the situation there and what we need to do with Admiral Seamons."

There was still danger, but they could resolve it.

"Okay. We'll take care of the weapon and be right behind you. Leave someone with a vehicle for us. I'm exhausted." Jessie smiled at her cousin.

He saluted her. "Gotcha. Good job here today."

"I didn't do anything," she said, still awed and grateful for what she hadn't done.

"Yes, you did. You listened to the spirit and made the right decision at the right time. You did perfect." His smile was huge. "You were the perfect person for Secret Keeper, Jessie."

"Thanks, Aiden." She'd always had her family's support, but

there were times she imagined everybody had second-guessed Papa's decision. She knew she had.

"Thank you." He turned to go. "Oh, also reactivate the mist as you leave. We turned it off once Jake found me and talked the special ops teams down. It was such a pain in the butt to get through it and find everybody."

"All right," Jessie said.

Aiden walked out, and Jessie wanted to stay in Zander's arms. She was feeling immensely better but weak from everything they'd been through recently and all the stress. She leaned against Zander and silently prayed in gratitude. The situation had been diffused. It was over ... for the moment.

"Thank you, dear Father above," she whispered.

"Amen," Zander echoed, his breath warm against her forehead.

She clung to him. It was over. Zander's arms were all she needed now.

An impression filled her, stronger than even when she'd known they needed to head to the cave at that exact moment or when she'd known she shouldn't fire the weapon.

Her hand flew to her mouth and her stomach turned over with the implications of what she'd just felt. Would her family understand?

"Really?" she asked aloud.

"What?" Zander asked, pulling back slightly to focus on her face.

A warm peace came over her, and she knew exactly what they had to do. She was going to have some angry and upset family members, but this impression was the exact reason she Secret Keeper.

She opened her eyes and focused on Zander. This was the reason he was here as well. "We have to blow up the cave."

His eyes widened, but he immediately nodded. "Okay. I have enough C4 and can easily blow it." He looked down at the weapon they were still kneeling by. "That's smart, Jess. We'll move the weapon. Too many people know about the cave now. Really smart. Do you have any ideas where to relocate the weapon to, or do you want to meet with your family about it first? We might need a temporary hiding spot, at least."

He pushed to his feet and reached for the backpack that contained the C4 and his detonators.

Jessie also stood, but she grabbed his hand. "We're leaving the weapon in the cave."

Zander whipped around to stare at her. His dark eyes were full of surprise and questions. "But ... Jess, it's never even been fired."

She shrugged. She knew that. It seemed like such a waste, from the people who created it and were killed for it, to her Papa giving so many years of his life and dying because of the weapon.

But she could not deny the prompting and also the relief. The Deltas would finally have peace.

"Jess." He squeezed her hand and looked deeply into her eyes. "Your Papa and your entire family have dedicated their lives to this weapon. Admiral Delta gave his *life* for this weapon."

"No. Papa gave his life to protect Hudson."

He said nothing more but held her gaze, obviously concerned about her decision.

She wavered, thinking about Papa and her family and all they'd done to keep this weapon safe. But Papa had never fired it either. Each of her family members' faces and blue eyes flashed through her mind. All of them giving so much time, energy, and devotion to this weapon. Its creators who'd been killed for it.

It was tragic, but she knew this was what Papa wanted. Knew it deeply. She wondered if this wasn't why she'd been made Secret Keeper. Papa couldn't destroy it because of his allegiance to the people who'd created the weapon, entrusted him with it, and given their lives for it. But he wanted her to finish this and put this chapter of instability and worry and fighting behind her family. The Deltas would be stronger for what they'd been through, and they would finally have peace.

She could see Papa's smile and almost hear him say, "Good job, my girl." Her guardian angel was watching over her.

Resolve filled her, and she'd never felt so determined about a decision in her life. "The weapon will never be fired, and that's the way it has to be. Think about it. Too many people know about it. The weapon will never be safe after all this, and our family will never have peace." She smiled, relieved and growing more excited about her decision with every passing moment. No matter what she would face when her family members found out. "I got the inspiration, Papa agrees, and this is what needs to happen."

"Okay." His smile was shaky, but then it turned into his normal incredible grin.

Man, she loved that grin.

"All right." He blew out a breath. "Let's blow up the most important weapon in the world that your family has dedicated their lives to." He pointed at her. "I'm a hundred percent with you, Jess, always." She felt that radiate through her. "But you're telling everybody the news, not me. I can't afford the negative publicity when I need your family to approve of me."

She smiled. She liked that he wanted her family to approve of him.

"Let's do this." Zander gave her a quick kiss and then grabbed his backpack again.

Jessie looked from Zander to the weapon and then back again. She felt light and happy. Her family would finally be free of the weapon. And she could be with Zander.

Chapter Sixteen

Zander quickly wired the C4 explosives. Jess brought the case, removed the weapon, and set it right next to the charges. Nobody would ever access it again. He could hardly believe it, but he knew Jess was not only right that it needed to happen, but she'd also received the inspiration from above. He trusted her.

He glanced over at her and she met his gaze, her beautiful blue eyes as peaceful as he'd ever seen them. He hurried faster; he could set up this charge in his sleep. Soon, he and Jess would get out of here. They would walk away arm in arm like in a movie scene with the mountain exploding behind them. This cave would be buried under the granite cliff.

He smiled. He wasn't the dramatic type, but he liked the image. Most of all, he liked the image of him and Jess together. He wanted to be with her. Always. Would she relocate to his home base in California? Maybe he'd ask for a change of assignment.

Were there any instructor opportunities for EODs in Colorado? Was he ready to be an instructor and not on the front lines?

Finishing, he strapped on his backpack, set the timer, and wrapped his hand around Jess's. "Time to go."

"Thank you, Zander." She squeezed his hand as they hurried into the exterior cave.

"Of course. Hey, should we grab a couple of these gold bars rather than blow them all up?"

He was teasing. Mostly.

"Sorry, love. I feel like all of it needs to be buried. Papa's legacy, buried and secure. Is that weird?"

They reached the exterior door and exited into the crisp, early morning—or was it night?—air. His watch said eleven-forty-three p.m. Night, then. It was a different scene than the fog and the fear of coming into the cave. They both changed back to their night-vision goggles, then continued walking.

"Not weird," he reassured her. "I think it fits. But a gold brick would be kind of cool."

He winked at her and upped his pace. He wanted to make sure they were well clear of the cave before it blew. Where had Aiden left someone waiting for them?

"*Love?*" he added, grinning happily at her. Did she really love him? Was the entire crazy ordeal over? Were they finally safe and going to be together? How soon could he hold her and kiss her for a long time like he'd been dreaming about?

"You okay with that?" she asked quietly.

"Oh yeah." He grinned, pulling her into his side and squeezing her waist. "More than okay ... love."

Jess gave the cutest little laugh. Zander had no idea the last time he'd been so happy.

Until a man sprang from behind a tree, ripped Jess from him, and shoved a gun into her neck.

"Seamons," Zander growled. "Let her go, or I'll rip you apart." He couldn't draw his own weapon and put her at risk.

"Give me the Delta weapon."

"It's in the cave. Go get it," Zander told him.

Seamons looked at them, obviously realizing they weren't carrying anything large enough to be the weapon. He looked at the open cave door and his eyes narrowed. Greed filled his gaze.

Jess elbowed him and dodged away. Zander leaped to her, pulling her behind him as Seamons fired his pistol. Liquid heat seared through the side of Zander's abdomen. The force of the bullet threw him back against Jess.

"Zander!" Jess screamed.

Seamons ran for the cave entrance.

"I'm okay," Zander grunted out, regaining his footing and yanking out his own pistol. Blood streamed down his hip. He felt a little lightheaded. He shoved his other hand into the wound to slow the flow, then yelled to the retreating figure, "Don't do it, Admiral!"

Seamons ducked into the cave.

Jess ripped her backpack off and pulled out the first aid kit. She yanked out some squares of gauze. He lifted his hand from the wound and she shoved gauze pads into the flow of blood and pressed. Hot pain stabbed at him. He was losing a lot of blood, but he would be okay. He holstered his pistol. They needed to move.

"It's clean. It passed through," she said. "Are you okay?"

Her beautiful face was swimming in and out of his vision.

"Zander ... Zander!"

"Jess, we've got to ..."

They weren't far enough away from the cave and it was going to blow. He wrapped her up and pushed off with all the energy he had left. The explosion ripped through the night and all he had the time or strength to do was tackle her to the ground, cover her with his larger body, and pray he took the brunt of the debris and rock that would shower down on them.

"Zander!" Jess screamed.

Debris, rock, tree branches, dirt, pine cones, and even shards of the granite wall slammed into his back as he cradled her beneath him. Pain ripped through him.

And then mercifully everything went black.

Chapter Seventeen

Jessie screamed Zander's name as the mountain exploded behind them and she was buried under Zander's body. Rocks, pieces of granite, branches, and other debris pelted them, stinging any exposed parts of her arms and legs that Zander hadn't managed to cover as he wrapped her up and took her to the ground.

The debris stung like a hundred wasp stings. Some of it cut her, but it was nothing compared to her stress over Zander. *Please say he's alive*, she begged heaven above. She'd asked heaven for far too much lately, but this was the one miracle that had to happen.

Tears streamed down her face as Zander's blood covered her back, warm and sticky and far too much of it. The scarier thing was he was not moving, lying on top of her like dead weight. She was having a hard time catching her breath, but she didn't care about herself.

That stupid nightmare. Had it been a premonition? No! She wouldn't believe it. He would live. He had to.

"Zander," she panted. "Oh, please no. You promised not to leave me!"

But he hadn't promised. Not really. He'd said he'd do everything in his power... and he'd used that power to protect her. He'd stepped in front of her and taken the bullet from Admiral Seamons. He'd covered her with his body like a shield and taken the brunt of the explosion.

No, no, no.

"Jessie! Zander!" Thor's voice. Oh, thank heavens.

"Thor," she tried to scream, but her lungs were compressed from the man she loved literally smothering her. Was he breathing? Could she feel his heartbeat? Everything was too loud and chaotic from the explosion and in her own mind to slow down and determine that.

"Zander!" Thor's voice was full of concern. She'd never heard Thor's voice sound like that. He was always teasing, laughing, trying to get a rise out of somebody, or he was gooey sweet with his beautiful wife Shelly.

She peeked out from under Zander's arm and could see Thor. He rolled Zander off of her, catching him before he hit the ground and supporting him on his side. Jessie pulled in a full breath and scrambled up.

"Let's get some clean gauze on this wound on his side and ..." Thor cursed.

"What?" She pushed her night vision goggles back into place and followed Thor's gaze. She wanted to curse, too. A wide spike of granite was embedded in Zander's back. Nausea rose in her throat, and she turned and vomited.

"Jessie." Thor's voice was semi-level. She could tell he was trying to calm her. "Get the gauze and then you've got to radio for help." His blue gaze met hers and he nodded to her. "You've got this."

She stood on wobbly legs and hurried over to where she'd dropped the first aid kit. It was buried under some rocks, but she saw the edge, pushed the rocks off, and yanked it out. Hurrying back, she pulled out some large squares of gauze, dropped to her knees, and pushed it into the wound on his side. Thor held Zander on his side with one hand and grabbed some of the gauze with his other, carefully wrapping and pressing it into the wound on his back.

"Can't we take that out?" she begged.

"Not yet. It can make the bleeding worse and cause more internal damage."

"But what if ..."

If they shifted him wrong and that spike embedded deeper and killed him or severed his spinal cord. It might have already nicked his spinal cord. It was so close.

"Does he have a pulse?" Thor interrupted her fears.

She lifted her free hand and pushed it against his warm neck, staring at his handsome face, his eyes closed, no smile at all.

She felt his pulse and at least they had that. "Yes, the pulse feels strong," she reported to Thor.

"Okay. Can you reach the radio in my pocket?"

She nodded, determined to get help as fast as possible. But what if he lost too much blood before then? What if he was already paralyzed or dying? Where was the team who should be monitoring the cave?

Please, she begged her Father above. *Please spare him.*

She fumbled with Thor's pocket, trying to pull the walkie talkie free.

The low rumble of motors sounded in her ears. She looked up at her cousin. "Thor?"

"Oh, thank heaven," Thor said. "They must've heard the explosion. What happened?" It seemed like an afterthought. The cave had blown and the weapon was gone, but Thor was a hundred percent focused on Zander, just as she was. What would he say when he knew she and Zander had buried the weapon on purpose?

The worst part ... it was all her fault. She'd told Zander to blow the cave and now he might die because of it.

She shook her head at her cousin. She could tell everyone later. Right now, she had to focus on Zander living through tonight.

Chapter Eighteen

Jessie paced the hospital waiting room, gnawing at her thumbnail, praying constantly, and avoiding the probing glances of all her family members and Zander's SEAL buddies. They'd all arrived over the past few hours to support and pray for Zander.

Various special ops medics, Blackhawk pilots, and his own SEAL friends had pulled off an amazing hoist operation in the dark and had gotten him in the air twenty minutes faster than Life Flight could have reached their location. Every second had felt like an hour as she'd watched the lifeblood of the man she loved oozing out. Transporting him had been a nightmare, and she thought she would have a heart attack as they carefully positioned him and took his body up in a basket. If he shifted wrong in the improvised litter, she knew that spike of granite could kill or paralyze him.

But Zander had made it to the hospital alive. The receiving hospital staff had been stunned to see a Blackhawk land on their helipad, but they'd loaded Zander and whisked him inside. A nurse had explained that they were pumping him full of fluids, would do a blood transfusion, and had taken him into surgery to stabilize him and attempt to remove the granite. If he survived that, they would see what damage had been done to his internal organs or his spinal cord. If there wasn't further repair needed, they would close up both wounds and see how his recovery went. His parents had been called and were being flown in by the Navy. Apparently the Navy, especially Admiral Gusbane, blaming himself that he hadn't recognized Admiral Seamons' deception and hadn't trusted the Deltas, had been extremely accommodating and willing to do anything the Deltas or the SEALs needed.

"Jessie." Her mom grasped her arm, pulling her to a stop. "It's going to be hours until they're done with surgery and even longer until he's awake. Can you please stop pacing long enough to tell us what happened?"

Jessie looked around at all the interested, concerned, loving faces. Her family. Would they be upset with her for what she'd done? She'd been so certain it was the right thing, but now Admiral Seamons was dead and Zander might not survive. Emotion filled her throat. She needed another minute.

She sank into a chair and looked around again. It was crazy that they were all here. Family, future in-laws, Zander's SEALs. Only little Mo, Kelsey's mom Lori, and Granny Vance had stayed back at the house. The sheriff's deputies had stayed with them, just in case. Nobody was monitoring the cave and only one of the sheriff's men was monitoring the cameras and sensors in Papa's house, just in case a mercenary hadn't gotten the message that Frederick was dead and the weapon blown up.

Thirty-two well-loved faces looked back at her. Thirty-two people who had risked life and limb, sacrificed careers, and supported Papa, and her, with everything they had. For the weapon ... or for Papa ... or because it was just who they were? Loyal, devoted, hard-working, incredible people who would never get a reward or recognition for their sacrifices. A hardened military family who trusted each other and trusted in heaven above. They'd been literally to purgatory and back.

Would they thank her for making it possible for them to finally have peace and rest? Or would they be livid with her for destroying not only Papa's life's work, but theirs too? Would they all be lost without that focus?

"Can you tell me what happened in the valley after we left?" Jessie asked instead, trying to buy some time.

Bailey stood up. "Me?"

Colt and their dad smiled at her. "Sure," Colt said.

"It was crazy, absolute bedlam," Bailey started the tale, making it overly dramatic and terrifying. Blackhawk helicopters had swooped down, soldiers spilling out of them armed to the teeth, barking orders at the family as the Deltas' SEALs escaped. The family tried to distract and keep those troops occupied and then even more troops rolling up the canyon. No way to fight or win without losing many of the Delta family and loved ones.

Jessie found herself smiling and saw many other smiles or sometimes eye rolls as Bailey over-exaggerated the story. Being herded into Papa's house and kept prisoner like a bunch of cattle. Admiral Seamons admitting that he'd sold out to Frederick years ago and even his wife Olivet hadn't known. He'd set it up for Olivet to get in with Frederick as well, to get more money and to assure she took the fall with the military or police if anything came out.

Bailey told how he'd used the zip drive to set up people he wanted Papa Delta to investigate and to gain the Deltas' trust. He'd even set up the shooter at the outdoor restaurant with Maddie and Braden who had shot him in the leg. The gunshot and the injury had been a complete fake. That made sense how he had run at the cave with no crutches.

He'd separated the Deltas back at the house and questioned each of them, grilling them, desperate to find out what they knew about the weapon and how to access it, telling them he already had special ops forces who had overwhelmed the family members who were missing and the weapon would soon be in his hands.

"He questioned everyone but Kylee ..." Bailey's voice trailed off and she looked guiltily at Chandler's fiancée. "Sorry, Kylee."

Kylee smiled sadly. "At least the bullet he took for me at the party was real."

"He truly cared for you," Joseph said firmly. "He told me that."

"Thank you." Kylee nodded to him and snuggled into Chandler.

There was silence for a few seconds, and then Kylee gave a slight smile and gestured to Bailey. "It's all right. Finish your story."

Bailey continued, talking about the troops camping all over the lawn. None of the family being allowed to leave the house and poor Granny Vance about going insane and Mo not wanting to go to sleep and Hudson carrying him around for hours singing to him before he crashed.

"It was a crazy and terrifying night, but as you can see, we all survived and I have lots and lots of good story fodder." She bowed. "The end."

Jessie smiled and wondered if she should clap. Bailey sat back down. Colt kissed her softly and drew her against his side. The simple affection made Jessie long for Zander. Would she ever know that level of comfort and familiarity? Would they ever be able to be together without stress and angst? He finally wasn't fighting against his feelings for her, but now he was lying on a cold hard operating table fighting for his life, not even able to use his strength or all the impressive skills he'd mastered over the years to help him.

He has his faith.

She teared up again, appreciating the reminder. *Please heal him.*

"Okay," her mom said. "Time to tell us what happened. Thor told us about you not firing the weapon and the news of King Frederick's death coming at just the right moment. Good job listening to the spirit, love."

Jessie nodded. That's what it was all about, right? Her listening. Her being the one chosen to make this decision, possibly because she *would* listen. Her boy cousins used to tease her when they were younger that she was small in stature but big in spirit. She hadn't minded the tease. It had helped her today.

"But Thor has no idea how the cave exploded and what happened to the admiral," her mom said.

"And I usually know everything," Thor bragged.

Jessie smiled at him while Aiden groaned. Most of the family simply studied her.

She wasn't a storyteller or given to dramatics, but most of all she didn't know how her family would react. She tightened her jaw and her resolve, but she also twisted her hands nervously.

"After Aiden told us that Frederick had been killed and everyone cleared out of the cave, it was just Zander and me. He was holding me close and suddenly I knew ..."

Everybody leaned forward. So many blue eyes focused on her, with a few deep-brown and green mixed in. Sweat popped on her forehead, but she had been brave in that cave and she knew she'd done the right thing. She straightened her shoulders and raised her voice. "It was one of the strongest promptings I'd ever felt in my life. I *knew* the weapon had to be destroyed."

There was a collective suck-in of breath.

"Wait a minute ..." Colt stared at her as if she'd lost her mind. "That wasn't a mistake? You had Zander wire the cave and blow up the weapon? On purpose?"

"Yes." She tilted her chin up and met her brother's blue eyes. He was confused and probably angry. All of them had taken the Delta Protection Detail seriously, but nobody more than Colt. He'd seemed to live and breathe it, had even built a special room off his garage with all his equipment. Most of her life she had wished Colt was Secret Keeper, and the past couple of weeks when she was designated Secret Keeper by Papa, she had really wished she could let her brother take the responsibility.

But not any longer. She'd done the right thing and she would take their anger, censure, questions, whatever they threw at her. They were all probably questioning their support of her being the Keeper about now. She looked around the room. Cousins, siblings, in-laws, future in-laws, parents, uncle and aunt, the elite

SEAL team. Everyone looking at her as if all the stress might have been too much and she'd lost her mind.

Little Jessie. Against all these brave, tough, accomplished people.

"Why, Jessie?" her dad asked, his voice gravelly, his elbows braced on his thighs.

Hudson jumped to his feet and started pacing. He had a lot of energy and it was obvious it couldn't be contained right now. She waited for him to say something, and he didn't disappoint. He stopped in front of her and then kneeled and grabbed her hands, his blue eyes intense. "Jessie ... Papa gave his life for that weapon."

"No." Jessie felt strength course through her. She smiled at the cousin she'd been closest to growing up. "No, Hudson. Papa gave his life for you."

He blinked at her and then he released her hands, jumped up, and paced some more. "You're right. Of course you're right." He gestured with his hands. "Why does it feel like we just lost him all over again?"

Tears stung at Jessie's eyes. He was right. The weapon, the cave, the secret, the patrols, the special conference room and monitors at Papa's house, all of it was so ... Papa. His life's work. His life's focus. And now it was gone. Useless.

No. Not useless. It had all served a purpose and could continue to do so. She slowly let her gaze travel around the room, focusing on each face that she loved and that Papa had adored. The most important parts of Papa's life had been her cousins, her siblings, her parents, her uncle and aunt, and her. All of them and so many others in the valley and those Papa had served through his military service. That had been his life's focus.

"I hope you can all forgive me," she said, her voice quavering. "Zander also tried to talk me out of it, but I felt the prompting deeply, and I couldn't deny it. I was meant to destroy the weapon and the cave. It *is* the reason I was made Secret Keeper. Because I don't know if any of the rest of you would've done it." She maybe shouldn't have had added that last line. It wasn't meant as a shot, but she knew it was the truth.

There were some murmurs, exchanged glances, and Maddie stood, her mouth working soundlessly as she tried to make sense of the information. Jessie knew Maddie was involved with helping to infiltrate and take down some seriously bad people. She probably had a list of people she would like to use the weapon on. In an emotionless tone, she muttered, "You're right, sis. You are absolutely right. There's no way I would've destroyed it."

Jessie shrugged. She didn't think Maddie was criticizing or approving of what she'd done. She was simply stating a fact.

The room was almost buzzing with energy and whispers in pockets around the room. Some of her family members looked at her as if they hoped she was pranking them.

"Huddy." She looked at Hudson. He stopped walking. "I know it feels like we just lost Papa again, but the truth is ... it was a proper burial for his legacy and it was the right thing to do." Her voice got stronger, and she stood and walked up to her cousin, tilting her head back to focus on his face. "This is the only way the Delta family will ever have peace. Too many people knew about the weapon and there would be no shortage of mercenaries, military, dictators, treasure hunters, and opportunists who would be after it. Including our own government."

She looked around the group and could see it was registering with some of them. She wished Zander was here to back her up. He'd believed her so quickly. Was it simply that he trusted her or because he'd felt it too? He'd been there. By her side. Right where he should be. Tears pricked her eyes, missing him, worrying about him.

Please let him live, she begged heaven above. *I need him.*

Her family loved her, and she thought they trusted her, but this was something none of them would have done and it would take a while to gain their understanding. Some might never approve, but they wouldn't question her insight from heaven above.

"Think about the past couple of weeks. All of us," she gestured to Zander's SEAL buddies who hadn't said much, "and Reed's men, trying to keep the weapon safe. I was so impressed with all of you, all the hard work and dedication to our family and Papa and the weapon. We would've had to keep that up ... for how long? Could we have? Eventually, one of you would've been killed or some evil dictator would've stolen the weapon. Papa was already killed ... Zander might be dying as we speak ..." Her throat clogged up. She coughed, tried to clear it, but then had to croak out, "When would it ever stop? When would our family ever have peace?"

There was silence in the room.

A side door opened, and a male voice said, "Jess is right."

Jess?

She whipped around to face him. It wasn't possible, but there he was. The man of her dreams.

Zander slowly walked out, wearing doctor's scrubs and a big smile. Oh, how she'd missed his smile. His skin was sallow and his dark eyes looked tired, but he was as handsome and irresistible as ever.

Jess's eyes widened as she heard "Zander!" echo through the room.

She ran to him, wanting to fling herself into his arms but not wanting to hurt him. "You're okay?"

He nodded and gently wrapped his arms around her and ushered her into his right side. "Just a little tender on the left and apparently I've got a stitch or two on my back as well."

"Oh, Zander." She laid her head against his shoulder. "I can't believe you're just ... walking around. Why didn't they come tell us?"

He smiled. "Since I was passed out and they were worried about a head injury, they only gave me local anesthetics to stitch up my side and to remove the granite and sew that up. Luckily, the gunshot was clean and the spike didn't hit anything vital. I woke up while they were closing me up about an hour ago. Freaked them all out. I begged them to let me walk out here and shock you all. Actually threatened to leave against medical advice if they didn't allow it. Once the blood transfusion was complete, I got some clear juices down and they'd already pumped enough fluid into me with IVs when I was originally brought in and throughout the surgery. They agreed if I *could* walk out here, they'd let me." He grinned. "Nobody knows how tough and resilient EODs are. Are you shocked?"

"Yes!" Shocked in the best possible way. *Thank you*, she prayed silently, tears of gratitude stinging her eyes.

Her family and his friends gathered around. They started

asking questions, all talking at once. Everybody was relieved Zander was okay.

The Delta weapon's destruction and her ruining Papa's legacy seemed forgotten. For the moment.

"Everybody, everybody ..." Colt hollered above the news.

The family finally calmed and turned to him.

"I agree with Zander. Jessie is right. She did the right thing. She was the right choice to be the Secret Keeper."

Jessie's chest filled with warmth. The oldest cousin, her big brother, was backing her up. She wasn't surprised. Colt was loyal to family above all else and would always have her back. She met his gaze, and he smiled and nodded to her.

"I would've been too prideful to listen to a prompting to blow up the weapon," Colt admitted.

Aiden and Thor exchanged a glance and shrugged and nodded at each other at the same time.

"And think about the pieces that fell into place, orchestrated from above," Chandler piped in. "Zander being the one by Jessie's side, the expert at exploding things."

"That's right," Cap crowed. "Taught him all I know."

Everyone laughed.

"They don't know I was only at your side because of how good you kiss," Zander whispered into her ear.

Jessie giggled.

Uncle Keith nodded to her. "Thank you, Jessie, for being humble enough to listen. You did exactly what Papa would have wanted."

"Thank you for giving our family peace," her dad said.

"Speak for yourself," Thor said. "What am I going to do in my spare time?"

"Kiss your wife," Shelly said.

"Oh yeah!" Thor grabbed his wife and started kissing her.

The family laughed and teased and the SEALs even joined in. Jessie wondered if it would take some of them more time to come to terms with it, but she had done the right thing. And they'd all have to figure out how to live with it.

Hudson and his wife Kelsey approached them. "Hey," Hudson said. "You two need some privacy?"

"I thought you'd never ask." Zander grinned at her, and her knees went weak.

Privacy? *Yes, please.*

Hudson's wife Kelsey escorted them through some double doors while Hudson stayed behind to chat with the family. She took them down a hall and then into a classroom of sorts. "I spent some time working here when I was in school. They do first aid and Lamaze classes in here." She winked. "Enjoy." Then she was gone.

Zander gently cupped her face with his hands. She clung to his biceps. It felt great to hold onto those beautiful muscle bumps, and she didn't have to worry about touching any of his recent wounds.

"You're really okay?" She could hardly believe it. "I thought I'd lost you."

"Lucky for you, you didn't." He grinned.

"So lucky. Actually so blessed and grateful." She fought the sting of tears and wanted to gush how much she loved him and pray her gratitude aloud. "How did you know I was right when you walked into the room earlier? You couldn't have overheard that discussion."

He laughed. "I heard you talking when I walked in, and I figured it was the right thing to say. You're always right in my mind."

"I like that."

"Jess … we haven't had much time together, and I have no clue what's going to happen with my career and assignments after this mess, and I don't want to be presumptuous, but …" He grinned at her.

"Oh, using that smile to get your way now?"

"You know it." He looked over her face. "You did call me love earlier today, right?"

"I can't recall that." She pursed her lips. "I'll have to think about it."

He leaned down and she went onto her tiptoes, clinging to his biceps.

"Well, this is risky, then …"

Her stomach pitched happily. "I can't imagine something risky could scare *the* Zander Povey."

"I can run into enemy fire or fight any insurgent, but asking *the* Jessica Delta to date me is terrifying."

"Date you?" Dating sounded so normal and basic and perfect.

"Well, I'm hoping for some serious dating, but fun too," he clarified with a smile. "Lots of kissing and hopefully a commitment to figure out how to be together always. And soon, a huge diamond ring. I might've snuck a gold bar out of a certain cave and think I could trade it for a pretty impressive diam—"

Jessie pressed her lips to his, cutting him off. He smiled against her lips, then proceeded to kiss her, holding nothing back. Wow, did he hold nothing back! She thought of those tortured, beautiful kisses from before. She'd loved them, but the purity, commitment, and dedication in this kiss blew everything they'd previously experienced away.

They pulled apart to catch a breath and Jessie said, "Yes, I would love to date you, Zander."

"Perfect. Now maybe we should find a chair. I'm about to pass out."

"Zander!" she scolded and hurried him over to a chair. He sat down. "Are you really okay? What do you need? I'll get your doctor or Colt or Kelsey. A drink? Some food? Another IV or more blood? Do they need to reevaluate you?"

Zander grinned up at her, wrapped his arms around her waist and pulled her onto his lap. "I'm fine, Jess. A little lightheaded from that incredible kiss and the happy future I'm planning with you. Sitting down is all I need. With you in my arms. Avoiding my left side. And some more kissing."

Jessie tried to protest that he needed help and that she would call a nurse for help, but he wrapped his arms around her and kissed her. She had no way to protest as she melted against him. On his right side.

Epilogue

It was Halloween, and it was a chilly and odd day for a wedding, but Maddie had never done anything traditionally, so why start with her wedding?

The crowd of friends and family filled the new addition to the ski lodge that Alivia and Klein had recently finished for Jace and Ammon Jardine. It was beautiful, a wide-open room with wood beams and floor-to-ceiling windows overlooking the sweeping Summit Valley below. No snow yet, but it was a crisp, clear fall day.

Jessie appreciated each clear, peaceful day, and today was a great one to see so many friends and family members. It had been over a month since Papa's memorial service. An emotional event with a massive crowd. He'd received full military honors and nobody left without shedding a few tears.

The family was healing, though it was impossible to replace the hole a man like Papa left behind. Jessie missed him. More now than ever, as her family were all busy with their own families. She'd been busy catching up online with all the school she'd missed during the Delta weapon drama, so that helped a little. She'd graduate in December and then ... she wasn't sure.

A few mercenaries had shown up over the past month, found the exploded and burned-out cave, and left. King Frederick's regime had been dismantled after he died and there were only about a dozen of his top leaders who hadn't been captured and arrested. Who knew what hole they were hiding in? The people of Banida, Poland, and Germany were rebuilding their lives. That would take time, but at least the war was over.

Admiral Gusbane had apologized to the Delta family and offered prestigious assignments to Braden, Aiden, Zander, and their SEAL buddies. Her dad and Uncle Keith also apologized for ever mistrusting him. Braden had chosen early retirement from the Navy. He and Maddie were working with Jasmine Quinn and Sutton Smith to continue fighting against human trafficking and drug lords. Jessie was very proud of them. Zander, Aiden, and the SEALs had only asked to go back to work. Aiden and Melene were making things work with her being in Virginia whenever he was home, but when he went on missions, she'd join whatever humanitarian group needed her anywhere on the globe.

Jessie and Zander talked through FaceTime, text, and email every day, unless he was on an assignment that prevented it. She'd been able to go visit him in Coronado, California and he'd come to visit her twice in the past month. There were some advantages to having a high-up admiral feeling beholden to you.

Jessie focused back on the happy couple. They beamed at each other and were such a perfect fit. She didn't judge Braden and

Maddfor their choice of wedding day, but it sure wouldn't be hers. She fantasized about a Christmas wedding, but she hadn't told anybody that. She wasn't even engaged. Despite Zander's tease about stealing a gold brick to buy a diamond ring, she hadn't been given a big, shiny diamond yet. Zander was on a special ops mission currently, so she wouldn't be getting engaged for Halloween either. Maybe Thanksgiving?

Jessie stood in the lineup of bridesmaids with Alivia and Braden's sister Isabelle. She liked Isabelle a lot. It was nice to have a new friend who didn't have a significant other. She kept in contact with her friends from school, but with Zander not here in the valley, being alone was an acute pain. She'd hoped he'd make it back for his close friend Braden and her sister's wedding. He hadn't dared commit one way or another as he'd gone undercover for a mission somewhere in Russia. The mission must've taken longer than he'd planned. There was always that fear pricking the back of her mind that he'd get killed on a mission, but he'd made it through the Delta mission, so she kept focusing on faith that he'd keep coming back to her.

"Do you take this woman to be your lawfully wedded wife, to have and to hold, to love and to cherish, for richer or for poorer, as long as you both shall live?" Pastor Sam asked Braden.

"I do." Braden's teal-blue eyes twinkled at Maddie. He looked very handsome in his dusky blue suit and burnt orange tie. Not as handsome as Zander would've looked, but was it fair to compare anyone to Zander?

"Do you take this man to be your lawfully wedded husband, to have and to hold, to love and to cherish, for richer or for poorer, as long as you both shall live?"

Maddie tilted her head, took her time looking Braden over, winked at him, and then said, "I guess he'll do."

The crowd tittered with laughter.

"Just teasing. Of course I do. Have you not checked out this fine-looking male specimen who can kiss better than Westley from Princess Bride?"

Pastor Sam shifted, but he was used to the Deltas' teasing. Everyone else laughed.

"Well, then," the pastor said. "We'd better see this kiss. I now pronounce you man and wife. You may kiss the bride."

"Yes!" Maddie cheered.

Braden simply grinned, wrapped his bride up tight, and gave her a kiss that looked Oscar-worthy.

The crowd cheered, and Jessie cheered with them. She could picture her and Zander kissing passionately like that. Someday. Hopefully soon. She wanted to be married, though she had no idea how it would go with him gone a majority of the time. That would be rough. But she would never tell him to give up his hard work and specialties. He had given it up for a while to protect the Delta secret weapon. She was grateful he could get back to doing what he loved, grateful he was healthy and whole and hadn't given everything for the Delta weapon. Like Papa.

She could bet Papa and Granny were watching over them on a beautiful occasion like this. Actually, as she thought about that, she could almost feel Papa smiling down on them, so happy for Maddie and Braden.

Braden lifted Maddie into the air, and everyone cheered.

The crowd surged to their feet, and the congratulating commenced. Jessie chatted and hugged and laughed and kept

Thor and Aiden from wrestling during Maddie's wedding and enjoyed the delicious chicken and salmon teriyaki dinner. She wished Zander was here, but she couldn't waste each day pining for him. She would stay positive and happy and hope that someday it could work out for them.

Dinner and dessert and toasts wrapped up. Jessie had given the last toast to the beautiful couple. She finished with, "And Braden, please train diligently so someday you can best my feisty sister in a fight. I've never accomplished such a grand feat yet."

Everyone laughed.

"That's 'cause you're too sweet to pick a fight," Thor called. "You could easily win."

Maddie called out her protests and Aiden threatened to fight Thor on the dance floor.

As Jessie went to interrupt yet another brawl, her mom wisely started the music and the dancing. Thor and Aiden happily went off to dance with their wives.

Jessie didn't want to dance with anyone, but she chatted with many people that she loved. Hudson and Kelsey sidled up next to her. Mo was dancing with Thor and Shelly. He was adorable. The entire Delta family spoiled him.

"Hey," Hudson said. "Can we ask a favor?"

"For sure. Anything for the people who gave us Mo."

Hudson's blue eyes twinkled. "Can I tell her?"

"We haven't even told our moms," Kelsey said in a falsely shocked voice. She pushed at his shoulder, her dark eyes all lit up. Jessie loved seeing all the couples in her family together and these two had gone through years coming to their happily ever after.

Jessie pressed closer to them. The music covered a bit of the conversation. Hopefully no one would overhear. "Are you two expecting?" she whispered excitedly.

"We aren't saying." Hudson grinned happily. "But the fact that Kelsey is extremely fertile bodes well for my chance at those eleven boys. It'll be a full a lacrosse team, so Chandler will be ecstatic."

"Brave!" Kelsey cried out.

He grabbed her and kissed her while Jessie clapped her hands happily together.

They pulled apart and she couldn't stop smiling. Mo was the cutest ever. She could hardly believe they were already expecting again.

"How do you know?" she asked quietly. "You've only been married five weeks." She blushed at what she was asking.

Hudson chuckled easily. "I had her take a test last week, just hoping. I'm the luckiest guy in the world." He picked his wife up and swung her around.

"Yes, you are," Jessie agreed. She was thrilled for them and wished Zander could share this moment with all of them.

"So here's what we need." Hudson got semi-serious.

"Okay ...?" She was intrigued. Hudson always had some kind of crazy plan. She'd often been part of them growing up. It made her feel young and carefree to be in on something with him. Papa had often known about their plans. As long as they didn't hurt anyone or damage someone else's property, he had rarely stopped them. She smiled just thinking about it.

"Do you remember Jason Spackman?"

She nodded. Jason had been a little too flirtatious and cocky in high school, but he'd never bothered her too much. He bothered her a lot now. He'd lied to Hudson and claimed Kelsey's baby was his and caused them four years of separation and pain.

"He had the nerve to show up."

"Here?" That was crazy. The guy must be clueless. "Seriously?"

"Yep. He's over at the refreshment table, pounding shrimp down his ugly gullet. Can you ask him to dance?"

She cringed. "Just don't leave me dancing with him for too long."

"Twenty seconds. Promise." He crossed his heart. He was such a kid at heart.

"Okay. I'll do it for you, but only because I found out about ... the best secret first."

"You're the best." Hudson hugged her.

Jessie waved to them and sauntered around the edge of the dance floor. She saw Jason by the refreshments. He was chatting with Ammon Jardine, who owned the ski resort with his brother Jace.

Ammon saw her first as she walked their way in her silver high heels in the clingy burnt-orange dress Maddie had picked out for all the bridesmaids. He grinned. "Hey, Jessie. You look great."

"Thanks, Ammon. The resort looks amazing."

"Thank you. Alivia and Klein outdid themselves with this room and the suites we added on to the hotel. We're excited for ski season."

"Me too." She gave him a quick one-arm hug. He was a great guy. She'd thought he was after Alivia at one point, but Klein had won. They'd found out Klein had always had Alivia's heart, though her older sister was too tough to let even Maddie or Jessie know that.

"Jessie Delta." Jason gave a low whistle. "Dang, girl. You grew up to be a hottie!"

Jessie grinned when she wanted to cringe and shove a shrimp into his ugly mouth to shut him up. Actually, she'd prefer using some of the debilitating moves Papa had taught her. Forget being kind or a peacemaker with a guy who had hurt her cousin and Kelsey like this loser had.

"It's been a long time, Jason. How have you been?" She blinked up at him as if she were flirting.

"Not as good as you, beautiful. Do you want to dance?"

"I thought you'd never ask."

He shoved his plate of food at Ammon, who raised his eyebrows and set the plate on the table. Jason grabbed her hand and tugged her out onto the dance floor. Whirling her into his chest, he wrapped her up, his sticky hands lower than they should've been on her back.

20, 19, 18 ...

She counted down in her head. Hudson had better keep his end of the deal. This guy was just gross.

"Man, if I would've known how fine you were, I wouldn't have stayed away from home for so long." He pulled her even closer and whispered, "You want to get out of here?"

... 3, 2, 1.

If Hudson didn't show up right now, she was kneeing this guy and letting Hudson rewrite his plan. Her cousin was a master at ad-libbing when necessary.

"Excuse me." Hudson tapped hard on Jason's shoulder. "Can I cut in?"

"Buzz off, dude. She's mine." Jason didn't even turn to look at him.

"I don't think so." Hudson grabbed Jason's shoulder and ripped him away from Jessie.

Jessie helped, shoving Jason away and telling him, "You're way out of your league, dude."

"H-H-Hudson," Jason stuttered. He looked around at the circle of Delta men who had moved into position while Kelsey danced with him, and his chin quivered. Then he held his hands in front of his face. "Don't hit me. Please don't hit me."

Kelsey held Mo in her arms and sauntered up to them, looking gorgeous and confident.

"Kelsey. Um ... wow. I'm sorry. I'm really, really sorry."

"Not yet," Hudson said, grinning. "But you will be." He folded his arms across his chest, showcasing his well-defined biceps, and cocked his head to the side. "What did you think would happen showing up here?" Hudson didn't wait for an answer but called to his brothers, "Bros?"

Aiden, Thor, Chandler, and Hudson's brother-in-law Sheriff Reed all stepped closer. They yanked Jason off his feet, tipped him upside down, and hauled him ingloriously off the dance floor.

"You have the right to remain silent," Reed began.

"What did I do?" Jason whined, his face turning red as all the blood rushed to it.

"Really?" Hudson asked. "What *didn't* you do?"

The men disappeared out the door. Kelsey and Mo stood close by Jessie, watching them go.

"Who was that dude?" Mo asked.

"Nobody, love." Kelsey kissed her son's cheek. "Let's dance. Thanks, Jessie." They danced off, and Jessie waved. She knew they could've done much worse to Jason with Hudson's fame, money, and talent. She was glad they could close that chapter and move past it.

"Those boys." Her mom came up, laughing. "Do you think they'll hurt him?"

"No." Jessie's cousins were too honorable to thump a loser like that, even if he did deserve it. "He might spend a few minutes in a jail cell, though." They both laughed. "Aren't you glad you had girls?"

Her mom hugged her. "I had Colton."

"He doesn't count. Too serious." She winked at Colt as he and Bailey danced by.

"You look beautiful, sweetheart." Her dad approached with a drink for her mom, handing it over.

"Thank you."

"I'm sorry Zander couldn't make it," her mom said.

"Me too." Her dad's eyes twinkled happily. Was he sorry or not? "Do you want to dance?" he asked Jessie.

"You should dance with Mom."

"He will. Soon. I'm going to enjoy this strawberry lemonade. This marrying off a daughter is a lot of work. Maybe I do wish I had all boys." She winked and walked over to sit by Aunt Holly.

Her dad took Jessie's hand and put his other hand formally on her waist. She rested her hand on his shoulder. They waltzed around the dance floor, which was a little weird as "Can't Stop the Feeling" was playing. Of course Maddie would have upbeat songs at her wedding. She and Braden were dancing happily, seeming unable to take their eyes or their hands off each other.

"It's great to see her so happy," her dad said, following her gaze.

"For sure. Braden is definitely the right man for her."

He nodded in agreement and asked, "Are you happy, sweetheart?"

"Of course," she said. "I've got all my family around. Nobody has persecuted me for blowing up a legendary weapon, I'm graduating with my master's soon, and my boyfriend is a super talented special ops hero."

"Who you wish was here."

"I always wish it, but I'll be happy and make things great, even if my lover isn't here."

"Your lover?" Her dad wrinkled his nose, obviously not liking that wording.

"Sorry. My super-stud who can kiss better than Westley from the Princess Bride." She stole Maddie's line, making her dad groan. "Chief Petty Officer Zander Povey, Master EOD," she clarified. "Have you ever met him?"

"Once or twice." Her dad shook his head at her. "Have you two talked about how to be together? Aiden and Melene seem to make it work."

"They do." She didn't love the idea of leaving the valley, but it would work out. Somehow.

"Excuse me." A male hand tapped her dad's shoulder. "Can I cut in?"

Jessie looked over her dad's shoulder and cried out, "Zander!"

He stood there in his dress blues, which were actually black, looking irresistibly handsome with the biggest smile for her. "Hi, Jess."

"You going to wield that smile like a weapon?"

"If it gets me a kiss."

Her dad let out a long-suffering sigh, but put Jessie's hand into Zander's.

"Thank you, Dad."

"Be good to her," her dad said. It was a standard dad warning, but her dad knew that Zander could and had protected her with his life. He'd never not be good to her.

"Always, sir." Zander nodded respectfully.

Her dad clapped him on the shoulder and walked over to find her mom.

Zander tugged her close, lifted her off her feet, and swung her around. She laughed happily and wrapped her arms around his neck. He lowered her to her feet, holding her scandalously close. "Ah, Jess. Do you have any idea how much I've missed you?"

"Not near as much as I've missed you. Now stop complaining about it and kiss me."

"Gladly." He grinned and then he kissed her. Wow, did he kiss her! He bent her back and took full and complete control of her lips. She adored him.

"Come on, you two. Trying to take all the attention on *my* day!" Maddie's teasing voice was much too close.

Zander lifted her up, turning her to face her sister and Braden.

"Hey, man." Braden and Zander embraced. "Sorry I missed it. I traveled as fast as I could."

"You're here now," Braden said easily, never one to hold a grudge. "Thanks for coming. It means a lot."

"Congrats." Zander hugged Maddie. "You are one lucky woman."

"Don't I know it?" Maddie smiled happily at her husband. "Buff, Beautiful, Not-too-Bad-at-all Braden is the best husband in the world."

Braden laughed and hugged her.

"You two go dance and smooch." Jessie shooed them with her hand. "We won't steal your thunder."

"Thank you. You know how I love to be the center of attention." Maddie blew them a kiss and whirled off with Braden. She couldn't have cared less about the attention, hyper-focused on her husband. Jessie wondered how she'd even noticed them.

Zander pulled Jessie in close again. Slow dancing with her to "Marry Me" by Train. Jessie's heart leapt. He was truly here.

"How'd you get here?" she asked.

"Pulled a few strings." He grinned and tenderly ran his hands along her back, making her tremble. "Told the Rangers I was with that if they didn't finish the job and get me to the most beautiful woman in the world, I'd have Hudson Delta tell the entire world on all of his social media that SEALs were far superior to Rangers."

She laughed at that.

He directed her to a quiet corner of the dance floor and then suddenly they were behind a half-wall and a large potted plant and floral arrangement she hadn't even noticed.

"Zander?" she asked.

He dropped to one knee and grasped her hand, singing along with the song, "Marry me ... today and every day." He grinned and pulled a ring from his breast pocket. It wasn't even in a box, just a gorgeous princess cut diamond with smaller square diamonds embedded into the band.

She was stunned. They hadn't even talked about logistics of where they'd live or when they'd get married or ... who the heck cared?

"Yes!" she cried out.

Zander stood and kissed her deeply and then pulled back, grinning, and slid the ring onto her finger. He tenderly kissed her finger and then pulled her in and kissed her long and thoroughly. Very, very thoroughly.

She was flushed and so in love as they pulled back.

"I love you, Jess," he murmured.

"I love you, too, my frogman who's better than any prince." She wrapped her arms around his neck and they swayed in their private spot, flush with love and the future spread out before them.

"What do you think of living in Coronado and whenever I go on extended missions, we fly you home or to a humanitarian mission with Melene? She told me they have a lot of need for speech pathologists."

Melene had mentioned that option to her as well. She liked it. With her degree, she could help children and have the flexibility to be with Zander whenever he was home.

"Whatever gives me the most time with you," she said.

He grinned. "A Christmas wedding? Right after you graduate?"

"If you can wait that long," she teased him.

He hugged her tighter and whispered huskily in her ear, "I'd get married tonight ..."

A delicious shiver ran through her.

"But your dad threatened me with making me live in that spider-infested cabin up by the cave for a year if I didn't let your mom plan a Christmas wedding."

"A Christmas wedding it is."

"I think all of our SEAL buddies can come."

"Oh, good. We can make my mom hug Van and Cap. Those two have issues."

"Don't we all?" He grinned. "Except you. And lucky for me, you're willing to put up with me."

"You are pretty tough to handle."

"Oh yeah?" He cocked an eyebrow and kissed her softly. "That's tough on you?"

She moaned. "So tough. I can't believe I'll be expected to do that over ..." She kissed him briefly. "And over ..." She kissed him longer. "And over ..." She wrapped him up for a long, delicious kiss and didn't plan to ever let him go.

"Sheesh!" a little voice piped up from down low. "I thought my mama and daddy kissed too much."

"Mo!" Jessie bent low and he gave her a squeeze around the neck. "Sorry. I haven't seen Zander in a long time, and I missed him."

"Hey, tough guy," Mo chirped. "Why ya kissin' my Aunt Jessie?"

Zander laughed easily, swooped Mo up, and tossed him into the air. Mo squealed happily.

"I'm gonna marry your Aunt Jess," Zander confided to the little boy after he caught him.

"Zander and Jessie's getting married!" Mo squealed right as the song finished.

A cheer went up in the room, though nobody could see them.

Hudson poked his head around the corner. "Sorry. I'll just take my loudmouth son." He splayed his hands. "Toss him here."

Zander easily threw the boy in the air and Hudson caught him.

"What'd we talk about not sharing the secrets?" Hudson asked in a stage whisper.

"What, Daddy?" Mo asked loudly. "I didn't tell nobodys about the baby!"

"Did he say *baby*?" her mom said, coming around the corner to congratulate Zander and Jessie.

"Baby?" Aunt Myrna's voice. "Hudson? Kelsey?"

Pandemonium broke out.

"You better kiss me quick," Jessie told him. "Mo just bought us some time."

Zander grinned down at her. "I love that kid." He brushed her hair away from her neck. "But I'm not going to kiss you quick." He bent down low and kissed her neck.

She shivered at the beautiful sensation.

"Really, really slow," he said, taking his time trailing kisses up her sensitive neck.

Jessie wrapped her arms around his neck and held on. Kissing slow? That sounded wonderful. Zander in her life always? That sounded perfect.

She had felt Papa's presence tonight, but she sure hoped he wasn't watching right now as Zander cradled her close. His lips met hers, and the world exploded with joy.

* * *

I hope you loved the Delta Family Romances as I much as I loved writing them.

I wasn't ready to let this family go so I set my Christmas series - Summit Valley Christmas Romances here with the Deltas. If you were intrigued by the tough, hands-off, Captain Zeke Hendrickson read on for the first three chapters of his book.

Hugs and thanks for the support,

Cami

Delta Family Romances

Deceived

Abandoned

Committed

Betrayed

Devoted

Compromised

Endangered

Accepted

Returned

Devastated

His Perfect Match for Christmas

FIRST THREE CHAPTERS

Chapter One

Captain Zeke Hendrickson, elite Navy SEAL, the guy who no man could best and no person dared touch, balled his hands into fists to hide the fact that they were shaking. He could storm through any insurgents' camp, take a bullet without flinching, breach a door that had dozens of unfriendlies aiming machine guns at him behind it, and stay calm and focused. Not since escaping from home the day he turned eighteen had he noticed his hands shaking.

Coming back to the Delta families' valley high in the beautiful Colorado mountains to discuss "helping" Holly Delta protect a young woman, and "of course you're staying for Christmas, you're one of the family" had him experiencing nerves he didn't know he had. One of the family? That was a laugh. Why then did it make him strangely happy and not feel like laughing at all?

He rubbed at the back of his neck as he wavered on Joseph and Holly's front porch for far too long. All seemed quiet, but there were eyes, and possibly a scope, on him. He casually catalogued the scenery while looking for the source of his impression.

The valley was vastly different than when he'd left it in late September. First, it was covered with thick, white snow, the lake a slushy grayish-blue and the pine trees loaded with blankets of fluff. He couldn't wait to take a dip in that freezing lake. It had been cold when he'd done his therapy in the middle of the night in September. It would be an iceberg now. The sun was slanting down from the southwest. It would set soon. There was greenery dotted with red berries wrapped around the porch poles and railings.

The second thing he instantly noticed was the silence. Last time he'd been here as part of the Delta Protection Detail. The valley had been invaded by troops and Delta family members, his own men, and the local sheriff's department were everywhere.

Where was everybody and why did he sense they had security watching him when the Delta secret weapon was no more? He rubbed at the back of his neck again. He could really use Preach, Chaos, and Wolf watching his back, the goofball, cowboy Thor teasing him about something, or his good friend Zander Povey giving him that big smile and quietly protecting him from anyone inadvertently touching him. Zander was an EOD and on an assignment, but preparing to marry Jessie Delta this Christmas. Everybody else was apparently working or busy on this bright December day. Except whoever had eyes, or a target, on his back.

A slight movement and sound and he pinpointed the man's

location to Papa's front porch, the house next door. He focused in on it, issuing the challenge for the man to show himself or Zeke would be coming for him.

A security guard he didn't recognize stepped out from the cover of Papa's front porch, answering his question about who was watching him, but creating a whole new list of questions.

They studied each other for a couple of beats. Zeke's mind did its normal cataloguing: Former military, early thirties, blond, blue eyes, six-two, two-thirty, built but Zeke could easily take him, high-quality clothing and gear, comfortable with the L129A1 sharpshooter rifle in his hands. Possibly British? If not it was an interesting choice of weapon for an American.

The man simply glared at him and then stalked off around the back of the house. Hmm. What was that all about? The guy wasn't a threat to him and he was obviously a hired security guard, but Zeke could sense the guard's animosity from here and he instinctively didn't like him. Lieutenant Van "Chaos" Udy would say the guy had a very "punchable" face. Zeke smiled thinking of his teammate and friend and not minding the idea of punching the security guard.

He could go after the guy for information and maybe a decent fight, or he could knock on the door and he would probably get the entire spiel from people he trusted and was excited to see. Well excited was stretching it. Zeke didn't let himself get excited about much. Emotion and excitement were not a soldier's friend. Either could get a man killed.

Answers and a warm hug that he'd neither initiate or ask for, but somehow appreciated and didn't hate, would happen as soon as he lifted his fist and rapped. It was easy. He just had to knock on this door. He was semi-surprised Holly Delta hadn't been watching for him to pull into their quaint valley and ran to meet him as he exited the rented Accord. Was she simply focused on whatever woman they wanted him to help? With anybody else he might presume they were icing him or testing him but with Holly ... the older woman was tough, brave, but too kind and warm for his comfort level.

He flexed and released his fists, rolled his shoulders back, and prepared for battle. He wanted to laugh at himself. This wasn't battle. Yes, Holly would give him a "Mama" hug when she saw him. The contact always made him extremely uncomfortable, but at the same time he craved the human connection and feeling of unconditional love Holly somehow bestowed upon him with the hugs she insisted on.

Besides the hug that was coming, he couldn't put a finger on what else was making him nervous. That bothered him. Zeke was always in control of the situation and his men. Nerves got men killed quicker than emotion did.

He could blame the security guard putting him on edge but he'd felt it before the guy showed his ugly face or before Zeke arrived in the valley. He thought it might be the fact Holly was asking for help when she was surrounded by impressive Delta family members. These men and women were exceptionally trained and could protect the lady in danger from any threat. Why Zeke? He confidently knew he was one of the best-trained, highly-decorated, and able-to-execute special ops soldiers in the world, but he didn't know if that was the reason Holly wanted him here or the excuse to get him to come for Christmas.

It was also uncanny how Holly knew he had leave, and unless something huge broke, another assignment for him and his four-mean SEAL team wouldn't be coming until January. He'd planned to custom-make a bunch of new axe-handles to sell on his website, under an identity nobody would ever know about, and spend a lot of time in the gym during the Christmas holidays. Instead ...

Lifting his fist, he rapped hard on the glass front door before he could second-guess it, or twenty-two guess it as the case may be.

Footsteps came much too quickly and he could see the beautiful fifty-something Delta Mom coming into the foyer. Her face broke into a radiant, welcoming smile as if Zeke were the person she had been waiting to see for weeks. He knew that wasn't accurate. Holly made everybody feel special. He was nothing special. Unless you needed a tried and proven soldier.

He shook his head, blew out a breath, and steeled himself. His own mother had hit and belittled him more than his father. They both put on a persona for the church community that they were pious, kind people. He had seen his dad treat his older sister kindly on occasion and he'd heard other soldiers claim their parents were loving and kind. But he had never personally experienced a mother in their own private sphere, where no one else was watching, who was as warm, welcoming, accepting, and loving as Holly Delta.

The door flung open and Holly rushed at him. He instinctively edged to the right, his body already moving to incapacitate her with one quick hit to the back of the neck. No! He forced himself to stop, clenched his fists and his teeth, and impressively didn't react at all as she flung her arms around his neck and hugged him fiercely. At least he didn't react physically.

"You're here! Yay!" She kept right on hugging him. Despite his lack of movement, Zeke closed his eyes, cataloguing the moment for future reference. Nothing was as comforting and like the home he'd never known than Holly's "Mama" hugs. "Now hug me back," she encouraged. "You can do it cute boy."

Cute boy? Zeke had broken men's arms for much less, but from Holly it wasn't demeaning. She saw something in him that he doubted was actually there. She somehow saw him—hardened, battle-tested, emotionless, untouchable Captain Zeke Hendrickson as "cute" and as if he had warmth, depth, and ... worth. Worth beyond being an elite, fearless weapon and brilliant and tactical leader of the best SEALs in the world. In his not-humble-at-all opinion.

He shook off the introspection and forced himself to lean into her hug and wrap his arms around her back. He clasped his hands together at her mid-back. He hadn't been able to release his hands and place them palms down on her back yet. That was a step in the hugging process that he wasn't sure he'd ever get to. He kept his eyes closed, savoring the solace of her touch. All the hidden anger, remorse, and pain didn't matter when Holly held him tight.

"Good job, my sweet boy," she said softly.

Zeke should've laughed out loud. He didn't. He'd been through more elite trainings than anyone he knew, received commendations and praise constantly, and had been awarded many distinguished awards including the Navy Cross and recently the Medal of Honor, but Holly Delta telling him he did a good job hugging her, and intoning she was "his" sweet boy, a part of the family, seemed like the best reward he could imagine.

"And there he is, the elite Navy SEAL captain, hugging my wife again," Joseph Delta's voice came from the foyer.

Immediately Zeke released her and drew back. Holly smiled up at him and kept her hand on his arm as he extended his hand and shook Joseph's.

"Nice to see you, sir."

"You too, Cap, you too." Joseph luckily didn't touch him beyond the handshake and released his grasp quick. He somehow instinctively knew Zeke's hugs with his wife were unique and nobody else in the world would get away with touching him like Holly did. Or maybe his future son-in-law, Demo, had explained to him.

Joseph gestured into the house. "Come in. It's bitter cold out here."

Zeke shrugged. He was wearing a long-sleeved black shirt and black cargo pants. He didn't notice extremes in temperature much, trained to perform in extreme hot or cold situations and used cold therapy whenever he could to stay in top physical condition and heal some of the strain his constant physical training brought on.

"You have a bag?" Holly asked.

"In the car."

She gave him a look, seeming to sense immediately that he wasn't a hundred percent committed to staying. Captain Zeke having a jolly Christmas with a bunch of warm, friendly Christian believers was a bit of a stretch. Now if this young lady had a vicious killer after her, that would be more up his alley.

"We'll get it soon," Holly said.

He actually wanted his duffel within reach. He'd forced

himself to leave everything but his knife and utility tool in his bag and in the truck. It was unsettling not to be armed with at least his Sauger. Especially with the security guard out there. He looked again but the man wasn't in sight. It rankled at him that he'd forgotten about the guy while he hugged Holly. The man obviously was employed by the Deltas so it shouldn't have bothered him, but he didn't let his guard down. Ever. And he just had.

The family and this valley should be safe and at peace. The danger to the Deltas was gone now that the youngest, Jessie, and his friend Demo, the best EOD he'd ever worked with, had blown up the Delta weapon most of the world had been after. They had lost their patriarch, the impressive and renowned Admiral Davidson Delta. He knew that still pained Jessie and he was sure the rest of them. It was impossible to fill the hole of losing a great man like their "Papa Delta".

So why the unfamiliar guard? Something to do with the woman they wanted Zeke to help?

"Thanks for coming," Joseph said.

"Of course." He would do almost anything for the Deltas. These people were as unselfish, cohesive, and extraordinary as any family he'd ever met. The American public at large had no idea, but the Deltas keeping their weapon safe from King Frederick had stayed the man from raining nuclear weapons on America. The elite special ops Delta Force had thankfully taken out Frederick and things were somewhat calm on the international front. For the moment. There was always some terrorist or insurgent ready to stir up trouble. Weirdly Zeke liked trouble. Trouble kept him busy and not thinking. Thinking got men killed.

Holly kept her hand on his arm. He didn't know if she was

aware it was making him uncomfortable. She had some theory that she could acclimatize him to touch. He almost smiled at the thought. Maybe if Holly had been around a few years ago, his fiancé Rachel wouldn't have dumped him while he was on a mission with no outside comm. By the time he'd seen his phone again she'd blocked his number, relocated from Virginia Beach, and left no forwarded address. Rachel had a lot of issues with his lack of emotion or "romance" and she hated his phobia of touch. Who could blame her? Being engaged to a man who never instigated and barely tolerated kissing? Anybody who'd known about the relationship and his lack of dating since would think he was heartbroken. Zeke thought it was more learning a lesson. Romantic relationships weren't in the cards for a tough old frogman like him.

"Come back and meet our darling Mia." Holly finally lifted her hand but gestured him through the entry. The sweeping staircase had decorative greenery wrapped around the railing and a variety of tall, skinny, decorated with silver balls and other junk, fake pine trees arched almost the height of the two-story entry.

Darling? He glanced sharply at Holly. "You said this was a mission." If she dared try to matchmake him with some girl. He'd have to bug out quick.

She smiled at him. "It is." Her smile disappeared. "I'll let her tell you about the mission, or rather nightmare for our angel girl. Come on." She reached out as if to grab his hand, but seemed to think better of it.

Zeke's shoulders relaxed a fraction. He'd had about as much touch today as he could handle. When he was here fighting with the Deltas to protect the secret weapon Holly had forced him into one hug a day. He hoped she wouldn't try for more than that if they weren't all busy saving the world.

He followed Joseph and Holly through the entryway and into the sunny open living area with two-story windows overlooking the picturesque lake and mountains beyond. He remembered the scenic view. Even though it was now snow-covered, it was just as quaint. They had a huge gorgeous pine tree all decked out in the corner, Christmas-y stuff on any shelf, mantle, or wall that could be decorated, and a fire going. Most people would say the home and view were beautiful, perfect, and appealing.

He stopped walking and felt his jaw go slack as he took in a view more beautiful, perfect, and appealing than anything he'd seen in his vast world travels.

A woman stood from the couch as they walked in. Five-four. Athletic. Civilian. Blue fitted sweater dress with high-quality leather boots. Definitely wealthy. But there his usual analysis failed him. He somehow forgot analyzing and simply focused on the radiance of the woman herself. She had shoulder-length blond hair that framed the sweetest-looking face he'd ever encountered. Her smooth skin and rosebud lips were appealing, but it was the mixture of purity and happiness in her brown-sugar eyes that stunned him. Their gazes met and held and time ceased moving forward.

Suddenly she smiled at him. Warmth immediately filled his body and it felt like Chaos had gotten a lucky hit and slammed his powerful fist into Zeke's sternum. *Push out a breath. Okay. Pull it in. Now back away slowly.* He backed up. He needed to get away from this woman. Double time.

"Zeke ..." Holly was beaming at the woman and hadn't

noticed his signs of retreat. "This is Mia Burton. Mia ... Captain Zeke Hendrickson, elite and accomplished Navy SEAL and pretty much the toughest, most highly-decorated, and experienced soldier on the planet."

Zeke should pull his gaze from Mia to tell Holly to tamp down on the bragging, but he couldn't make himself do it.

"Sorry, Cap," Joseph said. "You know she loves to brag about you like you're one of her own."

At least Joseph got it. Zeke had no idea how to respond to the introduction. What was he supposed to say this captivating and stunning woman? He couldn't think of another option besides escape. This was not a good situation. Beautiful women didn't affect him. Emotions like warm flashes in his body and needing to breathe from a pretty lady's smile couldn't happen to him. He felt like he was soaring on some emotional high just having her smile at him. He couldn't complete a mission if this woman had anything to do with the objective.

Mia bounced across the space toward him and he should've either run or taken her out. He froze. Zeke never froze. It was as if she'd captured him in a snare he'd never been trained how to defend against.

She was pint-sized, but there was energy and power in that small frame that intimidated him.

Intimidated? Yeah right. Suicidal insurgents in Afghanistan hadn't intimidated him. This miniscule blonde was no match for his strength or skills. She couldn't capture or incapacitate him.

Not physically. But what about emotionally?

He pushed that away. There was no time to deal with it anyway as she was right in his space. Close. Far too close. She smelled like lemon candy. He absolutely loved lemon candy. Old-fashioned lemon drops. Pretty much the only good memory of his childhood. A grandma at his church would give him one every week if he'd sit still during children's class. She kept giving them to him even as a teenager. Grandma Hendrickson she'd asked him to call her. He'd stolen her name for his last name. He'd thought she was the nicest woman he'd ever met. Until he met Holly Delta.

The delicious-smelling woman standing in front of him stuck out her hand and used that smile on him. It made him feel strangely weak. He'd never felt weak before in his life. At least not since he'd escaped from his parents' house and joined the military. He'd had so many drill sergeants try to break him, but their belittlement and abuse was nothing compared to what he'd lived with throughout childhood and teenage years. He'd absolutely excelled in the military.

He looked down at the woman's hand and then back into those golden-brown eyes of hers. Were those long lashes real? They were pretty, that's all he knew. Not many blondes had brown eyes, but maybe her hair was dyed. His throat was dry and his pulse thrumming far too fast. He was trying to catalogue but the draw of her made everything off and his head feel too big for his body.

"Zeke," Holly said. "You can shake her hand."

That broke his concentration on the woman and he glanced quickly at Holly. He wanted to ask if he had to, but he could only imagine the answer and asking would make him look weak in front of this beauty. He never wanted to look weak in front of anyone, but the thought of this *Mia* thinking he was weak when he wanted her to listen to Holly's bragging about him and think he was a superhero had him sticking out his hand. Shaking hands was no big deal. He'd learned to do that as an adult and could get through it without making a fuss or obviously cringing and offending the other person.

Her hand slid along his so slowly he felt like the entire world had slowed down, except for his heart that was thundering out of control and a delicious tingling filling his stomach.

First her fingertips caressed his and then the fingers and finally the soft palm slid across his fingers and palms until they were aligned. Then she gently wrapped her fingers around the back of his hand and held on.

His breath shortened and he had absolutely no clue what he was feeling as he'd never experienced something like it before. He appreciated Holly's Mama hugs and they gave him that odd comfort that he somewhat liked. He could recognize accepting the hugs was a positive thing.

Holding this woman's hand had nothing to do with comfort. Her palm and fingers were warm and soft and it felt like his hand had found the spot it'd been searching for all his life. He didn't move as she held his hand and blinked up at him with those brown eyes of hers, but he realized something in that moment ... he liked her touching him.

That shocked him enough to pull away and clench his hand into a fist at his side. Crazily enough he could still feel the warmth and feminine softness of her much smaller hand. He hadn't really liked it, right? He'd just imagined he had because she was so pretty and seemed nice and soft and feminine and innocent ...

He took a step back. He had no choice. It was either that or he was going to touch her again and Captain Zeke Hendrickson never voluntarily touched anyone. Unless he was fighting them.

"Crikey," Mia said, shocking him yet again, blinking up at him with those big brown eyes and grinning invitingly. "You're a right big and tough one, aren't you now?"

She was British. That shouldn't have surprised him with the security guard outside's choice of weapon, but everything was surprising him today. He thought her accent was adorable. Adorable. Really? If Chaos could get ahold of his thoughts right now he'd never stop laughing. And then Zeke could pummel him. Chaos always put up a good fight. That'd be fun. A lot more fun than the discomfort of this moment.

He only raised his eyebrows. She'd probably think he was a mute but he didn't really care what she thought. Zeke didn't care what anyone thought. Caring what people thought only brought either pride or pain. Both could disable a man, and get him killed.

"He is big and tough," Holly said. "And more importantly he's experienced in all kinds of weapons, hand-to-hand combat, and defense. Zeke will keep you safe."

"Safe sounds ... lovely," Mia said but her voice quavered and her big brown eyes looked ... terrified. "Thank you, Auntie."

"Safe from who?" Zeke demanded, ripping his gaze from her to pin it on Holly. Auntie? They'd get into the relationship later. He needed to know who would dare endanger an innocent beauty like the one in hand's reach. Honestly it wouldn't take much effort at all just to reach out and touch her again. Just to see if it had truly been pleasant or if her appealing looks and smile had influenced him into thinking it was pleasant. He needed to do the research. Then he recoiled inside. Had he just wanted to ... touch someone?

Joseph stepped up and put an arm around Mia's shoulders.

She looked even smaller next to the tall, well-built Delta man and it thankfully distracted him from thinking about the unthinkable, willingly touching someone. Research or not, it was a stupid idea.

"Cap ..." Joseph said. "We asked you here hoping you could protect Mia from a vicious stalker. He's recently set his sights on Mia and promised to kidnap her and sell her to the highest bidder on the dark web. The terrifying thing is, we believe he's done the same thing to nine other women now."

If Joseph was hoping to coerce him into being invested, he'd done it. Sell this sparkling sweetheart on the dark web? Not on his watch.

He nodded to Joseph. "Thank you for giving me the opportunity. What details and information do you have for me? The past cases. The notes, threats, and contact the man has had with Mia, or anything else that will help. Do you want to text or email them? That might be more ideal so I can have the notes to refer to and not waste time talking about it right now. I'll hunt him down and have him to the authorities soon." He looked to Mia and nodded. Yes, he'd capture the refuse of humanity who'd kidnapped and enslaved other women and dared make this woman his next target. Zeke would make sure she was safe and he'd avenge the other women. Turning the spineless scum over to the authorities would be the only hard part. Vigilante justice sounded just right in situations like this. "Don't worry, Mia," he said. "You'll be safe."

He turned to go.

"Zeke!" Holly called to him.

"Cap!" Joseph joined her.

"What?" He turned back.

"The National Crime Agency in UK and the FBI here are

working together to track the guy down," Joseph explained. "There are two suspects but they've both completely disappeared. We don't have enough information to send you off hunting for either of them and that's not what we're asking of you. We'd like you to stay here, with Mia, actually at Papa's house where her two security guards are staying. They, and the rest of our family, will keep eyes on the cameras, sensors, and monitor the property. The man has found and taken each of the other women he's targeted. No matter what protection the police have provided or they've hired on their own. We can't have that happen to Mia. We want you to protect her, stick to her like glue, until the man is captured or your leave is up. At which point, we'll have to reevaluate the situation."

Zeke stared at Joseph then he looked at Holly and finally his gaze swiveled to Mia. For Joseph and Holly's parts they looked absolutely serious. Mia was biting nervously at her lower lip. Why was she doing that? He liked to understand why people had nervous ticks, his own was rubbing at his neck. He was surrounded by men most of the time and no man he knew bit at his lower lip like that. It was highly distracting. It made her look ... appealing.

A protectiveness filled him that he had no choice but to act on. He had to keep Mia safe, but he could do that best by tracking the guy down. He couldn't ... hole up in a beautiful house in a beautiful valley with a beautiful woman. He had to look at this mission objectively and unselfishly but he'd go absolutely insane not acting and not moving and ... being trapped with a woman as enticing as this one.

"You want me ..." He began slowly, still focused on Mia. For some reason those three words made her dark eyes light up in the most beguiling way he'd ever seen. She wanted him. Light, joy, and warmth seemed to crash into each other inside his chest. *She* wanted *him*? He'd met a lot of women who wanted him physically. Because of his hatred of human touch, he'd never been tempted to reciprocate. Rachel had broken down his walls but it had taken her years, and then she'd decided she absolutely didn't want him. But Mia seemed to want him, all of him.

He blinked to clear his vision and realized how ludicrous his thoughts were at the moment. He cleared his throat and pivoted to Joseph. What did Joseph want? "You want me to stay here and protect her like a glorified bodyguard?"

Joseph nodded. "I can't think of anyone I'd trust more."

"But she already has security with her and what about all your with-it and qualified nephews, niece, daughters, and son?" he asked. Joseph barely knew him. Sure they'd worked extremely well together those couple of weeks in September, but if this man had any idea how messed-up Zeke was on the inside he'd never want him alone in a house with his niece.

"Remember what you asked me to do with Zander and Jessie?" Joseph came back at him with. Kind of hitting below the belt honestly as Zeke knew exactly what he'd asked of this overprotective father and he didn't want to have to reciprocate the trust Joseph had granted Zander. "Despite how hard it was as a father to allow any man to be so close to my daughter, we both knew that Zander was the ideal choice to protect Jessie because he would stay by her side round the clock and he had a vested interest in her. Holly and I felt this situation could be just as … ideal."

Ideal for who? "But … but …" Zeke gritted his teeth. He hated stammering. He used to do it as a child because he'd been afraid. As an adult he either didn't speak or he made sure what he said was clear and concise. Stammering was for wimps. He rubbed at the back of his neck. He was feeling wimpy and backed into a corner.

He *had* asked Joseph to allow his friend and Chief Petty Officer, Zander Povey, Master EOD "Demo" to be Jessie's bodyguard because Jessie was the Secret Keeper, in extreme danger, and Demo had been head over heels for her. "Demo liked Jessie. I don't like ..." His eyes widened as he realized what he'd just said. He spun back to Mia and held his hands up. "Apologies ma'am. It's not that I don't like you, but I don't like anybody. Please don't take it personally."

For the first time her warm brown eyes weren't sparkling invitingly at him, they were flashing fire at him. He had the feeling he was about to hear an earful of British slang that would curl a proper Brit's toenails. He didn't like that he'd hurt her feelings. But this situation was not going to work out. It was better she knew now that he was cold and not interested in her as a woman. That always ticked women off so he found it was easier to get it out right up front.

He should probably back toward the door. One glance at Joseph and Holly said he'd upset everybody now.

He was a soldier. A human weapon. A man of action. He was not a stay by the beautiful woman's side or a bodyguard of appealing British blondes.

If he could only escape this situation and go find Thor or Greer or one of the Delta men. He'd love a good fist fight about now. Then he'd get back to the Air Force Academy and coerce some gungho pilot to fly him out of Colorado as soon as possible. He hated to let down Joseph and Holly but they could find someone to do bodyguard duty for a gorgeous woman in danger. Most single men in the world would jump at the chance. Not him.

The dangerous part? Hooyeah.

The being alone with a beautiful woman? Not acceptable.

Chapter Two

Lady Mia Burton could only stare at the handsome, too-tough, military machine in front of her. Machine fit much better than human. Captain Zeke Hendrickson couldn't be a mere mortal. More like Rambo, Thor, or maybe the Terminator had strutted into the living room. Just the way he moved was like he owned the world and could best any person in it. It was downright appealing, especially with the danger she had pursuing her.

The only time he hadn't seemed like a human weapon was when he met her gaze with his smoky grayish-blue eyes or when he'd shaken her hand. Then he'd felt real. Too real. The kind of real, flesh and blood bloke that could warm a girl up all the way through. Blimey. Was it stuffy in here?

He'd been stoic and quiet, until his impassioned desire to go hunt down the stalker and his equally impassioned refusal to be her bodyguard. Then the clincher when he'd said that he didn't like her. He'd amended it to that he didn't like anyone but it had felt personal. It had not made her feel too cheery. Had actually shocked her. Mia didn't like prideful people as she'd spent her life dealing with her Duke of a father and his pompous, elite crowd, but she had never had a man not be interested in her. She didn't know if it was her family name, her personal success, her looks, the smile she always wore, or her happy zest for life, but men simply liked her and were nice to her. What was wrong with this cheeky bloke?

In his defense, she hadn't acted like the successful designer and business owner she'd worked so hard to be, converting to a fan girl of the hot military man with her moony looks and stupid line about him being big and tough. Maybe that had been off-putting to him. She'd been overwhelmed by the sheer size and all the muscle on him. She'd been around all manner of sizes of men but he had to be a foot taller than her, twice as broad, and fit. His face and body were blindingly brilliant.

She'd like to touch some of those bulges and see what they felt like, but Holly had warned her he wasn't a touchy-feely kind of guy and she'd seen that as they'd been sharing a brilliant hand shake and then he'd yanked his hand away and clenched his fist. She wanted to know why he didn't like touch, and she wanted to help him like her touch. She'd felt a delightful spark and a warmth simply shaking his hand. It had been surprising, and made her want to feel it again. It didn't look like she was going to get that chance.

When he'd heard about the mangy git hunting her, Zeke Hendrickson had turned into Rambo, instantly in action mode and going to track the dodgy wanker down and tear him apart limb from limb. The man at that point had become human, all man. This American military genius, according to Auntie Holly, made her stomach fill with butterflies and her knees weak. His need to protect her had been ... blindingly appealing. This was a man who'd protect his lady. That was for certain. If only she could be his.

Okay. Mia bit at her lip. It was time to calm down and stop the fan-girling. Mia was a successful fashion designer and business-woman. Her company was flourishing, despite the fact that her father, the Duke, had never supported her dreams and would've preferred she not work like a "commoner". She loved her dad, but his theories were not hers. Her mum was as loving yet feisty as her dad was cool and haughty. How her mum adored her dad like she did Mia had no idea. He'd always been good to Mia and she'd caught glimpses of him feeling proud or warm toward her but he'd never acted on any of those feelings. Except when he heard about the stalker.

She didn't have the approval of her dad and she was fine with it. She definitely didn't need the approval of this hot captain. She had more men asking her on dates than she had time to give. They all thought she was fun, beautiful, lively, and some of them prob-ably liked the money and title she would attain some day. She tried to keep that information quiet, but men from England usually knew exactly who she was.

She thought most of the men she dated were ace. She'd just never met a man who captured her interest for longer than a few dates. Her mum either claimed she lacked commitment or she was meeting men who were "fun spunges" and "not equal to Mia's zest for life" in all the wrong places—church, the gym, the local café—great places to meet nice, lame, normal men obviously.

Captain Zeke Hendrickson wasn't a boring man. Nope. Nothing boring about him. But would he protect her from the famous stalker who'd left *the* letter on her pillow last night? She'd never forget the horror of that moment. Up to that point she'd taken the stupid love notes in stride, turned them over to the police, and promised to not ditch the security detail that her father had insisted watch over her since the notes had begun a month prior.

Last night she'd run out of her flat and straight into Commander Blaine Lewis's arms, rambling and scared and finally willing to take this stalking git serious.

Blaine had his partner call the bobbies and her dad, despite the fact that she'd dated and dumped him last summer he'd held her until she'd pulled away, and thankfully they'd made it to her parent's estate safely. After an elaborate ploy to throw the stalker off her path, she and her dad had taken one of his jets across the pond, running for her freedom, literally, to her mum's best college mate for protection. "If the Delta's can't keep your body safe, nobody can," her mum had declared. Her dad hadn't liked it, the trusting of Americans, but he agreed that the Brits hadn't kept those other girls safe and he'd succumbed to her mum's request, as he always did. The only time the Duke was ever soft was for her mum.

As Mia looked over the captain she thought this brilliant specimen of a man could keep her safe. But then she remembered that he didn't like her. A hot dose of anger, rare for her, made her want to flay him. As if she could.

"You don't even ruddy know me," she spit at him.

He gestured her down with his hands. It had the effect of making all those lovely muscles in his shoulders and arms flex through his fitted long-sleeved, black shirt.

"That's right, ma'am. I don't know you. So please don't take offense that I can't help you. I'm sure you'll be very safe with the

Delta family, and your bodyguards, and I'll just be on my way." He actually turned to go.

"Zeke," Holly's voice was sharp. "Sit down."

Zeke looked properly cowed. It was comical actually. His gaze swung for the entryway and then back to Auntie.

"Sit," she instructed and Mia thought even Auntie's wild nephews would obey that command. She'd only been around Auntie Holly and Uncle Joseph and their family for a few holidays throughout the years, but she sure fancied them. They were the kind of people you instantly felt comfortable around, and welcomed into their fold. Maddie had been her age and a hilarious friend who she still adored.

Zeke very slowly walked to the couch, and sat, on the edge of it as if he wasn't staying long.

Joseph and Holly walked to the couch opposite where Zeke sat and gestured her to sit next to him. Oh, he was going to go bonkers over that. The air in the room was tense as she stepped close to him and then gingerly sat on the next couch cushion. The muscles from his neck to his thighs visibly tensed.

Sheesh. She must really be off-putting to him. Had her antiperspirant or lemon body splash worn off? She should stop drooling over the handsome, fit stud. She had no need or desire to push herself on a man who was repelled by her. That hadn't happened to her before and she found it very ... disappointing. If she was honest with herself, she was gutted over his rejection. She wished she could believe it was because she hadn't felt rejection before, but she feared it was because this man was unique and intriguing and the kind of man who could capture and hold her attention like none other had succeeded to do.

"If this git doesn't want the job," she said, clenching her teeth. "I see no benefit in strong-arming him into it."

"Mia." Auntie gave her "the look". She and Maddie had found it hilarious that their mums weren't blood related but they had that same intimidating "Mama" look down pat. "Now, Zeke. Mia's mum was my college roommate and has been my best friend for life. I would do anything for her and her family. Anything."

Mia felt her bottom lip quiver. She knew Holly would, and Joseph as well. "Thank you, Auntie," she managed to get out without becoming emotional. Mia didn't think she was overly emotional as a rule but being targeted by the elusive "Sneaky Stalker" was terrifying. She'd think his barmy nickname was laughable, but there was nothing humorous about nine accomplished, well-known, and successful women from Britain over the past three years receiving "the note" and within days disappearing, still missing to this day. It hadn't mattered if the police had provided protection, or if they or their families had hired outside security. The bobbies were going insane. She wasn't far behind them.

She'd prefer death over being sold and enslaved as they assumed the women had been. Sheesh. That was a cheery thought. Merry Christmas with no peace for Mia right now. The only thing that felt like Christmas right now was Auntie's beautiful home and this picturesque valley. She prayed inside for faith and strength and for this blinding man to please, please protect her.

"Have you heard of the Sneaky Stalker?" Joseph asked Zeke. Both men were probably chafing with the sap of Mia and Holly's emotions.

Mia chanced a glance at Zeke and saw his eyes widen slightly as he bobbed his head. "The sicko that's targeted and kidnapped successful women in Great Britain." His gaze met hers and suddenly he wasn't the too-tough military chap who wanted to leave her as quick as he could march on. His bluish-gray eyes got darker and there was a fierceness in them that made her stomach do a little flip flop. This man would protect her and good luck to the stalker getting through him.

She felt Rambo's declaration of loyalty to her safety all the way through her body. A pleasant shiver traced down her spine and she was happier than she'd been since finding the note. Any barmy git who dared try and hurt her had better be prepared to get annihilated. Captain Zeke Hendrickson was going to keep her safe and nothing had ever sounded so soothing and stimulating at the same time.

"Yes!" She jumped up and threw her hands in the air.

He looked up at her, obviously confused. "Yes?"

"Mia?" Auntie questioned.

She sat down close to him, too close if the stiffening of all of his lovely muscles was any indication. She wanted to grab his hand to comfort him and because the first hand touch had been so lovely, but then she remembered that might put him off. They'd get into his aversion to touch, later. Right now she had to tell him how cheery he'd made her.

"I'm gobsmacked. So grateful. You are the toughest bloke I've ever laid eyes on, and Auntie and Uncle have told me about all your success and awards, and to think you're going to protect me. You really will watch out for me, won't you?" She blinked quickly to keep from crying. She'd been so terrifyingly gutted. Even with all her dad had done to throw up smoke and mirrors, even with his two best security guards, a former Royal Marine and a former

Royal Air Force, staying by her side. Even when she'd gotten safely to the Deltas's beautiful and peaceful valley, she still had this overriding fear and a pressure in her head that said that man was not far behind. That he'd track her down just like he promised in that awful note. Just as he'd found and kidnapped his other targets. Never to be found again.

"I ..." He shook his head and eased away from her. "I ..." He stood and paced away from them, turning around to face the three of them. He rubbed at the back of his neck and then clenched his hands into tight fists. "I completely agree that she needs round the clock protection and that psycho 'Sneaky Stalker' needs to be filleted or locked up, I'd prefer the former, but ..." He looked to Holly. "I'm not that guy. You know I'm not. I train. I fight. I train other people to fight. I plan and execute missions. I capture or kill the target. I can't sit around with ... her." He gestured to Mia as if she were a problem. A large problem if the angst on his face was any indicator.

Her happy bubble popped and she fell flat on her face. She hugged herself, chilled all the way through. The dry Colorado winter had nothing on the moist chill that penetrated to the bone in England, but she felt as cold as she had since finding that note on her pillow.

Run, beautiful. Run and hide. Because when I find you ...
The Sneaky Stalker

The other women had disappeared within days of receiving the now famous note. Some of them had even been in witness protection programs. The two that lastest the longest had hired private bodyguards and left the country. But he'd found them. He'd found every single one of the women that he'd threatened.

She could still picture her dad going to toe to toe with the lead detective, telling him he wasn't trusting his girl's safety to the "ruddy bloke" who'd let nine poor women be captured, sold like cattle, and never found, and the bobbies hadn't even caught the mangy git yet. Mia had never heard her dad lower himself to such common slang terms. Her mum ... most days of the week. Her dad ... too far above that. Not last night.

The poor man went red and blustered, already intimidated by who her dad was, and then to be called to the carpet must have dug deeply. In the end her dad had prevailed. As a billionaire and a duke he usually got his way. Unless he was fighting with her mum. Mia had never bested him in a battle of wills and she wouldn't even had told him about the stalker's original mailed notes but her mum and the bobbies had both informed him.

The Duke's already impressive team of twelve private security men, all former British military, had brought in trusted friends last night. They'd driven a dozen different motorcades out of her parent's estate where her dad had taken her after they left the station. Some of the teams headed for airports, others for yacht clubs, others for private estates far from Surrey. Her dad had stayed right by her side until he and four of his most trusted security guards had delivered her to Joseph and Holly. He'd told them he was leaving Commander Blaine Lewis and Lieutenant Charlie Portsmouth and he expected the Deltas to work with them to protect his little girl.

Mia had chafed at his tone and his terminology, she was not his little girl any longer, and the fact that Blaine would be part of her security detail. The Deltas hadn't flinched. They'd promised the entire family would watch over her and taken it a step farther.

They were bring in the most impressive military man they knew to ensure her safety. Her dad hadn't been certain an American would have training more impressive than his Commander or Lieutenant, but he'd surprisingly not only agreed, he'd assured he would pay any reward they named for them and the man. Joseph and Holly refused any kind of money, which surprised no one, but said they would pass a reward on to Captain Hendrickson. Her dad had agreed, and thanked them. Apparently his only daughter's life in danger had humbled him. She loved her dad, but humble had never been associated with his name and she could count on one hand the number of times she'd heard him say "thank you". Her dad had hugged her fiercely, the opposite of his usual crisp hugs done to please her mum, and he'd left, hoping to throw the Sneaky Stalker off even more by he and her mum being at their home this Christmas season.

Mia shivered and rocked slightly. It was all so heavy and serious and at Christmas time. She actually would be thrilled to spend a Christmas in the Deltas gorgeous valley with this fun and huge family, so opposite her own, but seeing her dad so intense, not proper or arrogant, had scared her almost as much as that note had. Tears pricked at her eyes. She was gutted thinking about that awful note, the poor women who'd been taken, her mum at home worrying night and day.

She and Mum should be organizing Christmas presents for hundreds of children who would go without if she couldn't deliver. It was the one time of year that Mia took off completely from work. Since graduation from university she'd spent the past six Decembers finding deserving families who didn't ask for aid but needed it desperately, shopping for the perfect presents, and then delivering them. She blinked quickly at the thought of those poor little ones, but the tears still trailed down her face.

Zeke's eyes widened and he backed up, holding up a hand as if to protect himself. "No. Please don't. Not tears."

Mia sprang to her feet and stormed up to him. He held his ground, but she could see how he was worried she'd touch him or something.

"What do you expect me to do?" she demanded, over-wrought with all the emotion. "Just let that murderer take me, sell me to the highest bidder and then ...?" She'd tried very hard to not think about the ... what then. Too horrifying and disabling.

He leaned toward her, which surprised her. His eyes got that fierceness in them again. "Nobody is going to take and sell you. Not on my watch."

His words rang in the air like the most beautiful promise she'd ever heard. Their gazes were caught, and she didn't want to ever look away. She found her hand raising toward him. She wanted to touch one of his muscles, reassure herself he was real and he really could protect her from a monster as depraved as the Sneaky Stalker.

Zeke flinched away from her hand and stepped back. That stung. He looked at Uncle Joseph.

"You're in?" Joseph clarified.

"Yes, sir."

Joseph stood and nodded to him. "Good man."

Mia thought normally Joseph would clap him on the shoulder. He looked like he was moving to, but thought better of it. The no touch thing was so foreign to her. It should be weird and it was off-putting, but she also found it intriguing. A challenge really. Not that she would admit that to anyone.

"Okay, let's talk logistics." Joseph escorted him over to the table and they sat, flipping open a laptop and started discussing security systems, how the stalker had followed his usual pattern of flirtatious or romantic notes mailed to the other women until the final note on the pillow that was the same in every case, the possibility of it being a copycat, what they knew about Thomas Pederson and Alden Wilson, former flings of hers who had both disappeared which was the only exception in this case, how the stalker found the other women, qualifications of her security guards, the extra help the Delta family would provide so her guards could sleep, eat, and exercise, which the Deltas were already prepared to do because of protecting the Delta "weapon", whatever that meant.

Auntie stood by her side, wrapped an arm around her waist, and they simply watched the two men discuss for a bit. It made her mind spin. She could design clothing that women and reviewers would go crazy over, and manage an international business, but security details? Not only out of her reach, but it made her queasy.

Holly inclined her head toward the kitchen. They walked together. Mia looked over her shoulder. Zeke was studying her. His expression was closed off and completely indecipherable. He was going to protect her. Nobody would get through that tank of a man.

But that didn't mean he was happy about it or that he "liked" her.

What would it be like to spend the holiday in that man's very un-Christmas-like presence?

She shivered again. Whether from concern or because of how intriguing he was, she wasn't certain.

Chapter Three

Zeke was reeling at what he'd agreed to. Protection detail. For a gorgeous British woman in extreme danger. The Sneaky Stalker was a filthy animal but he must be incredibly smart as well. It appeared to be a game with this guy. For over three years now he'd gotten around police protection, witness protection programs, and private securities. He'd captured every woman he'd threatened to, and the women still hadn't been found.

He snuck a glance at Mia as she and Holly pulled out some leftovers from the fridge and warmed them up. The stalker wasn't getting to Zeke's woman. His hand balled into a fist. Mia caught him looking at her. She gifted him with a smile. He didn't return it. Turning back to Joseph's schedule on the computer, he rubbed at his neck. Had he just thought of her as "his woman"? He needed to control his thoughts or he might stupidly act on them. Would he get the chance to touch her again in the course of protecting her? Probably. It would be good to know if her touch was truly unique and actually felt good to him, but he'd keep his distance like he always did.

"Thank you for planning this out," he said. Every hour was scheduled with either one of Mia's security guards or a Delta family member monitoring the exterior perimeter and the security sensors and cameras that were in a basement room of Papa Delta's house. Zeke remembered the setup and schedule well from being here in September. But now he wouldn't be rotating through the protection detail. Now he'd be shadowing a gorgeous woman. Hooyah. No. Not hooyah. The opposite of hooyah. Danger he couldn't fight or win against if he let her trap him with those deep-brown eyes of hers.

"Of course." Joseph focused the Delta blue eyes on him. "You'll stay by her side night and day and the rest of us will take care of everything else."

Night and day? *Night*? "Joseph?" His voice was sharper than it needed to be. Well, maybe he should've made it sharper. "Night?"

"Maddie's not here to stay in the room with Mia like she was with Jessie."

Joseph's daughter Maddie was an impressive warrior. Zeke wished she was here. He rubbed at his neck and snuck another glance at Mia. That dress fit her ... really well. Did she have her clothing custom made? Rich people anyway.

"We took the liberty of moving an extra twin bed into Papa Delta's master suite," Joseph told him.

They'd have their own beds but still ... Zeke closed his eyes. He'd slept in barracks, berths, racks, bunks, tents, caves, or open air with soldiers all over the world. Sometimes they'd been far too close and pushed against him while they slept. That had been rough but he'd gotten through. On military assignments. This was just another assignment.

He didn't let himself look at Mia. She looked and felt nothing like any assignment he'd been around before. Had he actually liked touching her hand? It concerned him, especially as he'd almost unwittingly touched her again.

"Come eat," Holly called. "And then we'll walk you over to

Papa's, introduce you to the security guys, and let you get settled in for the night."

Why were her eyes twinkling at him? Zeke's jaw tightened. This was a serious situation, but he had the uncomfortable feeling Holly was match-making him with her adopted niece. She wouldn't dare. Would she? Holly seemed to care for him and think the best of him, but first of all she'd know he wasn't interested, and second of all nobody would want to match someone they loved with him. Holly was a positive sweetheart but she was mature enough to know that damaged and intense warriors like Zeke would only hurt a charming woman like Mia Burton. Not that he'd ever hurt any woman physically, but emotionally he was stunted and he would have to be strong, and probably hurtful, to keep his distance.

He and Joseph stood, walked over to the long kitchen bar, and waited for the ladies to go first then they each loaded up plates with reheated roast, potatoes, veggies, and homemade rolls with butter. They sat at the kitchen table where Holly and Mia already had ice water, silverware, and napkins waiting.

"Thank you," Zeke said then dug his fork in. It smelled almost as good as Mia had, and he was starved. He hadn't eaten since he left Virginia Beach this morning. No peanuts on the military flight he'd hopped.

"Zeke," Holly admonished in a soft but firm tone. "Prayer." She held out her hand to him.

Zeke was chagrined and dropped his fork immediately. He hated prayer time. Growing up his dad had said every mealtime and bedtime prayer as the "patriarch" of the family. Zeke couldn't remember a prayer where his dad didn't beseech heaven for help for his wayward son and list all of Zeke's shortcomings. At least his family hadn't held hands during those never-ending sermon prayers.

He knew the Deltas were religious but he'd luckily escaped most of the group meals and family prayers when he'd been here before. He and the other SEALs had stayed at the Admiral's house, which had been stocked with lots of food options and quite often the family would bring them plates loaded with delicious food since his men were usually on patrol duty when the family had a joint meal.

He swallowed and looked at Holly's extended hand. She and Joseph and Joseph and Mia already had hands clasped and were watching him. Mia's brown eyes were intrigued, and concerned, by his reluctance.

Holly nodded to him and reached out, trying to help out obviously. Zeke gritted his teeth and quickly clasped her hand in his, tight.

"Okay, relax it a little bit," Holly instructed.

Shoot. He softened his grip and thought he could tolerate this much contact through a prayer, as long as the offering over this meal was a lot briefer than any of his father's had been.

"Now Mia's hand." Holly tilted her head toward Mia.

Blood pumped far too quickly through Zeke's body. He looked at the sweet, beautiful face of the blond woman at his side and then at her extended hand. Did they have to make this so hard? Couldn't people just bow their heads and get the obligatory ritual over with?

Mia's welcoming look started to slip. Holly squeezed his hand. Joseph looked at him as if he had some serious issues. He did.

They should know that. Their daughter was marrying his friend Demo. Demo or Jessie should've explained to them this was a bad idea to bring him here and thrust him in intimate and uncomfortable situations like praying and holding hands.

Don't show weakness, he commanded himself. He closed his eyes and reached out blindly for Mia's hand. He'd rather not look at the viper as it touched him.

Their hands connected and Mia must have been an expert on this hand holding thing. She confidently secured their palms together and wrapped her soft fingers around the back of his hand. His breath shortened and he realized instantly this was not a viper. This delicate but firm touch was the complete opposite of a viper. Unless it was being disguised and would bite and poison him soon.

Zeke didn't dare open his eyes, but the sensation of warmth and his hand being in the perfect spot against Mia's almost overwhelmed him. He had no idea what Holly said in the prayer. He had no idea what was happening to his hand or his body. Without thinking about it, he wrapped his own fingers around Mia's delicate hand and knew somehow ... it would all be okay. Maybe he'd even be okay. He'd never felt such peace and security.

The prayer must've finished because he heard amens. His eyes sprang open and he released both women's hands as quickly as he could. He tried to forget the sensation of touching Mia. It was probably over-inflated because she was in danger and he felt responsible for her. Plus, how often had he held hands with exquisitely beautiful women in his life? Not since Rachel. Rachel had worked at a supplement store off base that carried a few things he couldn't get on base. She'd chased him for almost two years, slowly wearing down his barriers until he'd gotten comfortable with her, and he'd eventually assumed that must mean he should date her. When she said they should get married after dating exclusively for a year, he'd been terrified but agreed. While he was on a two-month deployment she'd met someone else and changed her mind about him. He'd gone back to single status with a sense of relief he'd never shared with anyone. He was responsible for his SEAL team and he cared for those men as much as he was capable of caring. It was a sense of relief to no longer be responsible for Rachel and a future family. As he thought back he could never remember any touch with her feeling like the two times he'd held Mia's hand. He'd learned to tolerate Rachel's touch and it hadn't repulsed him but he'd never encouraged it. Mia's touch made him warm and happy and somehow looking for a reason to touch her again.

Picking up his fork, he concentrated on his food. Despite being reheated it was delicious. Everything was savory and well-seasoned, the meat tender, the veggies still firm but soft, the roll was what blew him away. He loved homemade rolls. His mom had always made gritty wheat bread that stuck with you for hours. He'd had to retrain himself to eat wheat as an adult. He still didn't like it.

Holly's roll with butter seemed to melt in his mouth. It made sense as Holly was as sweet, warm, and kind as his mom had been cold, belittling, and sadistic.

Luckily the other three were having a conversation about each of Joseph and Holly's children, getting Mia up to date. Colton and Bailey were just home from their honeymoon and happily settled in their house in the woods not far from here. Klein and

Alivia were busy with numerous homes under construction and helping take care of his Granny Vance who stayed alternately with them or Thor and Shelly who lived next door, both houses were up by Colton's. Braden and Maddie were traveling the world protecting families and children from crime lords and traffickers. Zander and Jessie would be married at Christmas. Currently Jessie was with Zander in California but she'd be home soon. Zeke smiled to himself. Happy for his friend Demo to have found his perfect match in the sweet but brave Jessie.

They moved on to asking about Mia's parents. It was a short conversation, "Mum's as feisty and fun as ever, rocking the pickle-ball court and the charity lunches. Dad's ... well you know Dad, he means well and we love him but he is a pompous Duke. You can't expect him to be fun or interesting."

Zeke paused in his eating and looked over at her. First, her family wasn't perfect like the Deltas and second, her dad was a pompous ... Duke? "Your dad's a duke?" he asked, thrusting himself into their conversation.

She looked at him with her golden-brown eyes. Why did she look embarrassed? "And proud of it."

"Do I call you ... Lady Mia?" He tried to tease but this piece of information made him even more uncomfortable. He'd protected some royalty at different times throughout his career. They were pompous and made sure he knew they were far below him. Mia didn't make him feel like that though.

"Please don't." She laughed. "My mum hates being called Duchess. But she and my dad fancy each other and he never reminds her that she doesn't have royal blood. Though he does expect her to attend certain functions with him, he doesn't even get upset when she 'acts like a commoner' or when teases him. Usually he's too busy to notice her."

His eyebrows lifted and he saw Joseph and Holly exchange a look. "That's ... nice of him to not get upset?" He often felt that people were from a different world than him as it appeared most people weren't raised by two-faced, hypocritical, narcistic, pathological liars disguised as religious zealots. But she had truly been raised in a world he could never comprehend.

Mia laughed harder at that. "My dad doesn't know the meaning of 'nice' but he's a good man, loves my mum, donates his fortune generously, as long as it doesn't affect his bottom line, and is respected and fair in his political and business dealings. Plus he plays a mean game of cricket." She grinned. Her grin was perfect in his mind.

It was a lot better than he could say of his dad, but it was telling she didn't say her dad loved her. She didn't look like she wanted to dwell on what her father was or wasn't, so he racked his brain for something else to ask her and came up with, "Do you help your dad with his ... business and cricket, or play pickle ball and attend charity lunches with your mom?"

"Mum," she corrected. "Neither actually." She took a drink of water as if trying to decide how to answer him. "Except for in December when I take the month off work and my mum and I buy and distribute toys to hundreds of children in Surrey," she looked sad to be missing out on that which made him like her even more, "I design clothing."

He looked over her sweater dress and felt his neck heat up. He'd already noticed how perfectly it fit her. Custom made. By her. Her career fit her. Unique, creative, and fun. "Good for you."

Which was obviously not the correct answer as she gave him a placating smile and focused on her dinner.

"Mia," Holly sounded exasperated. "You saying you design clothing would be like Zeke saying he's an enlisted soldier. You're the best designer of women's clothing in the world!"

"Ah, Auntie." Mia smiled. "You're such a love."

"Well you are. She is," she told Zeke. "The girls and I each have dresses from her for church and special occasions. And of course every bit of her active wear we can get our hands on. Sometimes it takes a while shipping it across, but most Nordstrom's and Macey's carry her dresses and business casual now."

"Auntie," Mia sounded exasperated with her, "if you don't buy direct from my site you can't use the discount code for friends and family."

"Well I don't use it anyway. Your biggest fans should want to pay full price. Discount code," she muttered then focused on Zeke again as Mia raised her hands helplessly to Joseph. "She's 'Mia Forever'," Holly continued. "Have you heard of the brand?"

Of course Zeke hadn't. "Um ..." He lifted his hands helplessly. "I just wear what the Navy gives me."

Joseph chuckled at that and Mia smiled but Holly didn't. "Well, let me show you." She hurried over to the desk Joseph and Zeke had been working at and plucked up the laptop.

She came back and sat the laptop between them on the table, sitting back down, clicking on Safari, and typing. Her face lit up. "Oh, Mia, that cashmere sweater is gorgeous. Ooh I need the pink one."

"Thank you. The pink would be gorgeous with your coloring."

"I'm ordering that." She gave her husband an imperious look. "Don't you tease me about it."

"I wouldn't dare." He smiled. "I'm sure I'll love it on you."

"Well you dang well better." She grinned and then turned the computer toward Zeke. "Look," she demanded. "Look at how gorgeous her designs are. Unique but flattering. Comfortable but classy. I'm just in love with everything you design, sweetheart."

"Thank you," she said again.

Zeke thought she might be blushing. He knew he was turning red. He tried to look at the pictures of beautiful, too-thin, tall women posing in different dresses, sweaters, clingy pants, and business suits. He was sure the designs were incredible but he felt idiotic and uncomfortable staring at all these women. He hoped he'd looked for long enough when he raised his eyes to focus on Mia.

"Very nice," he said.

"Very nice?" Holly repeated. "That's all you've got to say?"

He turned beseeching eyes on Holly. She'd always had his back before this moment. "Incredible, alluring, mind-blowing, outstanding, brilliant," she whispered out of the side of her mouth.

Mia laughed. "I don't expect a tough career military man to know or care about women's clothing design, Holly." She went back to eating as if it was no big deal.

Zeke looked at Holly and shrugged. Not sure why he even cared that he'd messed that all up. She patted his hand and he only flinched.

"Sorry, Zeke," Holly said. "I should know not to push you."

Zeke wished he wasn't such an obvious loser right now. How

could he be this elite fighter, confident to take out a dictator and his minions, but put him in front of a beautiful, accomplished woman and he flubbed it all up?

He concentrated on his food, wishing he'd taken more to keep him busy longer. He needed to focus on the job not the woman. That was the only way he'd get through this assignment.

Find *His Perfect Match for Christmas* here.

About the Author

Cami is a part-time author, part-time exercise consultant, part-time housekeeper, full-time wife, and overtime mother of four adorable boys. Sleep and relaxation are fond memories. She's never been happier.

Join Cami's VIP list to find out about special deals, giveaways and new releases and receive a free copy of *Rescued by Love: Park City Firefighter Romance* by clicking here.

cami@camichecketts.com
www.camichecketts.com

Also by Cami Checketts

Summit Valley Christmas Romance

His Perfect Match for Christmas

His Ski Resort Overrun for Christmas

His Cabin Invaded for Christmas

His Unexpected Wedding for Christmas

Delta Family Romances

Deceived

Abandoned

Committed

Betrayed

Devoted

Compromised

Endangered

Accepted

Returned

Devastated

Famous Friends Romances

Loving the Firefighter

Loving the Athlete

Loving the Rancher

Loving the Coach

Loving the Contractor

Loving the Sheriff

Loving the Entertainer

The Hidden Kingdom Romances

Royal Secrets

Royal Security

Royal Doctor

Royal Mistake

Royal Courage

Royal Pilot

Royal Imposter

Royal Baby

Royal Battle

Royal Fake Fiancé

Secret Valley Romance

Sister Pact

Marriage Pact

Christmas Pact

Survive the Romance

Romancing the Treasure

Romancing the Escape

Romancing the Boat

Romancing the Mountain

Romancing the Castle

Echo Ridge Romance

Christmas Makeover

Last of the Gentlemen

My Best Man's Wedding

Change of Plans

Counterfeit Date

Snow Valley

Full Court Devotion: Christmas in Snow Valley

A Touch of Love: Summer in Snow Valley

Running from the Cowboy: Spring in Snow Valley

Light in Your Eyes: Winter in Snow Valley

Romancing the Singer: Return to Snow Valley

Fighting for Love: Return to Snow Valley

Other Books by Cami

Seeking Mr. Debonair: Jane Austen Pact

Seeking Mr. Dependable: Jane Austen Pact

Saving Sycamore Bay

Oh, Come On, Be Faithful

Protect This

Blog This

Redeem This

The Broken Path

Dead Running

Dying to Run

Fourth of July

Love & Loss

Love & Lies

Five Free Books

Download the complete Echo Ridge Romance Collection here when you sign up for Cami's newsletter.

Christmas Makeover:

Chelsea Jamison has been infatuated with Drew Stirling longer than she's loved playing basketball, high-top sneakers, and the Knicks. Unfortunately, all Drew sees is the kid who kicked his trash in the high school free throw contest and not the girl whose heart breaks into a fast dribble when he's near.

Drew makes an unexpected visit home to Echo Ridge and their friendship picks up where they left off as they scheme to make a teenaged boy's Christmas dreams come true. When Chelsea realizes she's fallen for her best friend, she wonders if there is any hope of a relationship with Drew or if she's stuck in buddy-status for life.

Last of the Gentlemen:

Despite the hardships she's faced, Emma Turner is determined to make a good life for her three children. Working nights and struggling through life doesn't leave much time for romance, which is just fine as far as Emma is concerned. But when her son's good-looking lacrosse coach takes an interest in her children, Emma has to fight off the smolder in her stomach and banish her daydreams. This schoolgirl crush needs to end before she embarrasses her son and herself. If only she could tell that to her heart.

My Best Man's Wedding:

Jessica Porter made a vow to marry her best guy friend, Josh, when they turned thirty. When Josh calls with the news that he's coming home to Echo Ridge for his wedding, Jessica is determined to break up the happy couple and take her rightful place as his bride. Gentry Trine, a coworker, agrees to pretend to be her fiancé to stir up feelings of jealousy. However, Jessica didn't realize fake fiancés could kiss like champions, and make a girl smile nonstop. Can she figure out which is the right man for her before she loses them both?

Change of Plans:

Kaitlyn knows who she's destined to spend her life with, until superstar Axel Olsen turns her dreams upside down.

Kaitlyn Johanson is chosen by heartthrob, nationally-acclaimed lacrosse player, Axel Olsen, for a dream date. She didn't know a man touching her hand could feel like heaven, but she awkwardly blacks out then admits to him that she's in a relationship.

Kaitlyn comes home to Echo Ridge hoping to rekindle her relationship with her high school boyfriend, Mason. She never expects Axel to show up in her hometown, hosting a lacrosse camp with Mason and his stepdad.

When Axel steals her attention and possibly her heart from the man she is supposed to marry, she has to decide if she'll take a risk on new love or give old love a second chance.

Counterfeit Date:

Mason Turner only has eyes for Lolly Honeymiller. She's vivacious and hilarious and unfortunately thinks of him as her best friend's ex. Lolly's friends cook up a scheme: pretending Lolly is making him over for a special date with his dream girl. The more time he and Lolly spend together, the harder it is to keep his feelings a secret.

Lolly offers to help Mason Turner prepare for a date with his dream girl. Through makeovers, shopping, and practice kissing, she tries to keep her distance but finds herself falling for a man she can never have. As the date approaches, both wonder if they can keep things fake or if the farce will implode and shred both of their hearts.

Download your free copy here.

Made in United States
Orlando, FL
17 April 2023

32166991R00163